P9-DHD-138

THE SECRETS WE SHARE

Books by Edwin Hill

LITTLE COMFORT

THE MISSING ONES

WATCH HER

THE SECRETS WE SHARE

Published by Kensington Publishing Corp.

THE SECRETS WE SHARE

EDWIN HILL

www.kensingtonbooks.com

KENSINGTON BOOKS are published by

Kensington Publishing Corp.
119 West 40th Street
New York, NY 10018

All Kensington titles, imprints, and distributed lines are available at special quantity discounts for bulk purchases for sales promotion, premiums, fund-raising, educational, or institutional use. Special book excerpts or customized printings can also be created to fit specific needs. For details, write or phone the office of the Kensington Special Sales Manager: Attn. Special Sales Department. Kensington Publishing Corp, 119 West 40th Street, New York, NY 10018. Phone: 1-800-221-2647.

Library of Congress Card Catalogue Number: 2021949986

The K with book logo Reg. US Pat. & TM Off.

ISBN: 978-1-4967-3541-6

First Kensington Hardcover Edition: April 2022

ISBN: 978-1-4967-3543-0 (ebook)

10 9 8 7 6 5 4 3 2 1

Printed in the United States of America

To Frank

1995

Natalie Cavanaugh had a secret, one that made her stomach hurt, and one that she had to keep to herself till she could figure out what to do next. She rested her head against the passenger's-side door of the Caprice Classic station wagon, letting hot air blow over her. Her mother Ruth tapped a finger on the steering wheel, and Fleetwood Mac played on the radio.

From the back seat, Natalie's twelve-year-old sister Glenn said, "Old people music."

"Then call me old," Ruth Cavanaugh said.

"I'm going swimming when we get home," Glenn said, meaning she was hopping the fence to the next-door neighbors' pool.

"Be sure they ask first," Ruth said.

"It's an open invitation," Glenn said.

"Don't abuse it."

Ruth turned into Starling Circle and down their driveway. The Cavanaughs lived in a brand-new development on the outskirts of Elmhurst, where acres of forest had been clear-cut to build fifteen houses, though so far only two were complete. The others lay frozen in various states of construction. At the very center of the circle, the Cavanaughs—fourteen-year-old Natalie, Glenn, and their parents, Ruth and Alan—lived in a gray colonial. Right next door, Diane Sykes and her two kids lived in a nearly identical house, the one with the pool. They'd all moved to the circle in the spring expecting to hear construction during summer. So far, they'd only heard each other.

Ruth parked in front of the garage. Natalie swept damp bangs from her forehead and leapt to the shimmering asphalt, where waves of heat lapped at her knees. Glenn shoved her. Natalie shoved back.

"Girls," Ruth said. "Let's get everything inside before it melts."

Plastic grocery bags filled the station wagon. Natalie grabbed two and dashed into the house, through the living room, past the bourbon stain on the family-room carpet, and to the kitchen.

Her mother crammed ice cream and ground beef into the freezer. "Your father's probably still asleep."

Natalie's stomachache returned, with a vengeance. Usually after a night like last night, her father slept in the guest room. When he finally woke, he'd slump at the kitchen counter and apologize for the bits of memory that came to him in flashes. The knife wound in his arm should have crystallized those memories.

"Let's all be as quiet as we can," her mother added.

"I'll put things away," Natalie said.

"No, *I'll* put things away," Glenn, who could turn anything into an argument, said. "It's my turn."

"*I'll* put the groceries away," Ruth said. "The two of you can unload the car."

"Race you," Glenn said.

Natalie took off, slamming the door. Behind her, Glenn stumbled down the front stoop, losing ground, but when Natalie went to grab a bag, the plastic caught on a window crank and Glenn beat her inside.

"Cheater," Natalie said.

"You're the one who slammed the door."

"If Dad wakes up, you'll be sorry," Natalie said, her voice a whisper, the lie coming easily. "You should be quiet, especially after last night."

They deposited their bags on the Formica counter.

"Stay with me for a second, Glenn," Ruth said.

Glenn's face flushed, enough so that Natalie knew at once that her sister had done something she shouldn't have. Glenn was always getting in trouble, pushing boundaries, while Natalie spent her life inside the lines, fascinated by her sister's bold infractions. Now she lingered to see what Glenn had done, but Ruth said, "Those bags won't walk themselves in from the car," and waited for Natalie to leave.

By the time she returned with more groceries, whatever had happened between her mother and sister had already transpired. Natalie jabbed her sister with her thumb, but Glenn shrugged. A moment later, their neighbor, Diane Sykes, knocked at the back door and let herself in. "Pool party," she said. "It'll be hotter than hell today."

Mrs. Sykes had her dark hair styled like Rachel on *Friends.* She carried herself with confidence, and unlike Natalie's own mother, who worked from home editing textbooks, Mrs. Sykes worked in an office, so when Natalie remembers this day, she knows it must have been a weekend. That morning, Mrs. Sykes took a mug from over the sink and filled it with coffee. She and Ruth exchanged something unspoken, their own secret.

"How's Tonya feeling?" Ruth asked. "You mentioned she was under the weather. I don't want something sweeping through our little neighborhood."

"Whatever it was, she's over it."

Ruth nodded. "Get your suits, girls."

Natalie and Glenn ran upstairs to their room. "What did you do?" Natalie asked.

"MYOB," Glenn said, as she chose a one-piece to cover the bruises.

Natalie left her sister and hovered outside her father's office. On most mornings, even on a Saturday like this one, she'd hear the clacking of his typewriter behind the closed door. Today, she toed the door open. Stacks of paper littered nearly every surface. She slipped into the room. Index cards were tacked on a bulletin board with characters' names and plot points. Tersely written rejection letters papered the back of the door. "My wall of shame," Alan Cavanaugh named it, especially on nights when he teetered on the precipice of maudlin, when he tipped between jovial and dangerous. Alan called himself a writer, but mostly he taught English at the local community college, something he didn't like to remember.

Glenn had made him remember that last night.

"I don't think I'll ever make it through all these novels," Glenn had said, turning a page in *Crooked House.* She'd spent the summer discovering Agatha Christie, working through every title the local library offered. "She wrote, like, eighty books. Imagine if you had eighty books, Dad."

Ruth was in the kitchen washing dishes, and the TV was on. Natalie watched a rerun of *Full House* and willed her sister to shut up as the laugh track reverberated through the room. Alan swirled the ice in his glass. "What do you think it would be like if I wrote eighty books?"

"We'd have a pool like the Sykeses."

Alan waved Glenn over. She put the book aside and sidled up to him. He stroked her head. "What else?" he asked.

Glenn swallowed, as if she knew she'd crossed the line. "Maybe we'd live in a mansion."

"Would that make you happy?"

"Probably."

Alan drank down most of his bourbon. Then he punched Glenn in the stomach so hard she fell to the floor and curled into a ball. He stood, knocking over the bourbon so that the last of it soaked into the carpet. And he kicked her in the side.

Ruth ran from the kitchen, a sponge in one hand and a paring knife in the other. Alan kicked Glenn again, and Ruth stepped into him, and Natalie wasn't sure if she meant to or not, but the knife stuck out of his bicep, and blood ran down his arm and dripped onto the carpet where the bourbon had spilled, and all four of them froze for what seemed like hours but had probably only been a few seconds, and the only sound was the laughter from the TV.

"Get out," Ruth said. "And don't come back."

Natalie grabbed Glenn's hand and dragged her outside and into the woods. They ran along the path, over the brook, across the clearing, and to the copse of trees. There, they collapsed in the hunters' blind. Their secret place.

Or maybe not so secret.

Natalie held up a cigarette butt. "We're not the only ones who come here."

Glenn still had the library book in one hand. It was too dark to read, but Natalie had Glenn tell her as much of the story as she could remember. And she listened to be sure their father hadn't followed.

The door to Alan's office opened. Glenn stood in the hallway.

"You shouldn't be in there," Glenn said as she applied lip gloss from an orange tube that matched her ponytail. The scent of artificial citrus hung on the air.

"Where did you get that?" Natalie asked.

"It's mine," Glenn said, "and I'll know if you use it."

"You stole it from the A&P."

"Did not."

Glenn turned and ran downstairs. A moment later, Natalie heard a splash in the Sykeses' pool.

"Are you coming?" Ruth Cavanaugh shouted up the stairs.

"I'll meet you there," Natalie shouted back.

She changed into her own bathing suit. Unlike Glenn, she could wear a two-piece. At the Sykeses' house, Natalie's mother and Diane Sykes sat in the shade of an umbrella, while six-year-old Lindsey Sykes did a cannonball off the diving board.

Tonya Sykes was there too, with her dangerous black hair and nose ring. Tonya would be a junior this fall, a year ahead of Natalie in school. Ever since the Sykeses had moved to town in the winter, Tonya had stridden through the hallways of Elmhurst High School, her lips painted in a slash of burgundy, while students parted to make way. And even though Natalie was closer in age, it was Glenn, somehow, who'd become friendly with Tonya.

They lay on floats in the water, paddling to the edge to sip their Diet Cokes.

"Hi, Tonya," Natalie said.

"Oh, hey," Tonya said, before turning her attention back to Glenn. "We're going to see *Babe* tonight. Ask your mother if you can come."

"She can't," Ruth Cavanaugh said.

"M-o-m!" Glenn said.

"Maybe," Ruth said. "But only if your sister goes too."

The last thing in the world Natalie wanted was to play third wheel to her younger sister. Besides, she doubted any of them would be going to the movies tonight. She stood on the end of the diving board.

"Cannonball!" Lindsey Sykes shouted from the water.

Natalie bounced off the board and into the air, and Lindsey shrieked with delight.

Natalie would think about this moment for years to come, about these few seconds when she hovered in midair, about the summer sun and the stench of sunscreen and orange-scented lip balm, about Glenn and Tonya scheming and the stomachache that wouldn't go away. All the players were in one place.

All but one. Her father.

As she lifted her knees to her chest and closed her eyes, she saw her mother lean toward Diane and whisper again.

Natalie plunged beneath the pool's surface.

Here, the world was quiet. Natalie held her breath till her lungs felt as though they would burst, knowing that as soon as she came up to take a breath, the day would return to focus. She couldn't have known that this would be the last time any of them would ever truly be happy, or that within a week, news trucks would line Starling Circle, and her mother would be suspected of murder. She also couldn't have known that by this time next month, Diane Sykes would be dead.

What Natalie did know was that eventually she'd need to tell the police where to find her father. Natalie's secret, the one that made her stomach hurt, was that she'd already seen him early this morning when she'd gone to retrieve the library book that she and Glenn had accidentally left behind the night before. Alan Cavanaugh was in the woods, beyond the brook, through the clearing, behind the rotting hunters' blind. He lay facedown. Dead. The back of his head crushed. His blood splattered across dry earth.

Now
November 16

CHAPTER 1

I watch her through the window from outside the pub. It's past midnight. The November night is cold, rain imminent, but she'll stay till last call. She drinks vodka on the rocks and probably thinks it won't betray her secrets. Her wallet sits on the bar, where it could be taken so easily. A detective badge pokes from beneath her practical blazer. She'd be pretty if she wore different clothes, if she took her hair out of the tight bun that sits at the nape of her neck. Unlike me, she hasn't changed. At forty-two, she looks the same as she has since she was a teenager: rigid, strident, severe. She's the kind of woman men tell to smile.

The first drop of rain splashes off my coat. The bartender refills her glass and moves on. He must know not to bother trying to engage. One of the few remaining patrons tosses a wad of cash onto the bar and leaves. He stops at the threshold, cold air sweeping through the open doorway. "Storm's coming," he says to me before shuffling away.

Inside the pub, Natalie Cavanaugh turns on her stool, searching the cozy space for something she can't find. I wonder if she feels the chill of winter, or if she senses what's to come.

CHAPTER 2

MAVIS ABBOTT IMAGINES HER TWELVE-YEAR-OLD EXISTENCE AS A set of boxes stored in a closet. When she wants to ignore something, she stuffs it into a box, ties it with a bow, and shoves it to the very rear of the closet. When she needs to focus, she tears the box open and scrutinizes what she finds inside. Today, she's all about the algebra test that she has this morning, one that starts in twenty minutes, one that she studied for nearly all weekend and that she intends to ace, but Kevin Chandler seems to have other plans. He won't leave her alone as he trails her on her walk to West Roxbury Prep. "Come on," he says. "Are you afraid?"

Mavis keeps her head down and picks up her pace. It's pouring, the kind of cold and unrelenting rain that November brings to Boston. Cars speed by on the busy road, splashing dirty waves of water up across the sidewalk. Mavis is in the seventh grade, and this is *the* year she's earned the privilege of walking from her house to the school by herself. A single infraction, her mother has warned, and she'll lose the privilege. Mavis has three blocks to go before hitting campus: under the stone railroad bridge, past the abandoned factory, and across Centre Street. Once she gets to school, she'll be able to escape Kevin and find her best friend, Stella, and they'll talk about the party this last weekend or the cute detective Mavis's mother invited or that glass of eggnog they sipped in the dark till Uncle Bennet caught them. But Kevin is relentless.

"I'm telling everyone that you're a chickenshit," he whispers as they nearly make it past the factory.

Mavis turns on him. "I am not."

"Prove it."

Lately, Kevin has found any excuse possible to harass Mavis, sitting behind her in class, at lunch, on the soccer field, and Mavis suspects that if she tells her mother about it, her mother will say that Kevin has a crush on her and that she has to tell him to quit it, but the truth is that one of the imaginary boxes Mavis isn't ready to open is the one that tells her she doesn't *completely* want Kevin to stop, even though he's really, really annoying. She has a microscopic, almost nonexistent crush on him, too, one that she can barely admit, even to herself. And that's something she *really* can't confess to her mother because her mother would freak out. So Mavis shoves Kevin instead.

"Quit it," he says.

"Leave me alone," she says, but she doesn't turn, she doesn't stalk away, and in that moment, she gives Kevin a glimpse of what it feels like to win. He folds his arms.

The factory sits beside them, behind overgrown brush and a rusty chain-link fence with a TRESPASSERS WILL BE PROSECUTED sign displayed too prominently to ignore. Enough mortar has worn away that the bricks have disintegrated and threaten the foundation, and sheets of faded plywood shutter the windows. This building has been here for as long as Mavis can remember, slowly decaying. Each morning on her way to school, she dashes along the fence and imagines a hand reaching through the chain-link to cover her mouth and yank her to an unknown fate.

"I dare you," Kevin says. "Go inside. There's an old lab. Steal one of the wall tiles and bring it to me. And it's not that hard of a dare, anyway. Most of the tiles have fallen off the walls."

"I have an algebra test," Mavis says.

"The adrenaline will help you focus."

Mavis glances down the road toward the school. Above them, a train rumbles by, headed toward downtown Boston.

"Don't you want to see what's inside?" Kevin asks.

That's the problem. Mavis does want to see what's inside. She's wondered for years, even though her mother has warned of a lifetime grounding if she ever stepped foot in that dirty, disgusting building. "You'll keep watch?" she asks.

"Only if you hurry up."

Mavis waits for a break in the traffic before scaling the fence. Every door and window she can see is boarded up. "How am I supposed to get inside?"

"There's a broken window in the back," Kevin says.

"Where's the lab?"

"It's just there."

"What floor?"

Kevin doesn't answer quickly enough.

"You haven't been in there yourself," Mavis says. "Someone dared *you* to get a tile."

"You're a bitch," Kevin says.

"And you're the chickenshit."

She stares him down till he looks away. Then she turns and dashes across the rutted, overgrown parking lot.

Later, when she gets to school, she'll show the tile to everyone and let them know that Kevin was too scared to get one for himself. She skirts the building and finds the open basement window in the back. Peering into the darkness sends a shiver down her spine that she blames on the freezing rain. But she breaks this project down into tiny pieces that'll help her get through it as quickly as possible.

Step one: get inside. She ducks and slides through the window, clinging to the sill and dropping into the dark, where she lands on a damp dirt floor. Here, the raw air smells of mold. As Mavis's eyes adjust to the dark, she takes in the detritus of an abandoned business—stacks of metal office chairs, an ancient furnace coated in asbestos, a wall of gray filing cabinets. Wires and cords hang from the ceiling, and a steady stream of water trickles through the open window and pools on the muddy floor. She swears she hears the scurrying of a mouse, or worse.

Her phone beeps. It's Stella. *Where r u?*

Mavis doesn't answer.

Step two: make sure she can escape. She places one of the office chairs beneath the window.

Step three: find a stupid tile.

She uses the flashlight on her phone and heads up a set of rotting wooden steps, where a swollen door leads into a wide hallway. Weak winter light filters through the boarded-up windows onto walls yellowed from age. She follows the hallway into an expansive room that must have once housed factory equipment. That room connects to another similar one, and then to a third. On the other side of the last room, a set of stairs leads up to the second floor. Maybe the lab is there? As she crosses the floor, something moves in her periphery. She turns the flashlight. Hundreds of eyes glimmer as rodents scurry into the walls.

Yuck.

Why did she come in here? Because of a stupid crush on a dumb boy? Mavis doesn't want to be *that* girl, and suddenly she couldn't care less about doing Kevin Chandler's bidding. He can get his own tile if he needs one that badly.

B there in a sec, she texts to Stella.

Step four: get the heck out of here.

As Mavis begins to retrace the path to the basement stairs, something in the corner of the cavernous room catches her attention. A thick wave of rotten air flows over her. She covers her nose and mouth with a scarf and squints into the darkness. She lifts her phone and aims the light beam.

She forgets about Kevin Chandler. And the algebra test. And how angry her mother will be when she finds out about this excursion. Rats swarm over something in the corner. Hundreds of them. It's vile, but Mavis creeps toward them anyway. And the stench grows stronger.

CHAPTER 3

"ENVISION SUCCESS," DETECTIVE ZANE PEREZ SAYS TO NATALIE Cavanaugh as he maneuvers the sedan through morning traffic on the rain-soaked Jamaicaway. "That's what Glenn says."

He steps on the accelerator and glides through an intersection, only to stop short behind a wall of brake lights. "See? Success!" he says.

Natalie grits her teeth. Her sister, Glenn, runs a baking blog, one that she peppers with pop psychology. Zane, along with about a million other people, follows Glenn's every move on social media. He's already brought her up twice this morning. "She's having a prelaunch of the book this afternoon for influencers," he says. "If I wasn't on duty, I'd go."

"Are you an influencer?"

"Have you seen my feed?"

Natalie hasn't seen anyone's "feed" unless it's part of a police investigation. To her, social media is a cesspool. "Glenn bakes cakes," she says. "It's not as though she saves the world."

"Good enough for me."

Zane turns off the parkway and makes his way to West Roxbury. A moment later, he pulls up beside an Edwardian-style house on a quiet, tree-lined street. Glenn's house.

"By the way," he says, "you look like you tied one on last night."

Natalie cracks the car door open. Rain pelts her coat sleeve as a blast of November air sweeps through the overheated car. She closed the bar down last night and feels it this morning. "What's it to you?"

"Ask your sister for a glass of water. You need to hydrate."

"Thanks for the tip. If I'm not back in fifteen minutes, come inside and say there's an emergency. No matter what I do, insist that we leave. Understood?"

Zane salutes. "Tell Glenn I made the jam blossoms. They were awesome."

"Fifteen minutes," Natalie says. "Not one second more."

She steps into the rain. The house rises in front of her, yellow with black and green trim and a mansard-style roof. The driveway sweeps up from the street, ending at a similarly painted garage and a guest cottage in the back. Two bare beech trees tower over the corner lot, which is enclosed behind a brick and wrought-iron wall that makes it seem as if Glenn lives on an estate.

Natalie glances at the surrounding houses. Glenn talks about her neighbors, about the barbecues and the movie nights, as though Natalie knows these people too. She wonders if they're watching her now. Glenn's neighbors are the types who whisper when a detective with the Boston Police Department shows up. Even after two decades on the police force, Natalie feels conspicuous with her firearm under her blazer and her practical suit. People identify her as a cop at once, someone to be trusted and feared at the same time.

She skirts the side of the house to the kitchen door and cups her hand against the glass, only to see Glenn at the kitchen counter with a pile of dough in front of her and a mixer going at full speed. She wears Christmas ornament earrings and an apron with the name of her blog, "Happy Time," stitched into it. Lights set in the ceiling shine on her face and impossible-to-miss orange hair. As much as Natalie likes to blend in and disappear, her sister yearns to be seen.

Natalie raps on the glass.

Glenn glances toward her, holds up a finger, and says something. She waves Natalie inside, where the air smells of butter and almonds and vanilla.

"Here's a surprise!" Glenn says, waving her over.

Now Natalie spots the camera set up on a tripod. "Not a chance," she says, trying to duck outside and retreat, but Glenn dashes around the counter and drags her to where the mixer still goes at top speed. "This is my sister, Natalie! She's the one who loves almond croissants." Glenn smiles toward the camera and kisses Natalie's cheek. "Say hello."

Natalie keeps her eyes focused on the mixer and waves. "Hi."

"Natalie's a detective with the Boston Police. She's busy. Really busy!"

"So busy that I can only stay for a few minutes. My partner's outside waiting. He says the jam blossoms are awesome."

Glenn grins. "And you should see this partner. Cuter than a button!"

"Turn that off or I'll start swearing. You won't be able to use any of the footage."

"Back in a few to finish up!"

Glenn smiles for a few seconds. The smile disappears the instant she stops recording. She switches the mixer off, too. "I'll have to do some edits," she mumbles. "Coffee?"

"Please don't post any of that. I hate being on camera."

Glenn takes a mug from over the sink and adds a touch of cream. She puts the mug on the counter and steps in, forcing a hug while every muscle in Natalie's body seizes up. Glenn is nothing if not passionate. "I thought you might cancel again," she says.

Passive-aggressive, too.

"I'm on duty," Natalie says. "Zane's outside waiting for me, and I'll have to book out of here if something comes up."

"I know. He texted to tell me you were nearby."

"What are you doing texting my partner?"

Glenn holds her at arm's length. "We need to do something about your hair."

Like most days, Natalie had tied her dark hair into a tight and practical bun that sits at the nape of her neck and tugs at her brow. "My hair?" she says. "I'm surprised there are any chemicals left on planet Earth after what they've done to yours."

Glenn fills a plate with almond croissants that she's already baked and waves Natalie to the kitchen table. "The publisher wanted something that would stand out in photos. They got what they asked for. And I'm trying to make as many videos as I can before December. We're posting them on my YouTube channel."

That explained the Christmas getup in mid-November.

Glenn slides the croissants across the table. "I told the world that these are your favorite, so I hope you like them."

Natalie's stomach growls. She can't remember whether she ate breakfast this morning or dinner the night before. She tears into the buttery pastry and chews hungrily.

"How is it?" Glenn asks.

"It's okay."

"I'll take that as a ringing endorsement. Take the rest to the station." Glenn grins. "Or give them to Zane."

"Does your husband know about your little crush?"

"No, and Jake doesn't need to find out, either, not right now. Besides, I'm not the one who needs to get laid. You are. Why not Zane? The two of you are together all day."

"I don't date coworkers. How many times do I have to say that? It never goes anywhere good. Besides, I probably have ten years on the guy."

"I bet he's about the same age as Jake."

"And I have two years on you. Besides, you're the Mrs. Robinson, not me."

"If you're not dating Zane, then who? What's his name? Or hers?"

Natalie isn't dating anyone, which only bothers her when Glenn brings it up. "I'm the older sister, and I'm the cop. I'm the one who's supposed to be bossy and meddlesome. Stop. And what's so important that we need to meet today? I have about ten seconds before I have to get back to work."

"I can't make plans with my sister?"

Natalie waits, like she would with a reluctant witness, letting the silence build till it threatens to fill the entire kitchen. Finally, Glenn breaks. "Do you want the easy one or the difficult one first?"

"Easy."

"Why didn't you come to my party on Saturday?"

"Are you kidding me?"

"You said you'd come, and you didn't. It hurt my feelings. The book launches next week, and it's a big deal."

Glenn started her blog, Happy Time, ten years ago as a hobby where she posted recipes and paired them with self-help advice. It sputtered along for years before going viral as people rediscovered baking during the pandemic. She spun the attention into a book deal and spent the last year "building her brand," as she likes to say. Now she makes regular appearances on local TV, and even traveled to New York recently to shoot a segment for a national show. The book is due in a week, and the publisher expects it to be one of their major pushes of the holiday season. As part of the marketing plan, Glenn threw a holiday bash this last Saturday so that she'd have plenty of photos and videos to coincide with the launch. And yes, Natalie had said she'd come but had finished off a fifth of Absolut and passed out in front of the TV instead.

"Who wants to go to a Christmas party in mid-November?" she says.

"My other fifty best friends who bothered to show up?" Glenn says. "They even wore velvet like I asked them to."

"Guess what? I don't own a velvet dress. And if you had fifty friends, you certainly didn't need me. Especially not with this hair. Besides, you're an overnight success."

"I suppose, if you can call working for almost no money for a decade an overnight success."

On the street, lights flash as a cruiser speeds by the house. Out of habit, Natalie dips her ear to her radio to see if she can catch what's going on.

"Try not being a cop for two more minutes," Glenn says. "Or be *my* cop. I need to show you something, and you can't freak out."

"You realize that when you say that it's a guaranteed freak-out?"

Glenn shoots her a glare as she opens her tablet computer. "You've been to the blog, right?"

"Of course, I have."

"I post recipes, and people post comments. Most of them are really nice. Sometimes I'll make a mistake in the directions, and they'll let me know. Or they'll post a query like 'Can I use dates instead of sugar?' or 'What if I substitute cashews for cream?' Once in a while, I'll get someone who probably needs a psych eval." She clicks through a few pages and opens a document. "And once in a long while, someone will post something angry or threatening, and usually I either delete it or ignore it, and my regulars will shame the person into trolling somewhere else. Happy Time is supposed to be a supportive community."

"Or you could report it to the police. Especially if it's a threat," Natalie says, though she knows that an anonymous online threat won't get much, if any, attention.

"Listen, okay," Glenn says. "It's usually not that bad. But on Sunday, someone posted this."

She spins the tablet around and shows Natalie a screenshot of a post from "BagelBoy." It reads, *I'm watching you.*

"Who's BagelBoy?" Natalie asks.

"He could be anyone. You have to provide an e-mail address to post, but when I wrote a note, the e-mail bounced back, so it's probably fake."

Natalie reads through the post again. "A lot of people are watching you because of the publicity. Do you have security cameras?"

"I don't want them."

"You should consider it. You're the one who's cultivating the brand, right? That can come with some risk. Has he posted again?"

Natalie hears footsteps in the next room. Glenn quickly snaps the tablet closed just as her husband, Jake, enters the kitchen. Jake is in his mid-thirties, tall and doughy, with unruly hair that sticks out in every direction.

"Natalie Cavanaugh," he says. "What a surprise."

"I thought you'd be at the office," Natalie says.

"Staying home." Jake nods toward Glenn. "I'm trying to help this one out as much as possible. Big day next week."

"He's a sweetheart," Glenn says.

Natalie catches her sister's eye; she gives an almost imperceivable shake of the head. "We can finish this later," Natalie says.

"What are you two scheming about?" Jake asks.

"We're talking about Mom's house," Glenn says, quickly. "It's been sitting there empty for over a year. It's probably time to sell."

Natalie and Glenn's mother, Ruth, passed away in the spring from early-onset dementia. They'd moved her into a nursing home after Natalie started finding notes around the house saying things like "Turn off the stove," "Buy Earl Grey," or "Schedule a neuropsych evaluation." Since Ruth's death, the two sisters have avoided doing anything about her assets. Natalie has a habit of ignoring things till they become a problem, or until Glenn takes charge, and she hopes her sister will do so with this too. Out on the street, another cruiser speeds by. Through the window, Natalie sees Zane jogging up the driveway. It's probably been fifteen minutes. He bangs on the kitchen door and opens it without waiting for a response. "Situation," he says. "Right down the road."

"Give me five minutes?" Natalie says.

"This is real, not a drill."

Natalie stands. "I'll call in a favor with one of the computer techs," she says, before hurrying outside and into the rain.

Glenn Abbott can feel her husband following her every move as she takes the bowl of puff pastry from the mixer and puts it into the refrigerator. The tablet sits on the kitchen table, calling to her. Jake leans against the doorjamb, arms folded, blocking her retreat. "What was she doing here?" he asks.

"She's my sister." Glenn retrieves the tablet and faces him. "And where did you go last night?"

"I needed some air."

"I didn't hear you come in."

"It was late. I assumed you were in bed. Were you? In your bed?"

Glenn doesn't take the bait. Jake is worried that she'll tell Natalie what he did last night. She can still see the stain on the wall from where he'd hurled a glass of bourbon before coming at her, his face twisted with rage. She'd nearly flinched as memories of her father had flashed through her mind. But she'd held her ground. "Go someplace else," she'd said, staring him down till he'd put on his coat and driven away.

Now she faces off with him again. "I have an event today. I need to get ready."

Jake doesn't move, and Glenn hopes that he'll offer an apology, or even a kind word.

"What was that about a computer tech?" he asks.

"Someone posted something on my blog that scared me."

He pauses a beat before responding. "I'm glad Natalie's on it, then."

He steps aside, and Glenn ducks past him and into the next room. Wide floorboards creak beneath her feet.

"Good luck with your event," Jake says.

Glenn turns to him, her palms out, her body language open. No longer trapped in the kitchen, she wants to find a way to connect again. "What did I do?"

Jake pours himself coffee and takes a long sip. "You tell me."

"I'm sorry."

"For what?"

Glenn starts to say something and stops. "I apologized," she says. "Now it's your turn. You scared the shit out of me last night. And I won't tolerate violence. Not ever."

When Jake doesn't say anything, Glenn says, "Up to you," and heads through the house, to her office in the back, her sanctuary. Here bookshelves line the walls, along with photos of Glenn with Ina and Martha and Deb Perelman and other cooks she admires. Glenn had earned an MBA and worked as a consultant for years. Once Happy Time took off, once she had her book deal, she'd felt comfortable taking a chance and leaving behind the security of her job. The next few weeks will show her whether she's placed the right bet.

Her desk sits in front of a rain-streaked window that overlooks the veranda and their cottage. Even now, she can't help peering through the glass, searching for Patrick Leary, who's been staying in the cottage for the last month. Patrick is Jake's friend from high school, and Glenn knows exactly what she did and why Jake's angry, and why her husband has stayed in the guest room since the party on Saturday night. Glenn flirted with Patrick, right there in front of the neighbors and Jake's clients, all the people they know. But Glenn flirts with everyone, men, women, gay, straight, standing too close, fingers in the crook of an arm, laughing. It's part of how she became who she is. And she's been married to Jake for more than six years, and surely he's come to terms with that part of her. But maybe, she reminds herself, she had too much to drink on Saturday night. Maybe she went too far. And maybe, if she's really being honest, she's more interested in Patrick and his treacherous grin than she wants to admit. She can own all of that, but no lines have been crossed. Not yet. Not on her part.

She hears Jake's footsteps as he heads up the front stairs and into the guest room. She opens the tablet and finds the discussion-board post she showed Natalie earlier.

I'm watching you.

What she hadn't shown Natalie was the second post. This one reads, *I know what you did*, and includes a photo. It's of a *bûche de Noël* surrounded by candles, the same *bûche* Glenn had made for Saturday's party. The photo had been taken here in the house and posted to the site as a warning.

Glenn suspects Jake is the one who posted it.

She glances out the window toward the cottage. She checks the street. Patrick's Audi is parked where he normally leaves it, and she wonders where he's gone. She needs to get to Elmhurst soon for the influencer event. Her mother's house is there, on Starling Circle, empty. *Meet me,* she texts to Patrick, adding in the address. *I need to see you.*

* * *

Upstairs in the guest room, Jake Abbott hears the kitchen door open as his wife lugs a cooler to her SUV and drives off. He gathers clothes from where he piled them last night after he finally came home. The scent of citrus lingers on his white Oxford. He takes the clothing down the hall to the hamper in their walk-in closet, and changes into a pair of jeans and a new shirt. In the bathroom, he brushes his teeth and runs a hand through his hair. Back in the guest room, he takes the suitcase from under the bed and checks it one more time. The money is there. So is the new passport. And the gun.

He moves the suitcase out to his car and hides it in the trunk beneath a tarp. He'll be ready to go, as planned. He loves Glenn more than she knows, and he wishes that he were leaving on better terms with her. To be honest, he wishes he didn't have to leave at all, but if the plan goes smoothly, by tomorrow Patrick Leary will be dead and the world will believe Jake is, too. In the end, he hopes Glenn will at least be grateful for the publicity.

CHAPTER 4

Natalie Cavanaugh surveys the crime scene through the rain-streaked windshield as Zane eases onto the curb beside an abandoned building about a half mile from Glenn's house. Crime tape has already been stretched along the chain-link fence. Lights on cruisers flash, and two uniformed officers direct traffic through the busy intersection. A third uniformed officer keeps an eye on a growing crowd of onlookers on the other side of the street. A single news truck has set up shop, too, though Natalie suspects there may be more soon, depending on what they find inside. Nothing good happens in an abandoned building.

"Find out what the unis know," she says to Zane. "I'll head inside and talk to the medical examiner."

Zane ambles through the rain to one of the officers. Glenn has one thing right about Zane: the man is attractive. Charming, too. None of the uniformed officers ever seem to mind when Zane shows up on the scene, even when they have decades more experience on the job. Natalie wishes she could master that same ease.

Cold wetness seeps into her shoes as she ducks under the yellow tape, slips on a pair of booties and gloves, and signs the log. A battering ram leans against the wall beside a heavy metal door. Inside, trash and debris litter a cement floor that's seen better days.

"You find much?" she asks one of the crime techs.

"We've only been here for a few minutes," he says, "but it's pretty clear people have been in and out, probably for years. We found some used needles and a sleeping bag on the second floor. There'll be tons of evidence, but who knows if any of it's useful."

"Where's the body?"

"Through there. It's dark. You'll need the flashlight. Keep going to the left. You'll know it when you see it."

Natalie follows his directions toward voices that echo through the large, interconnected rooms. The occasional spot of sunlight shines from cracks in the plywood-covered windows. In the last room, her flashlight beam lands on the medical examiner steadying himself. The distinct stench of human flesh beginning to rot—decaying chicken with a note of cheap perfume—lingers on the damp air. A pair of crime techs stands by, and a stream of what appears to be fresh vomit arcs across the floor. The ME opens his eyes as Natalie approaches. "That your barf?" she asks.

"One of the responding officers," he says. "A rookie. But you think you've seen everything . . ."

He nods to a darkened corner. Natalie edges across the floor, not sure if she wants to see something else that she'll never be able to unsee. She steels herself and aims the flashlight into the shadows, where the remains of—someone—sit upright on a wooden chair, arms and legs bound with zip ties. Rusty blood spatter covers the wall behind the body and part of the floor. Brain matter too. A knit Boston Bruins hat clings to the victim's skull, though the eyes and the flesh around them seem to have been gnawed away. From what's left of the clothing, Natalie assumes the victim was a man, though she'll need the ME to confirm. In fact, she'll need the ME to confirm a lot because not much is left to identify. She snaps photos on her phone of the scene and the surrounding room for her own reference later on.

"ID?" she asks.

The ME shakes his head. "No wallet. No keys. Nothing that we've found yet. And we're lucky it's cold out too. My guess is that the body's been here for at least twenty-four hours pending results back at the office. If this were July . . ."

"Nature's meat locker," Natalie says. "Can I assume cause of death?"

"Bullet to the brain. I'll give you that one."

Outside, an ambulance blasts its siren. A moment later, two EMTs roll in a gurney and await instructions. Zane follows, striding across the factory floor with a scarf tied over his nose. "Hot dog!" he says. "It's like a pizza party in here."

"Shut up," Natalie says, snapping a photo and blinding him with the flash. "What else can you tell us?" she asks the ME.

"Male. Early to mid-thirties. Caucasian. Nice teeth."

"Expensive dental work?" Natalie asks.

"Exactly. Not your typical addict, if that's the angle you were considering. The kid who reported it says rats were feasting on the body. That explains some of the tissue damage. The rest is from the gunshot."

"Where's this kid?" Natalie asks Zane.

"Neighbor's house, according to the unis," Zane says. "Blue bungalow, next door. Goes to West Roxbury Prep. The unis tried to get her to talk, but she won't say anything or give her name."

"Call the school," Natalie says. "The headmaster will want to know what's going on here. Maybe he can help with a name, too. I'll go over there and see if I can get her to talk."

Natalie leaves the scene and heads outside, pausing the moment she steps into the fresh air. She turns her face to the sky as rain washes away some of the stench of death. She's been a homicide detective for more than a decade now but still hasn't gotten used to sights like the one inside and hopes she never will.

Across the street, a second news truck has pulled onto the sidewalk. A correspondent stands beneath an umbrella, checking his hair while the cameraman sets up. One benefit to working with Zane is that the camera loves him. Natalie will happily cede any publicity from this case, even if she winds up passing on the accolades, too. She's had enough publicity to last a lifetime. She keeps her head down and goes next door. In contrast to the factory, the house is neat and well-maintained. When Natalie knocks, the man who answers is as well-groomed as his front yard.

"She's in the kitchen," he says, waving Natalie into the house. "Hasn't said a word since I found her screaming at the front door."

"Thanks for being a good citizen. Most people don't like to get involved. Do you mind answering a few questions?"

"Shoot."

"Did you see anything strange going on next door?"

"Nothing beyond the usual. Sometimes I'll see kids hanging out or some unfortunate vermin. I work at home, and my office overlooks the backyard, so I'd see anything that happens, at least during the daytime."

Natalie gives him her card. "Call me if you think of anything else."

He leads her down a narrow hallway to where a girl slouches at a kitchen table, her back to the door, the sleeves of her white blouse rolled to her elbows. An untouched glass of water sits in front of her, and a burgundy blazer hangs off the back of her chair. She spins around, sweeping unruly dark hair out of her eyes, and it takes a moment for the two sides of Natalie's life to converge. "Mavis?" she says.

The girl leaps from the chair and embraces Natalie.

"I missed my algebra test."

"You know her?" the man asks.

Natalie holds Mavis—Glenn's daughter, Natalie's niece—as tight as she can.

"My mother is going to kill me," Mavis says.

"Somehow I doubt that," Natalie says.

CHAPTER 5

"I didn't do anything," Mavis whispers.

"No one thinks you did," Natalie says.

"I shouldn't have gone into that building." Mavis punches her own arm. "Stupid, stupid, stupid."

Natalie steps away, looking at her niece with her dark, tangled hair tumbling around her shoulders. The two of them are nearly the same height now, which seems impossible. Natalie remembers meeting Mavis for the first time, taking her from Glenn's arms, and believing she might break the fragile-seeming infant. All these years later, the girl reminds her of herself at the same age a tomboy, embarrassed at success, relentlessly critical of her own every move, and desperate to please. Thankfully, Natalie knows what her own twelve-year-old self would have wanted to hear.

"You're right," she says. "You shouldn't have gone into that building. It's dangerous, and you never know who might be hanging around a place like that, but in the grand hierarchy of bad deeds, we have a homicide up here." Natalie holds her hand overhead. "And you going into that building is down by the floor. Murder always trumps trespassing. And the good part is that you might be able to help me figure out what happened. That's making good out of bad, right?"

Mavis wipes her nose with the back of her hand. The man who owns the house materializes at their side with a box of tissues. Natalie mouths, "Thank you," as Mavis blows her nose loudly.

"Do you want coffee or something?" he asks.

"No, thank you. We'll let you get on with your day," Natalie says. "Thanks for your help, especially looking out for this one."

"It's the most exciting thing that's happened to me in years."

At the front door, rain continues to pelt the windows. Across the street, more news trucks have arrived. "Put your hat on and your hood up," Natalie says to her niece. "Leave this house like you live here, then go straight home. If someone tries to ask you a question, keep moving."

"What do I say to my mother?" Mavis asks.

"Tell her you have a headache. I'll meet you there in about five minutes and do the talking."

Mavis stands at the door for a moment before plunging into the rainy morning and scurrying along the sidewalk, past the press corps.

"There'll be a lot of folks from the media around today," Natalie says to the homeowner, "and they may come knocking on your door. Can you keep what you saw to yourself? Just say 'No comment' when they ask. They'll probably find out on their own that Mavis is my niece, but I'd like to hold it off as long as I can."

The man grins. "We were all in seventh grade once. No need to make the experience any worse than it already is, right?"

"Thanks again for your help." Natalie hopes she can trust him to keep his word.

At the crime scene, she finds Zane, who says, "Still haven't ID'd the body, but we're looking." He glances up the road. "Did I see your niece walking by?"

"Maybe," Natalie says. "She goes to West Roxbury Prep. How do you know Mavis?"

"Your sister posts photos of her all the time."

And that's the problem. Glenn will make headlines if they don't manage this case carefully, and Natalie hopes those headlines don't connect to her. She's not quite ready to even tell her partner that Mavis found the body. She will soon, but not yet.

"What did you learn from the kid?" Zane asks.

"Still working it. Hold down the fort here. I'll be back in a bit."

She hurries to her sister's house. When she arrives, she finds Mavis by herself in the kitchen, sitting on a stool and staring at the countertop.

"Where are your parents?"

Mavis shrugs.

Natalie pours herself a mug of coffee. "What do you want?"

"Coffee," Mavis mumbles. "Black."

Natalie slides a mug in front of her. "I should find your mother and tell her what happened."

Mavis slouches forward. "Please don't."

"It's not as though I have a choice, but I'll see if I can take the brunt of whatever comes our way."

Natalie dials Glenn's number, but the call goes straight to voicemail. She hangs up without leaving a message. *Call me*, she texts. "When did you start drinking coffee?"

"Today." Mavis takes a sip and makes a face. "Right now."

"Do you like it?"

"Not really."

"Want to tell me why you went into that building?"

Natalie waits for her niece to get her thoughts in order.

"I walk by it every day," Mavis finally says. "It was there. And I was curious."

"That's fair. Any other reason?"

Mavis shakes her head.

"You sure?"

"Yes."

"This part might be hard, but take a deep breath and tell me what you saw. Anything you remember. It'll help to hear it in your own words."

"I climbed through a window in the basement. Upstairs, there were like three big rooms all connected, but the windows were boarded up, so it was really dark, and all I had was the flashlight on my phone." Mavis closes her eyes. "I heard this sort of humming sound, and . . . it was so gross."

"Take your time," Natalie says.

"Something was moving in the shadows in the third room. It was like a blob quivering in the dark, and I thought I saw a person. When I turned the flashlight on, there were like a bazillion rats all over . . . all over it. And its eyes weren't there anymore, and neither was most of its face. So I ran. I thought that if I tripped, the rats might do the same thing to me."

"I shouldn't tell you this, but the victim was dead before the rats found him. He wasn't eaten alive, if that's what you're worried about."

"Do you know who it is?"

"Do you?"

Mavis shakes her head.

"We don't either. Not yet, at least, but we're working on it." Natalie sips her coffee and thinks about where to go next with her questions. She needs to be gentle with Mavis. Otherwise, the girl will shut down. "What else did you notice? Did you see anyone? Even something small might wind up being important."

"I just ran."

"The building is close to the school. You can't be the only one who's curious about it."

"The headmaster says that anyone who goes near it will be suspended for a week. I guess I got caught."

"When I was in seventh grade, if you'd told me to stay out of an abandoned building, I'd have gone into it as soon as I could. Who's bragged about going inside?"

Mavis bites her lip.

"I'll need to talk to anyone who's been in that building in the last week. It'll help us establish a timeline. Remember what I said about helping us with the investigation. This is what I'm talking about."

Mavis turns to Natalie. She has the look most witnesses have when they're about to spill, but Natalie hears footsteps on the back stairs, and the look evaporates. Jake enters the kitchen and stops short when he sees them.

"Mavis?" he says. "Why aren't you at school? And, Natalie, I thought you ran off to play Nancy Drew."

Natalie almost misses the jab. She's too distracted by the need to tell her brother-in-law that his daughter found a dead body in a rat-infested building. But Mavis says, "Don't be sexist, Dad. It's not a good look."

"Right on," Natalie says.

"My bad," Jake says.

Natalie leads Jake into the next room, takes a deep breath, and dives into the basics of what happened.

"Why would she go into that building?" he asks.

"You could try playing Nancy Drew yourself and find out more. Or maybe Veronica Mars?"

Jake rushes into the kitchen. Natalie gives them a moment; when she returns, she hears her niece say, "I'm fine, Dad," complete with an eye roll in her voice that summons up all of her inner teenager.

Natalie's phone rings.

"Is that Glenn?" Jake asks.

"It's my partner. I need to take this." Natalie clicks into the call. "What do you have?"

"We found a wallet," Zane says. "Cambridge address. Name is Bennet Jones."

Natalie almost drops the phone. "Say that again."

Zane repeats the name. Natalie glances to where Jake sits with an arm over his daughter's shoulder while Mavis tells him what happened this morning. She's getting into the story now, as she recaps the part about the rats. "Disgusting," Jake says.

"I'll be there soon," Natalie says, letting the phone fall to her side.

Jake looks up.

"There's been a development," she says to him, "and I need to get back to the crime scene." She touches Mavis's cheek. "You okay?"

"I'll survive."

"You were brave today. We can talk more later."

Outside, in the rain, Natalie only makes it a few yards before she hears Jake behind her. "What's going on?" he asks.

"Did you tell her to go into that factory?" Natalie asks.

"What possible reason would I have to do that?" Jake asks.

Natalie wants the answer to his question, too, because whether he's figured it out or not, Jake has become a suspect in a murder, if not the prime suspect. Jake knows the victim. So does Natalie. Bennet Jones worked at Jake's company, and six years ago, Bennet introduced Jake to Glenn.

"This is a homicide." Natalie hopes her voice doesn't betray her. "Now, for whatever reason, your daughter's involved. Get ready. The questions have only just begun."

Jake watches Natalie as she sprints to the end of the driveway and turns the corner. He stands in the rain for a moment, till his shirt is soaked through and he's begun to shiver. Back inside, he tears into an almond croissant. He's barely eaten since Saturday, and he's grateful that Glenn is off, wherever she's gone. Mavis isn't his biological daughter, but that hasn't mattered to him, or to her, he hopes. And he wants these last hours together. He puts an arm around her and almost begins to sob.

"Am I grounded?" Mavis asks.

It takes a moment to compute what she's saying. She's too young to understand that today's infraction won't register in a lifetime of indiscretions. He ruffles her hair and manages to earn a smile. It's important to prioritize, to stop and have fun in life, to appreciate the things you have. That's one of the lessons he'd wanted to impart to Mavis. Now all he wants is to make these final hours with her last. He won't have many more of them.

Mavis can't possibly know how bad things can get or how small mistakes transform into larger ones. Jake works as a CPA. He also manages Mavis's soccer club, including the club's finances. Parents around here take sports seriously. Jake took over the role of team manager soon after he met Glenn and they got married. Soon after that, they moved into this enormous house and enrolled Mavis in a school that costs forty grand a year in tuition. He hoped soccer would help him bond with her, as her new father. He would never have guessed how much money goes through a kids' soccer club, but parents know that sports can be a gateway to later success, and they're willing to cough up the funds to be sure their kids get a piece of that success. The annual budget for the club is over two hundred thousand dollars. Jake also wouldn't have guessed how little oversight there was of those funds. For the last year, he's been creating false statements for board meetings, ones that he suspects most of the parents either don't bother looking at or don't know how to read. He's also dodged payments from various vendors till some have begun to level threats at him. It started with a bad decision, one that snowballed until he didn't have a way out, not till recently. Not till Bennet introduced him to Patrick Leary, who showed up offering a lifeline.

Now, here in the kitchen, Jake opens the chess set. "It's too wet to kick the ball around," he says.

"What about my algebra test?" Mavis asks.

"It'll be there tomorrow. And your teacher will understand."

"Don't let me win."

"I haven't let you win for a long time."

As Jake sets up the board, he remembers watching Patrick Leary with Glenn at the party on Saturday, the way the man ran his hand over Glenn's back, the way she stood too close and laughed at his jokes. Later, Jake followed Patrick to the bar. "What can I get you?" Patrick asked.

Jake leaned in close and whispered, "Stay away from my wife."

"Sorry, buddy," Patrick said, patting him on the cheek. "You don't call the shots. Not anymore."

CHAPTER 6

Lieutenant Angela White has the day off, and she's counting down the seconds till her wife, Cary, leaves with their eight-year-old son, Isaiah, and she can start her *Real Housewives* marathon. Isaiah's taking his own sweet time getting ready, though, like he does whenever he hasn't finished his homework. He has his laptop open and frantically works through an assignment while moving between tabs on his browser.

"You'll finish quicker if you stop multitasking," Angela says.

"Two-minute warning," Cary says as she shoves a lunch into his backpack.

Angela plops onto the sofa. She hasn't bothered to change out of her pajamas and doesn't plan to, not before noon, at least. George, their German shepherd mix, jumps up and burrows beside her. "Damn dog," she says, as she scratches his belly. "If you're lucky, I'll take you to the beach later," she adds, which earns her a face lick.

Cary makes one last sweep of the living room before grabbing her own bag. "Shut it down," she says to Isaiah.

"West Roxbury's trending," he says.

"You should not be on Twitter," Cary says, as Angela feels her day off slipping away.

"What's happening in West Roxbury?" she asks.

"Homicide," Isaiah says.

"Let's go," Cary says.

Isaiah shuts the laptop just as Angela's phone rings.

Glenn Abbott pulls into Elmhurst, a ten-mile drive from her home in West Roxbury, but a world away. Here, restaurants and independent businesses line a small downtown, complete with brick sidewalks lit by gas lamps. Glenn grew up in this town, one where she's remembered more for being the girl whose father was murdered than for captaining the debate team. It's not a label she loves, and she supposes it's one of the reasons she chose the bookstore here for next week's launch. Unlike Natalie, Glenn wants to lean in to that past and reclaim it. She wants the sad eyes and stares that she imagines whenever she comes to this town to be replaced with something else. She'd be satisfied with indifference. Maybe this homecoming will be the first step.

She parks on the street and checks her phone, hoping for a response from Patrick Leary, but the only text she has is from Natalie, asking her to call. Glenn suddenly wishes she hadn't shown her sister the posts on her blog. Natalie is a cop through and through, and if Jake did write the posts, Natalie won't be able to look at him anymore with any shades of gray.

Glenn gets out of the SUV and lugs the cooler from the back. It contains all the ingredients she'll need for today. The bookstore has a coffee shop attached to it and sits across the street from a real estate office. In the shop window, a poster for next week's launch shows Glenn wearing a Happy Time apron and slicing into a raspberry and chocolate baked Alaska. When Glenn looks at that photo, the only thing she can see is her bright orange hair and photo-corrected teeth. They sparkle white. And they feel like pieces of her that have been cut away and replaced, a feeling she notes and tucks away for later. She glances across the street. A woman with long blond hair and wearing a red raincoat stands under an umbrella in the doorway to the real estate office. "Nice poster," the woman calls.

Glenn puts on her public mask, waves, and steps inside. The bookstore manager greets her with a hug. "We have everything ready," he says, lifting one end of the cooler and leading her downstairs to where a mini kitchen has been set up, complete with a mixer and blowtorch so that Glenn can whip up the baked Alaska from the book cover. Today, she's hosting a gathering of fellow bloggers and Instagrammers from around the area who will hopefully post photos of the event and help drive interest in the book before it publishes next week. She's done the same thing for many of them at similar events. "How're preorders?" she asks the manager.

"You'll be happy," he says. "We're already at capacity for next week. You probably could have launched at a bigger venue."

"Then I wouldn't have supported my local bookstore," Glenn says.

The manager leaves her to get settled, and Glenn spends the next half hour going through her checklists of equipment and ingredients. She pre-made the components of the baked Alaska, including the base and ice cream. All she'll need to do for the event is whip up a meringue, assemble, and pose for photos. As she finishes, she hears the clatter of high heels on the stairs behind her and turns to see Charlotte Todd.

Charlotte is in her early thirties, a few years younger than Glenn. She has curly, honey-colored hair and a designer bag hanging from one arm. She's a lawyer, one who gave up practicing criminal law to go into PR.

"Big day," Charlotte says, enfolding Glenn in a hug.

"I never could have done it without you."

Jake introduced Charlotte to Glenn just as Happy Time took off, when Glenn needed someone to help build her public profile. Since then, they've become friends and associates. Charlotte helped Glenn navigate the world of media. Without her, Glenn isn't sure she'd have landed an agent or the book deal, and she certainly wouldn't have made any TV or radio appearances. She'd probably still be writing recipes and sharing them with the few hundred devoted followers she'd had up until about a year ago when the site started trending.

Now she extracts herself from Charlotte's embrace. The scent of perfume wafts around them—floral, citrus, familiar. Charlotte specializes in fixing things when they go wrong, and after the last few days, after those posts to her message boards, Glenn wants to be sure nothing goes wrong. At least not before the book publishes. "This is all set," she says. "We don't start till one. Let's grab coffee."

Upstairs, they take a seat in the window of the café and gossip for a moment. Rain pelts the glass. Charlotte tells Glenn about her yoga instructor who goes to BC Law. "He's giving me private lessons."

Charlotte lives the single life, cosmos and handsome men and spa retreats to the Berkshires, the kind of life that Glenn sometimes wishes for, even though she's been a mother now for more than a decade. "I thought you hit it off with Zane at the party on Saturday," she says.

"The cop? I gave it my best, but whatever I was selling, he wasn't buying." Charlotte rips open a wad of sugar packets and stirs them into her coffee. "What about you? That neighbor seemed a bit too keen."

"Patrick? It was nothing."

"Didn't look like nothing to me."

Glenn doesn't want to talk about Patrick, not yet at least. "I need to show you something."

"That's what I'm here for," Charlotte says.

Glenn opens her tablet and glances around the café before showing Charlotte the posts, including the one with the photo.

"*I know what you did,*" Charlotte reads. "We're back to the neighbor, right? Patrick? Did you two do something you shouldn't have?"

Glenn shakes her head.

"Then what is there to worry about?"

Glenn leans forward. She feels paranoid, which, she supposes, is what was intended by the person who posted those messages. She nearly tells Charlotte about the fight with Jake, about the glass he hurled against the wall. She nearly tells her that after Jake left, she stood with her feet rooted to the kitchen floor as the scent of bourbon transported her to another night, another time, till she finally mopped up as much of the liquor as she could. Afterward, she made her way through the house and out the back door. Patrick sat outside the cottage, smoking a cigarette.

"Everything okay in there?" he asked.

"He knows." Glenn's words froze on the cold night air.

Patrick dropped the cigarette and ground it out with his heel. "What does he know?"

Glenn pulled her cardigan closed. "You know too," she'd said before going inside and locking the door.

But Glenn doesn't tell any of that to Charlotte. Instead, she says, "I think Jake posted these messages."

Charlotte hands back the tablet. "Jake wouldn't do that."

"How would you know?"

"Because I've seen the way he looks at you," Charlotte says. "Jake's besotted. Do me a favor. Whatever happens, don't forget that."

Glenn reads through the posts again, but Charlotte's reassurances don't make her feel better. If Jake didn't post the messages, someone else did. And that means she might have a bigger problem than she realized.

When Natalie returns to the crime scene, she finds Zane chatting with two uniformed officers. The paramedics maneuver a gurney with a body bag on it out of the building and into the back of a waiting ambulance. Across the street, news cameras roll. Natalie can only imagine what they'll spin this story into once they learn that Mavis found her father's dead business associate, and whatever happens, she wants to control how that message hits the news.

"Can I take a look at the vic?" she asks the medical examiner as she steps into the back of the ambulance.

"Be my guest."

The ME unzips the top of the body bag. The victim still wears the knit Bruins hat over empty eye sockets and gnawed flesh. Natalie tries to see Bennet Jones's face in the bones of this ruined corpse, but there's too much damage. She reaches out to remove the hat. The ME stops her. "Evidence," he says.

That's right.

"Call me as soon as you confirm the ID," she says.

"Will do."

Natalie clambers into the rain, and the officers hold traffic as the ambulance swerves away. She beckons Zane toward their car. "Let's go," she says.

Zane puts a hand up to tell her to wait.

"Now," she says.

One of the uniforms shuffles his feet. The other one grins and mumbles something. Even from this far away, Natalie can tell they're calling her a bitch, or worse, but she's learned to ignore the comments. To his credit, Zane seems to admonish them before trotting to her side.

"The Cambridge PD are on their way to Bennet Jones's apartment," he says. "They'll let us know what they find."

"We should still be there. I'll drive."

Zane tosses her the keys and slides into the passenger's seat. Natalie blasts the siren and maneuvers around the line of cars waiting to get through the tight intersection. Zane reports in on the radio and rambles off an address in Cambridgeport that Natalie doesn't need. In front of them, most vehicles ease to the side of the road as she presses her foot to the floor.

"What do we know?" she asks.

"Maybe a drug deal gone bad," Zane says.

The Bennet Jones Natalie had met hadn't seemed the type to do drugs, but Natalie's also been a cop long enough to know that even the most straitlaced people have hidden lives. "My guess is that building is used for lots of things beyond drug deals," she says. "Teen drinking, sex, a shelter for the homeless. The question we'll need to answer is why the vic was there in the first place."

Ahead, the light turns red. She doesn't slow as she careens through.

"Bennet Jones is already dead," Zane says. "Let's not join him. It doesn't matter how quickly we get there."

Natalie ignores him and speeds through another light. Zane squeezes his eyes shut. "Did you get anything from the kid?" he asks.

"She said it was dark, and she didn't see much beyond the wall of rats."

"Doesn't your niece go to West Roxbury Prep, too? I bet the kids at her school know everything that goes on in that building."

Sooner rather than later, Natalie needs to tell Zane that Mavis found the body, but first she needs to know more about what they're dealing with. She speeds through another red light. "Why do I get the feeling that you've met Mavis?" she asks. Out of the corner of her eye, she sees Zane blush as she nearly crashes into an orange hatchback. She remembers Glenn saying that Zane had texted to tell her that they were in the neighborhood this morning, and everything falls into place. "You fucker," she says. "You went to my sister's party this weekend."

"I thought you'd be there," Zane says. "I showed up, and you never even came. Your sister tried to set me up with her friend Charlotte, too. Talk about awkward."

"You didn't think to mention it till now? We've spent nearly every waking minute together since Monday morning."

"There hasn't been a good time."

"You could have said, *I was here on Saturday for your sister's party* when you dropped me off this morning. Come to think of it, you could have told me the minute you got the invitation. Let me tell you something about my wonderful sister Glenn: she loves to insert herself into my life, and I don't like it. I want my personal and professional lives to be separate. And don't lie to me again. Ever."

Natalie careens across the BU Bridge into Cambridge as an awkward silence fills the car. She turns onto a narrow, tree-lined street and stops in front of a four-story brick apartment building. A young Cambridge cop waits for them at the building's front entrance.

Zane glances at his notepad. "Bennet Jones is on the second floor," he says.

Natalie suddenly regrets making such a big deal about honesty and Glenn's party invitation. She still needs to tell Zane about Mavis, of course. She also needs to confess that she's been here before, to this block, to this very building. She used to date Bennet Jones.

CHAPTER 7

Glenn had set Natalie up with Bennet a year ago. "He's nice," she'd said. "Have a drink. See if you have anything in common."

Natalie hadn't met many civilian men secure enough to date a cop. Maybe it was the gun, maybe it was the shield. She wasn't sure, and she couldn't begin to explain it to her sister. Instead, she said, "Jake's brotastic friend won't want anything to do with me."

"Bennet's not one of those guys," Glenn said. "He's in IT. Nothing brotastic about him at all." She plucked the pins from Natalie's hair. "And when you do meet, put on something... feminine. Please? Give yourself a fighting chance."

When Natalie met Bennet for a drink, she wore her hair up, along with a men's blazer and sneakers, but that drink turned into three drinks. He was geeky and eager, but he also knew to wear blue on a first date to make his eyes pop, and she said yes when he invited her over for a nightcap. "I hope you don't mind dogs," he said, as he opened the apartment door, and a black-and-white terrier mix ran into the hallway. "This is Rowdy."

Natalie lifted the dog and let him lap at her face. "I hope Rowdy's not the jealous type," she said.

"Maybe we'll find out."

When Natalie woke beside Bennet the next morning, Rowdy was balanced on her chest, his tail wagging. She watched Bennet sleep and told herself she could get used to this if she wasn't careful. Then she slipped out of bed and took Rowdy for a walk.

Now, in the car, Zane turns to her. "Next time Glenn asks me to a party, I'll let you know," he says. "We can't work together if we don't trust each other."

"Sorry, I overreacted."

"No more secrets," Zane says.

Every cop partnership has secrets, Natalie reminds herself. Every single one.

She gets out of the car and meets the Cambridge officer in front of the apartment building. He's young, maybe even a rookie. "Is Cambridge sending a detective?" Natalie asks.

"I'm all you've got. What's the deal?"

"Homicide in West Roxbury. Shooting. There were brains everywhere." Natalie jerks a thumb at Zane. "This one lost his lunch and contaminated the scene."

"Shut up," Zane says. "Someone hurled, but it wasn't me."

"I'm Aldrich," the officer says.

"I'm Perez. This is Cavanaugh," Zane says, while Natalie makes a show of finding 2B before ringing the bell. When no one answers, she rings all eight of the apartments repeatedly till a woman's voice comes over the intercom. "Fire department," Natalie says. "Can you buzz me in?"

The front door clicks open. Natalie takes to the stairs, flashing back to her first time here, to returning from her walk with Rowdy. She'd bought bagels and coffee and found Bennet in the kitchen wearing blue pajama bottoms and a Decemberists T-shirt. "I thought you'd snuck out," he said.

"You thought I ditched you and took your dog?" Natalie asked.

"Sometimes I think the worst of people," he said.

The woman who buzzed them in stands in the doorway to apartment 2A. She's twenty-something, with dark hair pulled into a messy ponytail, yoga pants on the bottom and business casual on top. "I'm on a conference call," she says, pointing to earbuds. "But I'm muted. What do you need? I thought there was a fire?"

"Would you have buzzed in a cop?" Natalie asks. "Bennet Jones. Apartment 2B. When was the last time you saw him?"

"Maybe over the weekend?"

Natalie pounds on Bennet's door. On the other side, Rowdy's nails clack on the wood floors. He yaps and paws at the door.

"Has he been barking much?" Natalie asks.

The woman sighs. "No more than usual."

"Do you have keys?"

The woman holds up a finger. She clicks off MUTE. "I can get you that spreadsheet by noon. Thanks." She clicks back onto MUTE. "We don't really know each other that well."

Rowdy barks again. The ME had estimated the time of death at twenty-four hours, or more. If the body is Bennet's, Rowdy will be hungry. Thirsty too.

"Mr. Jones," Natalie shouts.

"Did something happen to him?" the woman asks.

Natalie catches Zane's eye. "Why don't you go into your apartment?" he says, guiding the woman out of the hallway and through her door. "We'll let you know if we need you."

Rowdy barks again.

Natalie takes a step back.

"What are you doing?" Zane asks.

"We have probable cause."

"Do we?"

"The guy might be hurt."

"The guy's dead," Zane says.

"All the more reason to get inside."

Natalie kicks the door. It buckles. She kicks again. This time, the wood splinters. Zane takes his place to the side of the door, and on the third kick, the door flies open, and Rowdy rushes at them. Natalie scoops him off the ground.

"Boston Police," Zane shouts into the apartment.

Natalie holds Rowdy toward Aldrich. "Do you mind taking him?" she asks.

They're in Aldrich's jurisdiction. The officer has a vested interest in seeing what two Boston cops find at a scene he'll ultimately be responsible for, but he takes the dog and seems to defer to Natalie's experience the way she sometimes wishes Zane would. "Back in a few," she says.

She edges into the narrow front hallway, with Zane right behind her. The apartment hasn't changed since her last visit, with its sparse furnishings, enormous flatscreen TV, and a few pieces of art that dot the walls. In the kitchen, a coffee cup sits in the sink, and Rowdy's water bowl is nearly full. She toes open the bedroom door. Not much has changed here, either. The bed is made, and a few clothes—men's only, Natalie notes—lie across a chair. The room smells of fabric softener and sweat. In the bathroom, the toilet seat is up.

"What do you think this guy does?" Zane asks. "He has expensive taste. Look at the finishes in the kitchen and bathroom. None of that's cheap. And the artwork." He nods to an oil painting, abstract with planes of blue and circles of red. "That looks like a Philip Guston."

"A print?" Natalie asks.

"Seems original to me."

"I'll take your word for it."

In the second bedroom, an open laptop sits on a home workstation. Natalie taps the mouse. The screen lights up asking for a passcode. "Someone's been on this recently enough that it hasn't powered off," Zane says.

"Not if he changed the settings."

"Well, there's the coffee cup and the dog bowl. If the vic hasn't been here, someone else has."

Zane's phone rings. He listens for a moment and gives their location. "That was the lieutenant," he says. "She's on her way here. When she loses it, don't forget that you're the one who kicked in the door."

Natalie swears under her breath. The last thing she needs is to have Lieutenant Angela White involved in this case. She also bites her tongue before asking why the lieutenant called Zane instead of her. Natalie is the senior detective. The lieutenant should be calling her, but she knows the lieutenant and Zane are close.

"She wants to run interference with Cambridge," Zane says. "She's also worried the case might blow up in the press."

A voice echoes down the hall.

"Sir," Aldrich says, "this is an active crime scene."

Footsteps approach. A man turns the corner wearing a form-fitting blue sweatshirt. He's breathing heavily from a run. "What the fuck are you doing?" he asks.

"Ben?" Zane says.

Natalie steps around Zane and into the man's view. "You two know each other?" she asks.

"We met this weekend," Zane says. "At your sister's party."

"Bennet . . ." Natalie begins.

But he cuts her off. "Why don't you tell me what you're doing in my apartment."

"We thought you were dead," Zane says.

CHAPTER 8

At noon, Olivia Knowles steps out of the real estate office and into downtown Elmhurst. She tucks a strand of blond hair behind her ear, pulls her red raincoat closed, and dashes across the street to the café where Paul waits for her. Paul is trim and fit and approaching seventy. He owns the real estate agency where Olivia works. From time to time, he threatens to retire and sell the business to her, but she can't imagine that he'll ever actually make the move. She doesn't want him to, either. She'd much rather have Paul in the limelight.

She slides into the seat beside him. He's already bought her an Americano with skim milk. A single Splenda packet leans against the mug, waiting. She tears it open.

If Olivia has a best friend, it would probably be Paul, though she sometimes wonders if she'd make his top ten. The only time they see each other away from the office is during these coffee breaks, where they talk about work. Olivia likes it that way. Now they talk through the few remaining listings lingering from the fall. "That Mueller house is a hundred thousand over reality," Paul says. "Want me to have a go at them?"

"Sure," Olivia says.

He makes a few notes in his files.

By the register, a poster on an easel advertises Glenn Abbott's new book. She smiles beside a baked Alaska, her hair brassy and orange, and to Olivia, it feels as if Glenn is looking right at her. Paul follows her gaze. "She's here," he says. "Right now. She's doing an event downstairs. She went to high school in town, too. Her mother lived in that colonial over on Starling Circle."

Like all the best real estate agents, Paul knows nearly everything that's ever happened in this town, or at least he believes he does. It's why he's so much more successful than Olivia. Now he adds, "It was a shame what happened."

He probably wants Olivia to ask what he means so that he can fill her in on the gossip, but she makes him wait. Even Paul can't know *everything*. He doesn't know that Olivia knew Glenn's mother, Ruth Cavanaugh, and her story. She stirs her coffee and takes a long sip. Finally, she says, "I bet it was before my time."

Paul points to the poster, to Glenn's headshot. "Her father was murdered, twenty, maybe thirty years ago. Alan Cavanaugh. He worked at the community college teaching English. At first, the police thought Ruth Cavanaugh killed him. Why wouldn't they focus on the wife? But it turned out Alan was having an affair with the neighbor. A woman named Diane Sykes. She bashed in his head before killing herself."

"Sounds awful," Olivia says.

"It was. For a long time, it was the only thing anyone ever talked about around here." Paul leans back in his chair and glances toward the poster. "Some people still said Ruth did it, even after the police closed the case. I'm surprised Glenn wants to stir any of that up again."

"These little towns," Olivia says. "They always have their secrets."

"That's our biggest one," Paul says as his phone beeps. He glances at the message. "Duty calls."

After he leaves, Olivia sits for a while. As one o'clock approaches, a dozen or so women arrive, greeting each other with outsized hellos before heading downstairs. Olivia tries to shake away the feeling of being watched, but Glenn Abbott's eyes seem to follow her from the poster. She gets ready to leave but finds herself following the women instead, edging down the stairs to where Glenn stands at a makeshift kitchen with a mixer and a blowtorch. The women who'd come in earlier sit in rows of folding chairs, their phones out, snapping photos. "Join us!" Glenn says.

Olivia slides into a chair in the last row. The woman beside her smiles, mouths, *Exciting!* and snaps a photo.

Glenn turns on the mixer and pours in egg whites from a plastic container. She crosses her eyes as she tries to speak over the noise, and the women laugh. When the egg whites are whipped, Glenn holds the clear bowl upside down over her head and pauses to let them take photos. "Perfect!" she says. "And God help you if you're wrong."

Olivia takes a photo along with everyone else. Glenn goes through the steps of creating a baked Alaska like the one on the cover of the book, complete with vanilla and chocolate ice cream sandwiching a layer of raspberry purée. She encases the whole thing with meringue and uses the blowtorch to brown the billowy peaks. When she finishes, she poses with a chef's knife as she cuts slices. The knife is coated with raspberry sauce. "I can't tell you how much I appreciate your support," she says, putting the knife aside.

A woman with curly hair pops open a bottle of champagne and says, "Thanks so much for letting your followers know about the book, but enough photos, right? Let's hang out!"

That's Olivia's cue to leave, but before she can make her exit, someone touches her arm.

"Do we know each other?" Glenn asks.

"Sorry," Olivia says. "I didn't realize this was a private event. I'll get out of here."

"Don't worry about it. The baked Alaska will melt if we don't finish it."

Up close, Glenn's makeup looks thick, and her hair color brash.

"I was friends with your mother," Olivia says. She takes a business card from her purse and hands it to Glenn. "Let me know if you want to sell the house."

Glenn looks at the card and back at Olivia. "Oh," she says, the smile gone.

Bennet Jones takes his hat off and runs his hand through his hair, while Rowdy laps at his sweaty skin. He sets the dog down and keeps his focus on Zane, something that would normally set Natalie off. Today, she's happy to let her partner take the lead.

"Can you tell us if you've been to West Roxbury lately?" Zane asks.

"You kicked in my door," Bennet says. "Why don't you start with telling me why?"

Zane steps forward. He meets Bennet's eyes. "We're investigating a homicide, Mr. Jones. You're connected to the crime scene. You can see why we have questions." He waits a moment, letting Bennet absorb the information.

"Who was killed?" Bennet asks.

Zane ignores the question. "West Roxbury?"

Bennet glances at Natalie. "Yeah, on Saturday, when I saw *you* at Jake's party."

"I mean since then," Zane says. "It's Tuesday. What have you done between Saturday and right this very minute? And let me put it this way, the more time you can account for, the better it'll be for you."

"Do I need a lawyer?" Bennet asks.

"Tell us what you can," Natalie says, her voice soft. Bennet shoots her a glare.

"I didn't do much on Sunday. I was wrecked from the night before. Rowdy and I hung out and watched a game."

"Did you see anyone but your dog?" Zane asks.

Bennet shakes his head.

"Did you say hello to the neighbor or go to the dog park or talk to anyone on the phone? We'll be able to find out where you were anyway once we pull your phone records."

Bennet coughs. He crosses the kitchen, fills a glass with water, and drinks it down in one gulp. Natalie can see him starting to panic, like a witness caught in a lie. "Tell us what happened," she says.

"I did go back to West Roxbury on Sunday. I guess I forgot. I lost my wallet at the party. Jake and I looked for it. Afterward, I spent the day canceling my credit cards."

Zane flips his notepad closed. "And when was the last time you saw the wallet?"

"Saturday night. I must have left without it, or someone stole it from my coat pocket."

"Was there any activity on the cards?" Natalie asks.

He turns to her. "What are you doing here anyway?" he asks, and he's not talking to a detective.

Thankfully, Rowdy's ears perk up. A growl starts in his chest. He dashes out of the kitchen and down the front hall. A few seconds later, Lieutenant Angela White strides into the kitchen with Rowdy under one arm. "He's a nipper," she says.

"Only with strangers," Bennet says.

Angela looks him over. "Mr. Jones? We thought you might be dead. First good news of the day. Let's hope for more of it."

"Mr. Jones claims that he lost his wallet on Saturday night at a party in West Roxbury," Zane says. "He spent Sunday looking for it and canceling his credit cards."

Bennet's claims would be easy enough to confirm.

"Mr. Jones," Angela says, "have you ever been in an abandoned factory on LaGrange? It's over in West Roxbury. And don't lie. We'll find out if you've been there before."

Bennet's face has lost all color. He shakes his head.

"We'll need to find out who else was at that party," Angela says.

Zane clears his throat. "I was there."

Angela puts Rowdy down and folds her arms. "That complicates things. Please tell me you didn't know each other before."

"We'd never met before," Zane says, quickly. "But we chatted for a while."

"What were you doing at the same party? Who was the host?"

Zane starts to answer and stops. He glances at Natalie and then at Bennet.

Bennet holds up his hands. "Don't look at me."

Natalie needs to get ahead of this before she loses even more control of the situation. "Stop talking. Everyone. Lieutenant, two minutes. Please. It's important."

Angela steps right up to Zane, and Natalie can see that the lieutenant is tempted to tell him off for compromising the case, right there in front of a potential suspect. But she stops short of saying anything and waves Natalie into the hallway, where Aldrich, the Cambridge officer, still waits. Angela gives him a card. "You can head out. We're finishing up, but do me a favor. Call me if you notice anything here. And I'll take care of keeping Cambridge in the loop."

The officer heads down the stairs. After the door closes, Angela shakes her head. "I'm going to kill Zane one of these days. And don't quote me on that, but he's too hotheaded. He's the one who kicked in the door, isn't he? Also, you're the senior officer here. You know he asked to work with you, right? He said he needed a mentor, so take the lead. Zane's good, but he's been a detective for about five seconds, and he's green and would benefit from learning a thing or two about patience and being methodical, two of your best qualities."

Like Natalie, Angela White has been in Homicide for more than a decade. Unlike Natalie, though, Angela has risen through the ranks, replacing the former lieutenant last year when he re tired. Angela and Natalie used to be closer, if only by necessity as two of the few women in the department. Since this latest promotion, Natalie's sensed a growing distance between them. She suspects it will only get worse in about thirty seconds.

The lieutenant says, "What else do we know about this case? Still no ID? Do we have a time of death?"

"The ME estimated at least twenty-four hours," Natalie says. "He couldn't be more specific without an autopsy."

"That means it could be more, so this guy Bennet Jones could have killed the vic Saturday night while he was palling around with Perez, lost his wallet at the crime scene, and spent the last three days in a frenzy. A good DA will have a field day with a conflict like this one. This case is already all over social media and the news."

"Are you taking Perez off the case?"

Angela seems to consider the question for a moment and shakes her head. "Who knows? Maybe it'll get me in hot water. And I hate being second-guessed, but do you know what I hate even more? Making decisions based on PR crap. What do we know about Bennet Jones?"

Natalie takes a deep breath. She needs to get this over with. "He works with my brother-in-law," she says, closing her eyes and preparing for the barrage to come. When the lieutenant doesn't speak, Natalie opens one eye and then the other, only to see Angela staring at her. When the lieutenant finally speaks, she says, "I had a boss once who told me that as you get older, there's nothing sexier than competence."

"And I'm not sexy right now?"

"Not in the slightest."

"I could go to HR over that comment."

"Shut up. Let me guess the rest. That sister of yours, the one that's been all over TV lately—if I remember correctly, she lives in West Roxbury. The party was at her house, and you were there too?"

"I was not there," Natalie says, quickly. "I hate parties."

"We have that in common at least. Are you friends with Jones?"

Natalie grimaces. Now comes the bad part. "We went on a few dates about a year ago."

"You went on a *few dates*," Angela says. "You realize that Bennet Jones is our prime suspect, right? In a homicide. This can't get worse."

It can, though, and as Natalie puts the words together in her head, she realizes how bad they sound. "There's one more little thing. My niece was the one who found the body this morning. I interviewed her and didn't tell Zane, so don't get mad at him. I should have spoken up, but I panicked, and everything kept getting worse."

Angela starts to say something and stops. She takes a step away and returns. "Your niece found a dead body, and the only clue to identifying the vic was a wallet that belongs to someone who works with her father and you used to date. Did I get everything right?"

Natalie knows better than to say anything at this point.

"And is there anything else you're leaving out?"

Natalie shakes her head.

"Where's your niece right now?"

"With her father. At home."

"Why don't you wait for us outside," Angela says. "I'll finish up with Jones. And to be clear, you're off the case. Don't call your sister. Don't call your brother-in-law. Don't do anything. I'll be taking the lead going forward because this will be a shit show the minute it hits the news."

Back in the apartment, Angela notes Bennet Jones's stunned expression, his skin pasty-white against the black frames of his glasses. It doesn't look as though he's moved since she'd left the room. Zane stands by the window, peering out at the rain. Angela would almost have sympathy for Jones if she hadn't seen the same expression a thousand times before. This man hadn't woken this morning expecting his entire life to change. If he's guilty, he also probably hadn't expected to kill the man they'd found in that abandoned building. Most murderers didn't. Unfortunately for him, no matter what had happened, no matter how that wallet found its way where it did, Bennet Jones will be at the center of this investigation, at least till they find someone else to focus on. But the wallet won't be enough for a conviction. There are too many scenarios that a defense attorney could exploit to explain how it got there.

"You were at Jake Abbott's house on Saturday," she says. "How do you know him?"

"She told you?" Bennet asks.

"I'm asking the questions," Angela says.

"I work with him. We went to college together. We've been friends for fifteen years."

"What do you do?"

"Jake and I work together. He's a CPA, and I do IT."

"So you work *for* him," Angela says.

"Sure."

"Things good between you and your boss?"

"They're fine," Bennet says. "It's a nice place to work."

"How about his daughter? Do you know her?"

"Mavis, of course. She was at the party too. She was serving cocktails with her friend."

"Isn't she like ten years old?" Angela asks.

"Take it up with her parents."

Angela has about a million questions for this guy. She could ask him to come to the station, but she doesn't have enough for an arrest, not until they establish a better timeline. Besides, she wants to check to see that those credit cards have been canceled and get a look at Bennet Jones's phone records. Right now, the most important next step is to get to West Roxbury and talk to Mavis Abbott and her parents, and Angela will be curious to see if Jones makes a call to his boss after they leave. She crouches down and scratches Rowdy under his neck. "Don't go anywhere, Mr. Jones," she says. "Understood? We'll be back with more questions."

She nods to Zane. He takes the cue and follows her down the hall.

"What am I supposed to do about the door you kicked in?" Bennet asks.

"Believe it or not," Angela says, "there's a form for that. Someone will be around to repair it."

Outside, in the rain, Natalie waits by her car. She looks worried, and she should be.

"Sorry about the party," Zane says. "I met the guy that night. He told me his name was Ben, not Bennet. I didn't recognize him till he walked through the door."

Angela closes her eyes. One of the benefits of rank is having the weekends off, but weekends come with family responsibilities. She'd taken today off specifically to do what *she* wanted, and nothing else, and she should be on the beach right now tossing a ball to George. Instead, she'll be getting it from all sides soon enough. "Did you notice anything that night?" she asks. "Was Jones acting like he'd snuck back to the party after shooting someone in the head?"

"We were two single guys. We talked about sports, and Natalie's sister tried to set us up with one of her friends. I thought Cavanaugh would be at the party too. When she didn't show, I left as soon as I could."

"Any idea why she didn't go?"

Zane doesn't say anything, but Angela can guess for herself. Natalie comes to work with liquor on her breath some mornings. It's one of the reasons she hasn't moved up in her job. Another reason is that she can be exacting and hard to work with, and Angela had been grateful when Zane had asked to be on her team. Not many other detectives, certainly not many other men, would have made the same request. She looks over to where Natalie waits to be reprimanded. Angela wouldn't call her a friend—Angela's not sure if Cavanaugh has friends—but Natalie's a good detective, better than she realizes. She's a detective who doesn't try to stand out, for the right or the wrong reasons, but one who'll go the extra mile when necessary. And she's not the type of detective who usually makes mistakes.

Zane asks, "Why were you asking about Mavis Abbott in there? I saw her this morning heading to school."

Angela turns to him. "We need to go to West Roxbury and talk to her. Cavanaugh will want to sit in, but she'll do it as a civilian. Stay close to her. See what you can find out from her. Let's hope that she doesn't know more than she's letting on."

CHAPTER 9

GLENN RUNS HER FINGER ALONG THE CARD THE REAL ESTATE AGENT had given her. She remembers the woman now, standing across the street this morning in her red coat, watching and waiting.

"Who was that?" Charlotte asks.

"Some vulture trying to get me to sell my mother's house," Glenn says.

"Get used to it," Charlotte says. "You'll be famous soon and hearing from more than just real estate agents. You were awesome today, but I've got to run. You headed out?"

"I have something I need to do."

"Let's catch up tomorrow. This is going to be a big week."

Charlotte hurries up the stairs. Glenn thanks the bookstore manager before rolling her cooler outside to the SUV. She checks again for a text from Patrick Leary. He still hasn't replied.

Glenn should leave. Mavis will be home from school soon, and Glenn needs to talk to Jake. She needs to set things right and keep herself from careening over the cliff that she sees on the horizon, but she can also feel Patrick's touch, his breath in her ear as they stood in the dark, as she drew on every ounce of her resolve to keep herself from making a mistake she could never undo. She starts the engine. She tells herself to do the right thing and drive to West Roxbury.

But she doesn't.

Ten minutes later, she pulls into Starling Circle and down the long driveway leading to her mother's house. This is where she'd told Patrick to meet her, and Glenn had hoped to find him waiting on the front stoop, a cigarette dangling from his mouth. She loves that she can't scold him for smoking, that it's not her burden to carry. She wonders what it would taste like to kiss those lips. On her phone, she punches in, *I'll be here till 3,* and then deletes it. The text makes her sound like a woman she doesn't want to be.

She gets out of the SUV and crosses to where a fence separates this house from next door, where Diane Sykes and her kids used to live. Rain patters on the black tarp covering the pool. If Glenn closes her eyes, she can see Lindsey Sykes doing a cannonball off the diving board. She can also hear Diane Sykes gossiping about the day's news with her mother. Glenn remembers being enthralled by sixteen-year-old Tonya Sykes, who seemed to live without rules. Tonya had black hair cut in a jagged bob and a nose ring. At night, she snuck out of the house and disappeared into the woods, where she probably met up with friends to drink. Glenn remembers a specific day when she'd tried to act cool as Tonya snuck a bottle of Zima and twisted off the cap while crouching behind shrubs. "Come on," she said, waving Glenn over. "All yours."

The Zima tasted like rotten 7Up, but after one sip, Glenn felt as if she were floating into the sky. On the grass, far below, Tonya had lain back, her stomach exposed beneath her cropped T-shirt, and squinted into the sun.

Now a woman steps outside on the neighbor's back porch. She shields her eyes from the rain. "Can I help you?" she calls.

Glenn raises a hand to wave. She doesn't know this woman, and she doesn't want to, either. She doesn't want anything to do with this neighborhood anymore. Maybe she should call that real estate agent, after all. "We're listing the house," she says. "I wanted to let you know."

"Nice to meet you," the woman says, then she goes inside.

Glenn stares at the empty porch as the ghosts of her past whisper in her ears. How different their lives would have been had Diane Sykes shown the same indifference thirty years ago. Instead, Diane had offered a hand of friendship.

Glenn takes a step backward.

What has she done? Coming here, letting fantasy nearly morph into reality. She runs to the SUV, desperate to escape. She backs out of the driveway, her foot pressed to the floor. She speeds away from the circle. Somehow, she needs to undo the damage she's already done.

"You still mad that I went to your sister's party without telling you?" Zane asks Natalie as he joins her at the car. "God forbid we lie to each other, right?"

Zane is angry at Natalie, and he has a right to be. You can't work with a partner that you don't trust. Natalie wonders if he'll ask to be reassigned or if the lieutenant will take her off Homicide for good.

He holds out his hand. "And I'm driving. I'm tired of putting my life in your hands."

Natalie gives him the keys without comment and slides into the passenger's seat. He screeches away from the curb.

"Where are we going?" she asks.

"To talk to your niece and her parents. You can come and be a quiet citizen, or I can drop you at home. Your choice."

Natalie will come, but she suspects Zane already knows that. He drives in silence for a moment. Finally, he says, "Today wasn't the day to ream me out for going to your sister's party."

"I'm still mad about that," Natalie says, which doesn't earn the laugh she'd hoped for. "I know. It was stupid. I'm sorry."

Zane turns onto the BU Bridge and heads toward Boston. "I get it," he says, his voice softer this time, softer than Natalie would have offered if the roles were reversed. "You're protecting your niece. Maybe I'd have done the same thing in your place. But the lieutenant is out for blood now. She told me to watch you and report anything suspicious. And what about Jones back there? You dated him? Not to state the obvious, but that's a bigger deal than sipping your sister's eggnog."

Natalie remembers sitting in a bar with Bennet, and the way his fingers brushed along the back of her hand. "I like you," he'd said. She remembers being afraid of liking him too much.

She'd gone to his apartment again that night. Rowdy slept between them. In the morning, she went for a walk, this time on her own, and she kept walking till she got home. She also remembers ignoring Bennet's texts and phone calls till they finally stopped.

Now she says, "I went on two, maybe three dates with the guy a year ago. We didn't click, and I haven't thought about him since."

"That's probably a good thing. We found his wallet at the crime scene. What else do we need?"

"Where was the wallet, anyway? When I was there, they hadn't found anything."

"It was on the second floor, in an old lab."

"Like someone planted it there, at least that's what Jones's lawyer will claim, especially if he can back up his statement that he lost it at the party."

"You know as well as I do how dumb people are when they panic. They're still processing evidence, but my bet is they'll find Jones's prints all over the scene from when he spent hours looking for his wallet. We'll all be home at dinner tonight, all of us except Jones, who'll be sitting in a jail cell thinking about the rest of his life."

Natalie doesn't argue. Still, something about the crime scene doesn't sit right with her. Most murders are unplanned, and the dropped wallet makes this seem like an easy close, as Zane suggests. But when Natalie looks at the rest of the crime, it's anything but unplanned. The site was well chosen. And most people don't walk around with a gun and zip ties.

"Tell me about the party. How many guests will you need to talk to?"

"You know you're off the case, right?"

"Tell me anyway."

"Maybe fifty people. Most of them seemed to be from the soccer club. And really fancy. Much fancier than I realized. Your sister . . ." Zane shakes his head and stops talking.

"What?" Natalie asks.

"It was nothing."

Natalie waits.

"She was having a good time, that's all."

"What does that mean?"

"She was drunk. Flirty."

"That's nothing new. Did she tell you how cute she thinks you are, or how much she likes those photos you post on Instagram?"

Zane turns onto the Jamaicaway. "It was more than casual. She was all over this one guy, the one who lives out back in the cottage. Patrick Leary. Have you met him?"

Natalie shakes her head. "No, but Glenn flirts with everyone."

"I'm telling you what I saw. I doubt I'm the only one who noticed, and if we don't nail this to Jones, the next stops will be your sister and your brother-in-law."

Natalie's phone beeps.

"Is that Glenn?" Zane asks. "Keep what I said between us. And don't send her anything that'll get you in trouble. My bet is we'll be going over your sister's phone records soon."

Natalie glances at the screen. The text isn't from Glenn. It's from a number Natalie almost deleted from her phone a year ago. *Watch your back*, Bennet writes.

Mavis takes Jake's queen with her rook. Jake considers his options. He doesn't have any. "That's three in a row," he says, gathering the pieces. "And we missed lunch, too. What do you want?"

"Grilled cheese?" Mavis says.

"Then that's what we'll have."

Mavis seems to have forgotten about the events of the morning, for now at least. That doesn't stop Jake from hugging her till she shrugs him away. He releases her, even though he wants to stop time, to capture this moment together forever. After tonight, after he's gone, Mavis will be twelve years old forever. "Music?" he asks, his voice breaking. Thankfully, Mavis doesn't seem to notice. "Your choice."

"Taylor Swift?" Mavis says.

Glenn wants Mavis to be more confident, to stop phrasing everything as a question, to believe in herself. Jake likes his daughter exactly as she is.

Soon the music blares through the kitchen. Mavis stands at the stove, singing into a spatula. Jake sings with her, surprised by how many of the lyrics he knows. When the song ends, they sit at the counter and have lunch. "How are you feeling about everything that happened this morning?" Jake asks.

Mavis shrugs. "I'll survive."

"I'll need to tell your mother about it when she gets home. And the police'll be around to talk to you again, though I bet Aunt Natalie will handle it."

"I already told her pretty much what I could," Mavis says.

"Tell me."

"Who do you think that man was? The one I found?"

"Probably someone who sank too low to find a way out."

"Like an addict? Do you know anyone who does drugs?"

Jake isn't sure how to explain the world to his daughter, especially now that she's getting older and can understand nuance. Snorting coke in a dorm bathroom is a long way from shooting up in an abandoned building. But today isn't the day to start trying to impart that wisdom. "No," he says.

Mavis nods, accepting the lie as truth, or at least seeming to. Jake watches her as she finishes her sandwich. When another song starts, Mavis surprises him by taking his hand, something she hasn't allowed him to do in years. They dance for a few moments, and it feels like a gift. "Are you and Mom having a fight?" she asks. "You've been sleeping in the guest room."

It always surprises Jake how little he and Glenn can hide from their daughter. "I snore."

"That's all?"

"Absolutely." This time he isn't sure how much of the answer she buys.

She kisses his cheek. "I should study for my test," she says, running out of the kitchen and up the back stairs.

Jake listens to her footsteps overhead as he puts the dishes into the dishwasher. Sometimes he can't believe how much he loves Mavis, even if she isn't his biological daughter. Jake met Glenn six years ago when Bennet convinced him to go on a date with her. They hit it off right away, though Jake could tell she was holding something back. On their fourth date, as they strolled through the Public Garden and Jake hinted at taking her home, she told him about Mavis. "I had her on my own," Glenn said. "Have no idea who the father is and don't want to know."

Jake paused beneath a cherry tree. Its flowers glowed white in the moonlight. He took her hands in his.

"Most men bolt right about now," Glenn said.

Jake pulled her in for a kiss.

"The babysitter needs to be home by ten," she mumbled.

"We'll go to your place instead of mine."

They got married two months later at City Hall. Now Jake is thirty-four, and he'll do anything to protect Mavis.

Glenn too.

Are they having a fight? In a way, yes, but not for the reasons Glenn assumes. He remembers standing in the bathroom doorway on Saturday night and reminding himself how much he loved her. They were both still drunk from the party. She wore her flannel pajamas and had her newly dyed hair tied in a ponytail. She read with glasses balanced on the end of her nose. It was a look that worked. At another time in their marriage, the look would have led to good things. "Stay away from him," Jake said.

She took the glasses off and put the book to the side. "It was nothing."

"I know what I saw," Jake said before heading to the guest room, where he lay in the dark, staring at the ceiling, hoping she might come find him. If she had, he wonders now if he'd have told her the truth.

Last year, Jake got a stock tip. Glenn had quit her job to try to make the blog and the book work, something they'd both agreed to, but the house and the school and even the soccer club were bleeding him dry, and he thought if he invested a little cash from the soccer club's till, he could pay it back before anyone noticed. The board had approved new uniforms and building a new field, so the accounts were ripe with funds. Jake withdrew twenty grand in four installments and managed to lose it all. That's when he should have stopped, but when no one on the board noticed, he tried again, and again, and soon he owed the soccer club almost two hundred thousand dollars and had no way of paying it back. He created two sets of books and began falsifying statements. It was a story he'd heard a thousand times, one bad choice that led to another and another, but he'd never understood how easy it was to convince yourself that you were one step from success till you'd made so many false steps you saw no chance of escape.

In the evenings, he watched Glenn and Mavis moving through their lives, neither of them understanding that they were all careening toward disaster. He lay in bed and imagined going back in time and telling himself not to make that first mistake. He started hoping for a miracle.

That's when he told Bennet what he'd done. And Bennet introduced him to Patrick Leary. "He can help you out," Bennet said. "But don't ask too many questions."

Jake met Patrick at a bar in downtown Boston. Patrick seemed like a nice guy, if completely forgettable, with his neatly trimmed hair and checked shirt and jeans. He could have been any other office drone. "I have a friend with some cash that needs a good cleaning. Seems like your soccer club may be the car wash we're looking for. I'll need to stay close, though, at least till the project is done."

That night, Jake told Glenn that an old friend from high school needed help getting back on his feet. "Can he stay in the cottage?" he asked. "It'll only be a few months."

"As long as he keeps to himself," Glenn had said.

Jake puts on the yellow rubber gloves from under the sink and takes a key from where it hangs by the door. Outside, he edges around the house, under the pergola, and across the veranda to the cottage. His hands shake as he fits the key into the door. "Patrick," he calls. "You home?"

The cottage is small, a tiny living room with a stone fireplace, a kitchenette, and a single bedroom. It's furnished with castaways from their own house. He starts his search with the bookshelves, then moves to behind the sofa and around cushions. In the bedroom, he runs his hands through Patrick's clothing, beneath his sweaters and socks. Nothing. He finds the laptop under the mattress. It's the first place he should have looked. The laptop is where Patrick's kept a record of every transaction they've made. It also includes information on the offshore accounts Jake had set up. If the cops get ahold of it, they'll both end up in prison for a long time.

In the kitchen, Jake slips the laptop into his own computer bag and has taken off the rubber gloves when a car pulls into the driveway. A Black woman wearing practical shoes and a tailored suit gets out and looks up at the house. He recognizes her, but it takes him a moment to remember that she works with Natalie, that she's a cop. Jake realizes that he's sweating, almost gasping for breath, because he's expected this moment for months, and in a way, it comes as a relief until he realizes she's here to talk to Mavis about the body she found this morning. If anyone showed up to arrest Jake, it would be the feds, not the Boston police. He steps outside.

"Mr. Abbott," the woman says, walking toward him. "Lieutenant White. I work with your sister-in-law. My colleague will be here soon, and we'd like to talk to your daughter about what she saw this morning."

"I figured you'd be here. She's inside."

"Actually, there have been some new developments. Maybe I could talk to you first? I understand you had a party this weekend."

"A holiday party," Jake says. "It was a fundraiser for the soccer club."

"And for your wife's book, right?"

Jake nods.

"Let's get out of this rain. And any chance you have some cookies lying around? Detective Perez told me they were amazing, and I'm starving."

That earns a smile from Jake, one that reminds him not to trust this woman. He waves her into the kitchen, where he takes out tubs of cookies and hands Angela a napkin. "Cutouts, macaroons, jam blossoms, Russian tea cakes," he says. "It'll keep me from eating them myself."

He also pours himself two fingers of bourbon and lifts the bottle. "This makes them taste even better."

"I'm on duty."

Angela piles a half dozen cookies on her napkin. She bites into one that leaves a ring of confectioner's sugar around her lips that she swipes away. "Your associate Bennet Jones was at the party, correct?"

"Why?" Jake asks.

Angela breaks a jam blossom in half. "Zane told me these were the best," she says. "Do you have any milk?"

Jake fills a glass and slides it across the counter. Angela washes down half of the jam blossom. "I have a lot of questions. I usually do when I'm investigating a homicide. Some of them won't make sense to you, but I have my reasons. And it'll be easier if you answer."

"Fine, Bennet was here. But your detective could have told you that. What's his name? Perez? He was here too."

"Did anything happen with Jones? Anything out of the ordinary?"

"Is Bennet okay?"

Angela pushes the pile of cookies aside and waits. Jake sighs and says, "Not that night, but he came by the next day looking for his wallet. We couldn't find it."

"Good to know. When was the last time you talked to him?"

"Yesterday, at work. And before you ask, no, nothing stood out about yesterday. It was an ordinary day at work."

Angela takes a notepad from her pocket. Jake tries to read what she writes, but she closes it before he can. "We'll need to speak to everyone who attended the party," she says. "Did you have a photographer? I'd love to get my hands on those photos. We'll dive into social media, too, once we have the guest list. Everything's documented these days. You'd be surprised. Or maybe you wouldn't?"

"What could the party possibly have to do with what Mavis found today?" Jake can hear his voice rising in anger. He takes a deep breath and starts again. "A lot of the guests were my neighbors and my clients, and I'd rather not have the Boston police calling them without at least knowing why."

Angela bites the head off a snowman cookie. "Unfortunately, murder makes things uncomfortable."

"Listen, Detective . . ."

"It's 'Lieutenant,'" Angela says. "I'm the big boss. Your sister-in-law reports to me. So does Detective Perez—and the entire department, for that matter. But you can call me Angela if that makes you more comfortable. Some men don't like that I'm in charge."

"I'm not like that," Jake says. "Lieutenant."

"I need to talk to your wife, too. Would you tell her I'm here?"

"My wife isn't home. She had an event today for her book launch."

"She doesn't know what happened this morning?"

"Not unless Natalie told her," Jake says. "I didn't want to tell her about it till she got home."

Angela writes something else on her pad. "My son is eight now," she says, showing Jake a photo on her phone of a boy and a German shepherd.

Jake remembers Mavis at eight, walking her to school the first year they moved here, the first year he was her father. She was in third grade and held his hand.

Angela puts the phone away. "I dread middle school. All those hormones. All those smells. Isaiah's actually my stepson. My wife, Cary, is his mother, and she has an ex-wife, Brenda, who's his other mother. I can't stand Brenda, but I'll tell you one thing, when Isaiah is in trouble, the first thing Cary, Brenda, and I do is circle the wagons and make sure he's safe and absolutely nothing else happens to him." She glances at the clock over the stove. "Mavis found that body at about nine this morning. It's past three o'clock. You've kept this news from your wife for over six hours. Why?"

Jake meets Angela's eyes. He doesn't have an explanation for her, not one he can share, at any rate. He hasn't told Glenn because he wanted Mavis to himself today. Thankfully, he hears a car approach. "There's Glenn now," he says.

CHAPTER 10

When Glenn pulls into the driveway, she notes that Patrick Leary's Audi is still parked on the street, where he normally leaves it. Another car that looks like one of the unmarked vehicles Natalie usually drives for work blocks her path to the garage. Glenn swears under her breath. She expects to find her sister waiting inside, ready to follow up on the discussion-board posts, when all Glenn wants to do is forget the posts, forget the texts that she sent this morning, forget the last few days, and find a way forward with Jake. She pushed things too far with Patrick, and she came close, so close, to a place of no return. Now, she tells herself, all she needs to do is to get rid of her sister and make things right, so she stops short when she gets to the kitchen and Angela White comes toward her. She's met Angela a few times over the years, first as Natalie's colleague, then as her boss. Now Glenn really regrets telling Natalie about those discussion-board posts. The last thing she needs is for a BPD lieutenant to be delving into her marital woes. "Angela?" she says.

"Mrs. Abbott," Angela begins, in the way someone with bad news to deliver speaks. Behind the lieutenant, Jake stares silently at the kitchen counter, and Glenn's thoughts go straight to her daughter. "What happened? Where's Mavis?"

"Mavis is fine," the lieutenant says, quickly.

That seems to wake Jake up. "She's upstairs doing homework."

"Why is a police lieutenant talking to my husband?"

Jake glances toward Angela.

"Go ahead," she says.

Jake takes a deep breath. Glenn sees the bottle of bourbon on the counter and wonders how much he's had to drink at this point, and if she'll be dodging flying lowballs again. "Brace yourself," he says. "Mavis went into the abandoned factory on her way to school this morning. She found a dead body."

Glenn laughs. She knows it's not the right reaction, but she can't quite process what Jake said. She puts one hand to her hair, and another to the counter. She squelches the smile. "I'm sorry. That's terrible," she hears herself say. "Who died?"

Angela steps forward. "I know this must be a shock."

"I've told Mavis a hundred times not to go near that place."

Out in the driveway, another car arrives. Natalie climbs out of the passenger's side, followed by Zane. Detective Perez.

"Why didn't you call me?" Glenn asks Jake.

"I knew today was important," he says.

"Oh, Jake . . ." Glenn begins. The misplaced humor is gone. So is the smile that went with it. Glenn can't begin to tell Jake how much anger she wants to hurl at him. She remembers the text that Natalie sent, the one she ignored. "Does my sister know about this?" she asks, and when neither Jake nor the lieutenant answers, she leaves the kitchen without another word.

She can't face any of them right now. Rage gets her to the top of the front stairs. She rests a hand on the banister to steady herself as fear sets in. Down the hall, sounds of a television playing emanate from her bedroom, and when she bursts through the door, Mavis is sprawled among the pillows, her tablet balanced on her lap. She looks up, frozen. Terrified, even. And normally, Glenn would be annoyed to find her here, watching TV, but this is hardly a normal day.

Somehow, she finds a mask of composure. She kicks her boots off and slides onto the bed and pulls Mavis close. They watch the screen in silence as a woman in high heels chases a man through the streets. "Who's that?" Glenn asks.

"Ashley." Mavis's voice is small. "She's a detective."

"Do you like her?"

"She's tough."

Glenn inches closer to Mavis, who folds against her. "Sounds like you had a crazy day."

Mavis nods.

"Have you seen this show before?"

This time, Mavis doesn't answer, and Glenn wonders how often her daughter has snuck in here to watch these shows, what lessons she's taken from them, what other secrets she keeps for herself. Mavis is sitting on the precipice of being an adult, and Glenn can't protect her from the world, no matter how much she wants to. "I'll tell you a secret," she says. "I've seen every single episode of *The Bachelorette.* I watch them on my phone when I can't sleep."

Mavis smiles and burrows into the pillows.

"No one hurt you, did they?" Glenn asks.

"I banged my knee climbing out the window. But no one hurt me."

"You'd tell me if someone did, right?"

Mavis closes her eyes and rests her head against Glenn's chest. "Remember one thing," Glenn says. "If you're ever in trouble, scream your fucking head off. Your father, me, Aunt Natalie, one of us will find you wherever you are."

Mavis giggles.

"Are you laughing because I swore?" Glenn asks. "I know all the swear words. Every single one. Even the really bad ones."

A knock comes at the door. Angela steps into the room. Natalie stands at her shoulder. "We need you downstairs," Angela says.

Mavis's fingers dig into Glenn's palm.

"The quicker you talk to her," Glenn whispers, "the quicker this will be over. Just tell her the truth."

They walk together, through the hallway and down creaky stairs to the study. The last of the afternoon light shines through the room.

Angela waves toward a sofa and waits for Glenn and Mavis to sit before pulling up a chair. "Detective Perez is chatting with your father in the kitchen, so you have me."

Glenn places a protective arm over Mavis's shoulders while Natalie hovers in the doorway.

"I work with your aunt," Angela says. "And no one thinks you did anything wrong," she adds, "but I need you to be honest with me, okay? Just tell me everything you possibly can about this morning."

Mavis doesn't answer, even when Glenn squeezes her hand and whispers, "Go ahead."

"This is what I know already," Angela says. "It was dark, and there were rats everywhere, which, to me, sounds like a nightmare. I hate rats."

"Me too," Mavis says.

"Had you ever been in that building before?"

Mavis shakes her head.

"You can tell her if you have," Glenn says.

"I haven't gone in there before."

"Do you take the same route to school every day?" Angela asks.

Mavis nods. "Unless I go to Stella's house after school. Or sometimes we go to Centre Street, like, to Starbucks or something."

"Stella?"

"My friend."

"So you've walked by that building dozens of times. Why was today the one you chose to go inside?"

Mavis looks at her lap. "I was curious."

"For a specific reason?"

"Just because it was there."

"Did you see anyone near the building, maybe lurking?"

Mavis rolls her eyes. "I wouldn't have gone in then. And there's not much to tell. It was gross, and I ran as fast as I could. I already told all of this to Aunt Natalie."

Angela doesn't respond, not at first. "Sometimes we ask the same questions a few different ways. It can help jog the memory.

This next question is hard, and we may have to ask it a few times. Did you get a good look at the body?"

"It was dark."

A chill runs down Glenn's spine as she imagines Mavis so close to harm, so close to death. She runs a hand through her daughter's hair. "You watch those shows. You know that even the tiniest detail can help solve a murder."

"Police shows?" Angela says. "Which ones do you watch?"

Mavis shrugs. "All of them."

"What's your favorite?"

"*CSI: Miami.*"

"I've seen every episode."

"Me too," Mavis says before catching herself.

Glenn wonders how her daughter had managed to sneak in hundreds of hours of television without her knowing.

"Sometimes those shows get things right," Angela says. "Sometimes they don't. Like, it'll take a few days to get most of the lab results back. Things like DNA. The more you tell me now, the closer we'll be to solving the case." Angela leans forward. "You'd tell me if there was more to this story, wouldn't you? We'll find out anyway, but it's always best when a witness is honest from the start."

"He wore a Bruins hat," Mavis says.

"You knew the victim was a he? How?"

Natalie steps into the room.

"The clothes looked like something a man would wear." Mavis glances to her mother and then to her aunt. "There wasn't anything else."

"One more question," Angela says. "Was anyone else with you? Was Stella there?"

"No," Mavis says.

Angela holds her gaze for a moment. "Good job."

"I'll come check on you in a minute," Glenn says.

Mavis dashes from the room. The lieutenant watches as she leaves. "It would be helpful to have a list of the guests who attended your party," she says to Glenn.

"Why would this have anything to do with the party? It was three days ago," Glenn says.

"We don't know yet," Natalie says. "We're still trying to identify the victim."

"Go ahead," Angela says to Natalie. "Tell her the rest."

Natalie turns to Glenn. "We found Bennet Jones's wallet at the crime scene. We assumed he was the victim, but when we went to Bennet's apartment, we found him alive and well."

It takes a moment for Glenn to process what her sister has said. When she does, her blood turns cold. "You want to know why a wallet that was lost at *my* house was found at a crime scene by *my* daughter."

Glenn closes her eyes and rubs the bridge of her nose. For the first time since she's come home, since she heard about what had happened, she thinks about herself and what these events might mean. "I have a book publishing next week," she says. "I've been working on it for ten years, and it's getting all sorts of publicity and good reviews. I have appearances scheduled almost every day of the week for the next month. What will people say if the Boston police start calling around asking questions about the party?"

"We'll be as discreet as we can," Angela says.

Glenn stands. She moves toward the door. She's hosted enough parties to know how to get rid of an unwanted guest. "This is all very upsetting, to Mavis in particular."

"The list?"

"I need to talk to my lawyer first."

The lieutenant jots a note on her pad. She flips it closed and tucks it into her pocket. Finally, she stands and follows Glenn through the house to the kitchen, where Zane is speaking with Jake.

"Everything okay?" Jake asks.

Glenn doesn't bother to answer. "Thank you for coming by, Lieutenant. We'll let you know right away if Mavis thinks of anything else."

"I'll stay," Natalie says.

Glenn meets Natalie's eye. She wants them all out of her house, even her sister. More than anything, she wants to erase the last few days and start all over again. "You should go, too. It's been a long day."

The lieutenant doesn't move, not at first. "I'm sure we'll be back tomorrow after more evidence is processed. In the meantime, call me if you think of anything. Anytime. Day or night. And for the record, where were the two of you last night?"

Jake glances at Glenn.

"Here," Glenn says. "At home."

"All night?" Zane asks.

"All night," Glenn says.

Out in the driveway, Angela waits with Zane in the rain as Natalie speaks with her sister. "You get anything else out of Jake Abbott?" she asks.

"Not much," Zane says. "And we already corroborated Bennet Jones's story."

"I'll call the ME and see if he has anything new. We need an ID." Angela nods toward the house, toward where Natalie stands in the doorway. "Take Cavanaugh home. See what she'll tell you."

CHAPTER 11

At the end of the day, Olivia Knowles shuts down her computer, puts on her red raincoat, and leaves the real estate office, carefully locking the door behind her. It's still raining, and downtown is mostly abandoned. She clicks her key fob. The car beeps. She gets into her sedan and drives away from town, through the dark, winding streets. She moved to Elmhurst more than twenty years ago and has maintained as low a profile as possible since. Paul is the face of the real estate agency. Once in a while, he'll encourage Olivia to boost her public image, but she suspects he's secretly happy when she steps aside for him.

She turns on the radio. The announcer talks about a body found in West Roxbury.

Next week is Thanksgiving. Olivia suspects that her son, Jason, will stay out in California. He's in his mid-twenties now and forging his own life far from here, and far from the half-truths that Olivia fed him growing up. It's no wonder he rarely makes the trip home anymore and that their phone calls have grown infrequent. Still, she can't help but wish he'd make the trip. She misses him, even with his short fuse, the one that reminds her of his father. Olivia blames herself for Jason's temper. She kept too much from him about her life and her loves, and she suspects he's known it, or at least sensed it. Those lies are what he's tried to escape.

Paul will ask Olivia over for dinner on Thanksgiving, where he'll play host to an intimate gathering of thirty. Olivia will likely beg off the invitation and spend the day alone, the way she likes it now that Ruth is gone. Ruth Cavanaugh is one of Olivia's biggest lies. Her absence has left a hole in Olivia's heart that's seemed impossible to fill. They used to talk about spending the holidays together, about introducing their kids, and it had been easy enough for Olivia to play along with the charade right up to the last minute. She wonders if Ruth ever noticed that it was Olivia who always got cold feet first. "I'm not sure if I'm ready to meet your daughters yet," she'd say, and Ruth would cup her cheek in her hand and say something gentle and understanding like, "Next time," even as Olivia saw the relief in Ruth's eyes.

Of course, there are no next times now. Ruth is gone.

Olivia turns off the main road and onto a dirt lane that cuts through a section of trees, ending at the farmhouse where she lives, where she and Ruth used to lie under the stars, their fingertips touching, while Jason chased fireflies through the field. She parks in front of the barn and cuts the engine. Rain pounds at the car's roof and windshield. Olivia closes her eyes and allows the sound to transport her, to another rainy day, the last time she spoke to Ruth. By then, Ruth's dementia had taken root, and she'd moved to the nursing home. The girls had made that happen after Olivia had begun leaving notes around the house for them to find.

At the nursing home, Olivia didn't know which version of Ruth would greet her when she visited, old and confused or young and vibrant. On that day, Olivia left her car and ran through the parking lot and into the building. Upstairs, Ruth lay in a darkened room, her limp, gray hair fanning her face. On the TV, Steve Harvey reigned over the *Family Feud.*

Olivia had brought a box of Almond Roca, Ruth's favorite candy. She placed it on the bedside table and sat for a moment. "Did Glenn visit?"

Ruth turned to look at her, and it was clear that she was somewhere else, in another place and another time. Her eyes twinkled.

"Glenn's in her room. She stinks of tangerine. I let her keep that lip gloss she stole. She kept telling me that it fell into the cart, but it's better than having Alan find out, especially after last night."

"I'm sure Glenn didn't steal it. She's sweet."

Ruth had scoffed. "Sweet? I love Glenn, but she's not sweet. She's not very nice, either. Glenn would cut you off at the knees to get ahead in a three-legged race."

"I brought you some candy."

Ruth took the box. "I'll have to hide it," she said. "My own stash. Otherwise, the girls will eat it before I get any for myself."

Now Olivia cracks the car door. Rain pelts the armrest.

Ever since the poster for Glenn's book went up in the store downtown, Olivia has felt as if Glenn has been watching her, so much so that she'd assumed Glenn would recognize her this afternoon. Olivia had almost told Glenn today how much she loved Ruth, but she didn't. Instead, she gave her that stupid business card.

She nearly gets out of the car and heads inside. Instead, she drives toward Boston.

Angela White isn't the type of cop who needs to bother the medical examiner at work. In fact, on the occasions when she has, she's earned a reputation for puking, a reputation she'd prefer not to not cultivate. Still, when he calls, she comes. She takes the elevator into the bowels of police headquarters and hopes for the best as she steps into the morgue. She feels a gurgle in her stomach as soon as she sees the ME weighing a human liver.

"You holding it together?" he asks.

Angela ignores the dig. "What have you got?"

"I had another case to finish up, but we're running the prints. Let's hope there's a hit. Most of the rest is as expected. Cause of death is a gunshot to the head. Victim is a male in his early- to mid-thirties. Healthy besides the hole in his head."

Angela dares a peek at the body, with its Y incision and open chest. The face is as bad as she'd heard it would be, with the eyes and flesh gnawed away. She concentrates on the ME's face.

"We can talk outside," he says.

"Be quick," Angela says.

"This is the strange part." The ME uses a scalpel to point along where the eyes used to be. "I assumed this was blood, here, but it's not the right color or consistency. It's jelly."

"Petroleum?"

"My guess would be good old raspberry, though I haven't sampled it. There's peanut butter there too. It's like whoever killed this guy wanted the rats to have at it."

Angela manages to make it to the hall before the contents of her stomach empty onto the floor. The ME follows her. Angela wipes her mouth clean. "Reputation intact," she says. "Do me a favor and keep this to yourself."

"Don't worry. You're not the only one who hurls when they see me."

"I mean the PB and J thing," Angela says. "I want to make sure that detail doesn't travel anywhere."

Natalie looks toward her house in Jamaica Plain, a miniature one-bedroom Victorian on a dead-end street, as Zane parks along the curb. By now, the sun has set, and she hasn't spoken since the lieutenant grounded her, which means she'll be chained to her desk as of tomorrow. She'll even have to ask to go to the bathroom. "I'm watching out for you," Angela had said in Glenn's driveway, "but I'm also watching out for the department."

"And yourself," Natalie said.

"Fair enough," Angela said. "But let's keep your name out of the news if we can."

Now Zane turns toward her. "Cavanaugh," he begins.

"Shut up."

Natalie gets out and stomps away. At her front door, she fumbles for her keys as she hears Zane approaching from behind. She spins around as he leans a hip against the porch railing.

"I thought you'd live in a condo," he says.

"Too many neighbors. I don't like people."

"I've noticed. But let's grab a drink anyway."

"Don't you need to work on the case?"

"There's not much to do till the forensics start rolling in. I'm heading home after this."

Natalie turns the key. It will be good to keep Zane as close as possible, even if that means getting a drink with him while he tries to charm her into ratting out her sister. "Fine. Wait here," she says and slams the door in Zane's face.

She doesn't turn on the lights in the front hallway. Her house is less than eight hundred square feet, with a tiny parlor that leads to a dining room and kitchen, and a single bedroom at the top of a narrow set of stairs. The house has crown molding and a working fireplace and window seats overlooking the street, and when Natalie manages to keep the clutter from taking over, she marvels at how cozy her home feels. Lately, she hasn't kept the clutter at bay, and the last thing she needs is for Zane to see the mess. She drops her bag on the sofa. An empty wine bottle rolls off the cushion and across the floor. Upstairs, she locks her handgun in a safe. Then she joins Zane on the porch.

"What are you hiding in there?" he asks.

Natalie walks past him and down the sidewalk. He runs to catch up. Out on Centre Street, she leads him to the Brendan Behan. Inside, the pub's windows are steamy, and the air smells of Guinness and fryolators. Natalie waves to the hostess and gives the bartender a much bigger hello than she normally does. He pours her a vodka on the rocks without asking.

"Cosmo," Zane says. "Up."

"Is there such a thing as a cosmo, neat?" Natalie asks.

"They're delicious."

"Baking cookies, cosmos, feelings. You're like a girl."

"And you're like a guy. It's why we make a good team."

Natalie drinks down the vodka. The bartender refills her glass and delivers Zane's cocktail.

"How many guys order drinks like this one?" she asks.

"More than you'd think," the bartender says, before delivering menus and moving on.

"It matches your tie," Natalie says.

"I like pink," Zane says. "It's not a crime. I own a whole pile of pink shirts. Pink shorts, too. I even have a pink bathrobe." He raises his glass. "To crazy cases and great partners. You and your sister seem close," he adds.

Natalie takes a long swig of vodka. Zane wants to ferret out what he can about Glenn and Jake, and he'll take whatever he learns to the lieutenant. But Natalie can use him, too. If there's any evidence she doesn't know about yet, she'll make sure Zane tells her about it by the time they leave this bar. "You're asking about Glenn too quickly," she says. "You should try distracting me first. Ask about hobbies or boyfriends."

"You have a boyfriend?"

"Do you?"

"What about hobbies?"

"Macrame."

"That's what I'd have guessed."

The bartender swings by again. "Dinner?" he asks.

Natalie orders a cheeseburger. Zane scans the menu and opts for a salad.

"Girl," Natalie says.

Zane yanks up his shirt and shows off his abs. "Do I look like a girl?"

Natalie is surprised to feel her face flush. She hopes the dim lighting hides it. "You look as fine as you know you do," she says.

They sit quietly for a moment. Zane sips his water and tears a cocktail napkin to shreds. "Is that enough distraction?" he asks. "Should I go in for the kill? Get you to tell me all about Glenn and her deepest, darkest secrets?"

"That's what I'd do."

"The two of you seem close," Zane says, again.

"We're sisters, right. Sometimes we get along. Sometimes we don't."

"Did she bake a lot growing up?"

"Not really. She was a consultant before all this started. For her, the baking thing is more about being successful. I'm happy for her, though. She's excited about the book, and she's worked hard for it. But I'll let you in on a secret. Glenn doesn't eat gluten. Not even a slice of bread."

Zane laughs, and for a moment, the detective is gone. "I was wondering how she stayed so skinny."

"I hope all of this doesn't screw it up for her."

"What do you think is going on?"

"I wish I could tell you." Natalie swirls the ice in her glass. "Tell me about your own situation. We spend all day long together, and I don't know much about you. Do you have brothers and sisters?"

"One of each," Zane says. "Joe's my brother. Irene's my sister. We're best friends. We get together most Sundays and cook. We used to go to my parents' place in Randolph, but now we go to Joe's because he has kids. I bake something. Joe grills. Irene, well, she pretends to help but all she does is drink. She got married in September, so my bet is the drinking will stop soon."

Natalie spends most Sundays working, followed by a visit to this bar. She lifts her empty glass and clinks the ice toward the bartender. "Another round?" she asks Zane.

"Still working on this one."

"Doesn't sound like much goes wrong at the Perez house."

"We fight all the time," Zane says. "My sister's an alcoholic. My brother is on his third wife and fourth kid. My mother has a temper, but we survive it."

The bartender delivers their plates. Zane unwraps his silverware and goes at his salad, stuffing huge forkfuls of roughage into his mouth. Natalie douses her fries with ketchup. "Your sister's a drunk, and your brother has commitment issues," she says. "What do they say about you?"

"That I'll spend all of eternity in hell."

Natalie bites into her burger, and wonders what he means. Juice drips down her chin. Zane blots at it with his napkin in a way that feels intimate, and much more welcome than Natalie would have expected.

"What do you think is going on?" Natalie asks. "There are too many coincidences in this case for them to be coincidences."

"Done distracting me with personal questions?"

Natalie doesn't answer.

"Now we're playing chicken," Zane says. "Seeing who fills the silence first. I've seen you in the box. I won't win this one. So here goes. This is what I noticed today. Your brother-in-law has a secret. I don't know what it is, but he didn't call your sister when their daughter was in trouble. To me, that speaks volumes. Let's hope the secret has nothing to do with the body found down the street. What do you know about their marriage? Do they seem happy?"

"You'll have to ask them," Natalie says. "Any detective with a week on the job knows that all marriages are complicated, and this one isn't for me to speculate on."

"What does Glenn say about you?"

Natalie lifts her glass. "That I drink too much."

"And what do you say about your sister when she's not around?"

Natalie shouldn't answer. Zane is fishing, and he may be green, but he's a good detective. "That she's a controlling bitch," Natalie hears herself say.

"Is that what her husband says too?"

Natalie isn't drunk enough to take that bait. "Again, you'll have to ask him."

CHAPTER 12

SOMEHOW, GLENN MAKES IT THROUGH DINNER. AFTERWARD, MAVIS excuses herself. Glenn clears the plates, and when she feels a hand on her back, she turns toward Jake. Lines seem to have appeared in his face in the last few hours. He takes her hands. "I love you," he says. "More than anything."

Glenn yanks her hands away. "Whatever you did, Lieutenant White has us both in her sights now. And I know my own truth. None of this has anything to do with me."

"I'll take care of it."

Glenn shoves past him. She crosses to the kitchen door. It's dark outside, but the orange glow of a cigarette shines at the foot of the driveway. Glenn wonders if it's Patrick Leary, and she wants to tell him not to bother returning her texts. She wants to take out every bit of anger on him that she should be directing at Jake. She pulls the door open and steps into the night. The rain has finally stopped, replaced by frigid air that smells of fallen leaves and compost. She marches down the driveway.

The cigarette falls to the ground. She sees someone retreating in the dark. She runs after the sound of heels on asphalt, and she grips a shoulder, spinning the person toward her. For a moment, Glenn wonders if she recognizes this woman from the local news. She has the right hair, big and blond. Then she correlates the hair and red raincoat with her day and to the business card that still sits in her bag. What's this woman's name? Olivia something.

"What the hell are you doing here?" Glenn asks, and when the woman doesn't answer, Glenn's mind goes to last night, to the distance she's felt with Jake, the distance that drove her to send those texts to Patrick today. "You're having an affair with my husband?"

"I'm sorry," the woman says. "I shouldn't have come."

She gets into a sedan and drives away. Glenn stands in the dark as the cold worms its way under her skin and her doubts about Jake increase. The car stops at the end of the street, its brake lights glowing. It's only then that she thinks to note the license plate number, but the car is too far away.

Back inside, Glenn digs the card from her bag. OLIVIA KNOWLES. She shoves it toward Jake and waits for a reaction.

"Do you want to sell this house now?" he asks.

"I told those detectives we were home last night," Glenn says. "Together. I lied, and it didn't feel good. You went to see her, didn't you? You're having an affair."

"I don't know her."

"Where did you go, then?"

"Nowhere," Jake says. "Or nowhere that matters."

Glenn doesn't believe him. She doesn't know whom to believe anymore.

In the pub's bathroom, Natalie splashes water on her face to try to sober up. When she returns to the bar, Zane's looking at his phone. He glances up and smiles. "Where did you grow up?" he asks.

Natalie slides onto the stool. "Elmhurst."

"Fancy."

"Not the part where we lived," Natalie says.

"Are your parents still there?"

Natalie shakes her head. "My mother died last year. She had dementia."

"I'm sorry."

Natalie opts for a platitude. "She's in a better place now. And honestly, she went quickly. That kind of thing can drag on for years. And who wants that."

"Were you close?"

They weren't close, not since her father's murder. Natalie was never convinced that Diane Sykes had killed her father. For Natalie—Detective Cavanaugh—the more likely explanation was that her mother had bashed in her father's skull in a fit of rage. Natalie had spent almost thirty years believing in her mother's guilt, a belief that formed a wedge between them. She left Elmhurst as soon as possible and visited as little as she could get away with. Her mother carried the secret too, or Natalie believed that she had. She kept at a distance from both her daughters, as though believing that if she let them get close, her guilt might rub off on them. "We loved each other," Natalie says.

Zane goes at his salad again. He doesn't ask a follow-up question, and Natalie realizes it's because he already knows about her father's murder. She says, "Getting a new partner on the force is like going on a first date. You search the person's name and learn whatever you can."

"What did you learn about me?"

"That you swam butterfly in college."

"State champion," Zane says.

Natalie takes in the contours of his face, his gentle smile, even those dinner-plate–sized ears. She'd give anything for the touch of another human being right now. He meets her gaze and takes a fry from her plate. "Gotta live a little," he says. "And I'm sorry about your father."

Natalie shrugs. "I've had a long time to come to terms with it."

"You're drunk. You should eat some fries, too."

"You're nice."

Natalie swivels toward him. She tries to lean on the bar but misses and nearly falls off her stool. She's on her fourth vodka, and she's drunker than she realized.

"Steady there," Zane says, his face close to hers.

Natalie remembers Glenn's advice from this morning, to be bold, to take a chance.

"Finished?"

The bartender has a hand on her plate. The room sways, or maybe Natalie does. She hears herself ask for another round.

"We should get you home," Zane says.

Natalie touches his arm. She feels his bicep beneath his shirt. She imagines running her hand over those abs. She leans toward him and feels herself tumbling forward. When she opens her eyes, the bartender is staring at her. "You can't take her home like this," he says.

Zane pulls his jacket aside to reveal his badge. "I know."

Natalie takes in Zane's expression. He's more than uninterested in her. He's horrified. It's then that she notices the cosmo sitting on the bar, glowing pink in the dim light, completely untouched. He's been working her this whole time. The drunken fog lifts. "Fuck you," she says.

It's all she can do to walk a straight line out of the bar and onto the street.

CHAPTER 13

I CALL ON THE BURNER PHONE. IT RINGS FOUR TIMES BEFORE CLICKING through. No one speaks on the other end, though I can hear breathing. I can almost smell fear. "Everything's set," I say at last.

The voice that answers sounds defeated. "I'm not doing this."

The resistance doesn't surprise me. But the time for choosing has passed. "Then you know what will happen."

That's when the tears begin.

And I understand.

Maybe I'd feel that way too if the roles were reversed. If I were the one to have lost control.

CHAPTER 14

JAKE TAKES A DEEP BREATH BEFORE EDGING MAVIS'S BEDROOM DOOR open. She has every stuffed animal she owns piled around her and a copy of *The Hunger Games* balanced on her chest.

All the planning that has gone into tonight has seemed theoretical till now, but if he goes forward, this is it. This will be his last moment with his daughter. His last moment before their worlds change forever. He watches her, hoping to keep this image intact for as long as he can. A part of him wonders if he'll return one day to find Mavis grown up and with her own kids, probably calling some other man "Dad." He wonders if she'll find it in her heart to forgive him.

"Why are you looking at me like that?" she asks.

"I'm saying good night. And if I don't see you in the morning, good luck on that algebra test. You'll ace it."

"I know."

Jake crosses the room and kisses her forehead. "Want me to read to you? It'll help you sleep."

Mavis hands him the book, and he perches on the side of the bed and reads through a chapter till Mavis's eyes begin to close. He puts the book aside and turns the light off.

"Don't leave," Mavis whispers.

If he could, Jake would stay here for the rest of his life. He settles into an armchair and waits to hear his daughter's breathing grow steady with sleep.

"Can I tell you something?" Mavis whispers. "Something you can't tell Mom."

"I won't tell a soul." This once, Jake will keep that promise. "And I bet you'll feel better."

"Kevin Chandler dared me to go into that building. It was stupid. I shouldn't have done it."

Jake knows Kevin from soccer. He's a good kid, but needy. "Learn from the mistake, right?"

In the darkness, he hears his daughter roll onto her side. "I love you, Daddy," she says, her voice sleepy, and when he kisses her forehead again, it feels as if his heart is being torn from his chest. A moment later, her breathing grows steady, but he can't get himself to leave. He listens to the house. It's quiet. The whole world is quiet. He hears Glenn come up the stairs and go to their room.

He steps into the hallway. A shaft of light shines across Mavis's bed. With sudden clarity, Jake understands what he needs to do. And with that realization, his whole body relaxes for the first time in days. He hurries down the stairs, takes the laptop he'd hidden earlier from his computer bag, and heads outside. The rain has stopped, replaced with frigid winter air. He throws his arms out, lifting his gaze to a clear sky filled with stars. He sends a text to Patrick Leary, telling him to go to hell. In the garage, he lifts the suitcase from the trunk of his car and makes a phone call. "It's off. I'll turn myself in to the feds tomorrow," he says, before hanging up.

He closes the trunk. As he turns toward the house, footsteps cross the gravel, and a shadowy figure emerges into the moonlight.

"What are you doing here?" Jake asks.

At the station, Angela sits at her desk and dials Cary at home. "I'm waiting on some reports," she says, after her wife picks up. "Looks like it might be a late night."

"I figured that one out on my own," Cary says. "It's almost ten o'clock. Try to eat something besides pizza."

Angela glances at the pepperoni slices glistening in a box. "Give George a belly rub for me," she says, and hangs up.

A few moments later, Zane pops his head into her office. "Healthy dinner."

She waves him in and ignores the dig. Angela doesn't need a work wife. "The ME has narrowed the time of death to between seven p.m. and midnight yesterday, which means my theory about Bennet Jones committing the murder on Saturday night is out. Glenn Abbott claims she and her husband were home together, but wives lie."

Zane considers what she said for a moment. "If I were placing bets, I'd say Jake Abbott is good for this."

"Same," Angela says. "And Mavis Abbott was hiding something when I talked to her this afternoon. She knows something about her parents and doesn't want to say what it is. Maybe you can have a go at her tomorrow. Did you get anything out of Cavanaugh?"

Zane shakes his head. "Not much. She keeps things close to the chest. Did you know about her father? He was murdered by a neighbor when she was a kid."

Angela shrugs. "What about it?"

"What are the odds? Not many people know one person who was murdered in their entire lives. How often do you meet someone who knew two?"

Angela's thought about this herself. "Head home. Get some rest. There's a good chance we'll have an ID on the vic by morning, and neither of us will be sleeping much for the next few days."

"You too?"

"Soon."

Angela watches him leave as she finishes her dinner. She unlocks a drawer in her desk and takes out a file folder. Since Angela's promotion to lieutenant, she's kept a private personnel file on each of her detectives. Some of them are thin, others full of notes. Until recently, Natalie's had been empty. But last month, an envelope addressed to Angela arrived at the station. In it, she found a note and a newspaper clipping. The note was written in block letters and read, WATCH THOSE WHO WORK FOR YOU.

The clipping came from the *Boston Globe,* a mid-nineties article that detailed the murder of an Elmhurst man, Natalie's father, Alan Cavanaugh, and the subsequent investigation into the involvement of his wife, Ruth Cavanaugh. The article was standard crime-beat reporting, with quotes from the state police that dodged most of the questions. It even featured a grainy black-and-white photo of Natalie and Glenn clutching each other as they ran into the local school.

Angela had filed the envelope away and tried to forget it. Everyone had a past, and Angela suspected Natalie Cavanaugh wouldn't want to revisit this part of hers. In fact, the article helped Angela understand Natalie a bit better, to see why she avoided high-profile cases and trusted the press even less than the average cop. But the story nagged at Angela too, till, finally, she asked a librarian friend who works at Harvard's Widener Library to see what she could find on the case off the record, and had been rewarded with news articles, a *Dateline* exposé, and an episode of *Forensic Files,* complete with cheesy reenactments detailing how the focus of the case turned on a neighbor who'd been having an affair with Alan Cavanaugh, a woman named Diane Sykes. The case ended when the neighbor shot herself as the police arrived with an arrest warrant.

Now Angela wonders again who sent the envelope. More importantly, she wonders why it had been sent now. She tosses the pizza box into the trash. Just as she begins shutting down her computer, a text pops onto her phone. She reads it and calls Zane. "Are you close?"

"Just leaving the garage."

"Pick me up out front," Angela says. "We need to get out to the Abbotts'."

Mavis Abbott sits up in bed. She's still somewhere between sleep and awake, but she swears she heard a noise. She lies back down among her stuffed animals and listens, but the house is still. She rolls over and checks her phone. It's almost eleven. She's not supposed to have her phone in bed, but her mother won't notice, not after today.

You up?

Stella responds almost at once. *Where were u today?*

Did you hear about the body they found in the factory by school? I'm the one who found it.

Mavis holds her thumb over the SEND button, but she trusts Stella. Besides, Mavis suspects the whole school will know it was her by tomorrow anyway. She hits SEND.

What!?!?!

I had to talk to the police. It was a big deal.

Who was it?

Mavis starts to type and deletes her response. She knows that anything she types into her phone can be used by the police later. Instead, she writes, *No idea.*

Stella had been at the party on Saturday, too. She'd seen the same things Mavis had, though they hadn't discussed them afterward. The two girls had helped by serving hors d'oeuvres and eggnog, and Mavis had liked having a purpose. She'd also liked her blue dress, but what she really liked was that the detective came, the cute one who works with Aunt Natalie, the same one who'd come to the house tonight. During the party, Zane hovered on the fringes, observing. "Can I get you a drink?" she asked him.

"How old are you?"

"Thirteen," Mavis said, which was an exaggeration, but she would be thirteen in ten months.

"I'll get my own drink. And when do you think your aunt will show up?"

Mavis rested her back against the wall, as close to Detective Perez as she could get. He moved a half step away.

"Aunt Natalie won't come. She says she will, but usually she bails."

"Wish I'd known."

Later, when the party began to wind down, Mavis searched for Stella. She found her on the front staircase, texting. "It's time to set up the library for dessert," Mavis said.

Mavis and Stella had spent the afternoon decorating the library's bookshelves with white snowflakes and hanging glass balls on a vintage aluminum tree. Mavis's mother had baked towers of meringues, macaroons, and Russian tea cakes, and at the center of it all was a white chocolate yule log covered in meringue mushrooms. The last task of the night for Mavis and Stella was to light dozens of candles right before her mother revealed the room.

Stella covered her mouth, and Mavis could smell rum on her breath.

"I think I'm drunk," Stella said, as she retrieved a glass of eggnog from where she'd hidden it behind her.

Mavis glanced around. No one was watching them. She drank the rest of the eggnog and felt the rum flowing through her bloodstream. "I'm drunk too," she said.

Right then, Uncle Bennet appeared behind them, stepping out from her mother's office. Mavis tried to hide the glass, but he took it from her, and Mavis felt the blood drain from her face. Her mother would kill her if she found out they'd been drinking.

"I'll never tell," Uncle Bennet said, before returning to the party.

Mavis watched him disappear into the crowd. She hauled Stella to her feet and dragged her to the library. The door was closed. Mavis yanked it open. Light from the hallway streamed across the hardwood floor to where her mother stood, wearing a black velvet dress with long sleeves and an open back. Half of her hair had fallen from the knot she'd tied it in. Patrick Leary faced her, standing too close. Mavis sobered up instantly. She clasped Stella's hand in hers and took a step backward.

Mavis's mother turned slowly. Splotches of red erupted on her bare skin. "Is it time?" she asked, breezing right past Mavis and Stella and back to the party as if none of it had happened.

Now, lying in bed, Mavis contemplates the scene again. She doesn't know much about sex or dating beyond what she's learned from TV, but she does know how Kevin Chandler makes her feel when he sits behind her at school and whispers her name. She blushes, with splotches of red, like her mother. Mavis wonders what her father had witnessed on Saturday night, too.

Her parents think she doesn't hear things, that she doesn't notice, but Mavis hears everything. She heard her father throw that glass against the wall last night and drive away. She heard her mother on the veranda, whispering to Patrick. She also heard the lie they told the police today when they claimed to have been home all night. But Mavis hasn't been completely honest either, because the one thing she can't tell anyone, not even Stella, the one thing she almost manages to suppress herself, is that her stomach has ached since she fled the crime scene this morning, and it isn't because she saw a man being devoured by rats. It's because she recognized who was being devoured.

It was Patrick Leary.

And if Mavis knows anything, she knows that this singular fact will make her father the prime suspect.

She turns the ringer off and flips her phone facedown. She rolls toward the wall and takes everything that happened today and stuffs it into an imaginary box to think about later. She has that algebra test in the morning. She remembers a practice problem and starts working through it. She thinks about Kevin, and what a jerk he was to leave her this morning. She wonders if Stella will ask her to sleep over on Friday night.

Her eyes pop open.

She sits up.

This time the noise she heard was definitely not a dream. She gets out of bed and patters down the hallway. The guest room is dark, the bed still made. Her parents' bed is empty, though only her mother's side has been slept in. "Mom?"

No one answers.

She creeps down the back stairs and into the kitchen, hoping to find her father. He's not there, though a glass sits on the counter filled with ice melting around the last of her father's whiskey. Mavis drinks what's left of it, grimacing at the smokey aftertaste. She slips her feet into her shoes and puts a coat over her pajamas.

Outside in the cold, the door to the cottage is ajar. "Dad?" she whispers. "Are you there?"

She moves forward as if in a dream. She watches as her hand nudges the door. Somewhere in the distance, a police siren screams through the night. "Who's there?" Mavis asks.

An incessant ringing penetrates Natalie's restless, drunken sleep. She groans and fumbles for the phone, while managing to pry one eye open wide enough to see Glenn's photo flashing across the screen. She can also see that it's two minutes before midnight. "What?"

At first, she can't understand a word Glenn says, but her sister's tone sobers her up. "What happened? Is Mavis okay?"

Natalie hears Glenn take a deep breath. "Go to the house." Glenn's voice is steady and clear.

Natalie sits up. The blankets have fallen to the floor. She still wears the suit she wore to work and doesn't remember coming home or making it to bed. "Where are you? Where's Jake?"

"I'm in a squad car on the way to the station."

The clock on Natalie's bedside table clicks over to midnight.

"Listen carefully," Glenn says. "Someone shot Jake. He's dead. They're taking me in for questioning. Mavis found me holding the gun."

1995

THE RUMORS ABOUT DIANE SYKES'S AFFAIR WITH GLENN'S FATHER started in the first days of September, a few weeks after his death, when Glenn began eighth grade. At first, she wondered if anyone would take the rumors seriously. The police, after all, had responded to a domestic disturbance the same night her father was killed. The officer had found Alan Cavanaugh with blood dripping down his arm after Glenn's mother stabbed him with a paring knife. "It's nothing," Alan told the officer.

"Doesn't look like nothing to me," the officer said. His name was Tom O'Neil, and he was a year or two into the job. "And your neighbor reported shouting. She was concerned."

"Diane's a good friend," Ruth said. "I slipped when I was doing dishes. I was holding the knife. His arm got in the way. We thought it was worse than it turned out to be." Ruth smiled. "That's probably the shouting she heard."

"She's a klutz," Alan told the officer, his words still slurred, at least according to the police report.

It had been a logical next step for the state detectives to focus on Ruth Cavanaugh, to see if they could prove that she'd used a rock to bash in her husband's head soon after the local officer responded to the incident. There was blood all over the house, of course, but that was easy to explain away since the officer had seen the blood when Alan was still alive. The state detectives couldn't find the murder weapon, or any other evidence that linked Ruth to the crime scene.

"That's because there isn't any," Diane Sykes said to Ruth as they sat on Ruth's back porch drinking beers. Diane worked at a law office as a legal secretary, and she seemed to understand the nuances of criminal law enough to guide Ruth through those first weeks. She made sure Ruth didn't say anything to the cops that she didn't need to. That day, Natalie was in the backyard chasing Lindsey across the grass. "There are monsters in the woods," Natalie shouted.

"There is not!" Lindsey said, arms out, floating like a firefly.

Tonya, as usual, was somewhere else, somewhere Glenn wished she could be, while Glenn hovered on the edge of the deck, trying to absorb as much of the women's conversation as she could.

"If my boss didn't pinch my ass so often," Diane said to Ruth, "I might cross the line."

"You would not," Ruth said, swatting her friend's arm, seemingly grateful for the change of topic. "But that's why I like working at home. I don't have to put up with that kind of thing anymore."

"I can see it through his pants," Diane said. "I don't know if he even wears underwear! I felt it once, too, when I was using the copier, and he decided to brush against me." She shrugged. "But a girl gets lonely."

Ruth laughed harder than she had in days. She'd been married since she was twenty-two years old and a mother since she was twenty-four. Now, as she faced the uncertainty of her future, the uncertainty of widowhood and the possibility of a murder charge, she might have looked up to Diane as much as Glenn did.

Diane glanced to where Glenn sat quietly on the steps, hoping to linger long enough to absorb what it meant to be an adult, to be a woman, to live in the real world. "Whatever you do, sweetie," Diane said to her, "have your own money and your own bank account. Otherwise, you'll wind up working at a law office with an entitled prick like my boss. And you're much smarter than he'll ever be."

"What's 'the line'?" Glenn asked.

"The line?" Diane said. "It's something you don't want to cross, because once you do, you can't come back. And they win."

Within a few weeks of that conversation, Ruth and Diane stopped meeting on the back porch. They stopped drinking wine together. And Diane stopped offering legal advice.

Glenn walked into the cafeteria at school and kept her head high. It felt as if every single student stopped talking and stared at her like she was in a sideshow, even Kimberly Green, who'd been Glenn's best friend in seventh grade. It was early September, still hot, still a day Glenn would have liked to jump into the Sykeses' pool, if that were still an option. She kept her eyes focused straight ahead as she joined the line for lunch. She swore she heard whispering behind her but didn't turn toward it. That would give the source too much power. She bought a strawberry yogurt for lunch, which was all she could stomach. It wasn't till she exited the serving line and searched for someplace to sit that she saw Tonya Sykes at the back of the cafeteria, at a table by herself. Tonya's hair was still chopped into a black bob. She still had the nose ring that had seemed so cool, the one Glenn had promised to emulate, but the confidence she'd exuded had dissipated. Now that the news trucks had come to Starling Circle, now that the rumors about her mother had taken hold, Tonya spent her days scurrying through the halls like a rat.

The wave of silence followed Glenn as she crossed the cafeteria. It almost felt as though the other students were parting to form a path right to Tonya's table. There were three empty chairs. Tonya looked up, and something in her eyes told Glenn that she'd give anything for a kind word. Glenn remembered sharing that stolen bottle of Zima and how special it had felt when Tonya had said they might be friends.

"Do you want to sit?" Tonya asked.

Looking back on this day, Glenn now wishes that she'd been kind and offered a show of solidarity, but it was easier to let this truth about Diane ignite. It wasn't hard to fan the flames, either. Girls like Kimberly Green knew how to turn gossip into truth.

"Your mother's a whore," Glenn said, staring till Tonya let her eyes fall.

Glenn, after all, didn't believe for one second that Ruth Cavanaugh hadn't wielded that rock. She still doesn't believe it, even now.

Now
November 17

CHAPTER 15

Natalie is quiet. Her head throbs, and for a moment, she wonders if she heard Glenn correctly, or if it's the alcohol playing tricks. She swings her legs out of bed. She can hear Glenn breathing on the other end of the phone. "Don't say anything to anyone," Natalie says at last. Her mouth feels cottony, and her voice sounds thick. "I'll meet you at the station."

"My lawyer's meeting me," Glenn says. "Go to the house. Mavis is there. She'll need you."

Glenn hasn't been arrested, not yet at least. If she had been, there's no way she'd be on the phone right now. Still, her sister shouldn't talk much, Natalie reminds herself. She's in a squad car, and anything she says could be overheard and reported. Natalie tries to stand, but the room sways. "Don't trust the lieutenant," she says. "She's good, really good. Remember that you aren't friends with her, or Zane. It doesn't matter how many jam blossoms he's baked. This is an interrogation, and I can guarantee the wife will be the prime suspect."

"I'm well aware," Glenn says.

Natalie rests her head on her palm. The pounding abates, if only a bit.

"Why were you holding the gun?" she asks.

"I found it beside Jake. I shot it too."

Glenn could have gunshot residue on her hands and wrists, depending on the gun. Her prints will be on the weapon too.

"We're at the station," Glenn says, and this time Natalie hears a catch in her sister's voice, as if reality has finally begun to set in. "Take Mavis to your house. I'll call you when we're done."

"You'll be fine," Natalie says.

"Will I?" Glenn asks, and then clicks off.

Natalie imagines her sister stepping out of the squad car and into the station. Even this late at night, there'll be plenty of activity as officers come and go, and a section of society that Glenn never really knew existed, let alone imagined being part of, descends on the station. The officer will lead her through the smells and sounds of humanity. Someone might call out "honey" or "pretty lady" (or worse), and it'll take Glenn a moment to realize that this could be it, the rest of her life. That's when the weak break.

Natalie forces herself to stand. She takes a tentative step and trips over the shoes she'd kicked off earlier. In the bathroom, a glimpse in the mirror shows a woman still wearing the suit she'd put on yesterday and an ashen face surrounded by greasy hair. Natalie doesn't look like someone she'd trust to take care of herself, let alone a twelve-year-old girl. She cups water in her hand and forces it down. Then she strips off the suit and replaces it with a pair of jeans from the floor, a T-shirt, and a gray fleece, and ties her hair in a ponytail. After she chews on three aspirin tablets, her brain still feels foggy as she moves down the front stairs. In the darkened hallway, a dog barks as Natalie puts on a coat. The sound seems close, too close, and when the dog barks again, Natalie's head clears. Instantly. The sound is coming from inside the house. From the front room. She reaches for her firearm, only to remember locking it away in the safe upstairs. She presses against the wall in the foyer. "Who the hell is there?"

A light clicks on in the front room.

"Boston Police," Natalie shouts, grabbing an umbrella from by the door. "Don't move."

Two hands rise from behind the sofa, followed by two paws and a black and white snout. Rowdy barks toward the ceiling. Behind him, Bennet Jones sits up slowly, the hair on one side of his head flattened against his scalp.

"What the hell are you doing in my house?" Natalie says.

"Are you arresting me twice in one day?" Bennet asks.

Natalie steps toward him, brandishing the umbrella. "I might if you don't start talking."

"Can I put on my glasses? I can't see enough to be scared."

"Fine."

Bennet feels around on the side table and pushes on his thick-rimmed glasses. He focuses on Natalie, and she swears he almost laughs. It's a mistake.

"Start talking," she says.

"You stumbled home a few hours ago and could barely stand, let alone get the keys into your front door. I was worried that you'd drown in your own vomit, so I stayed to check on you."

Natalie has managed to block out what happened at the bar earlier in the evening, but as Bennet speaks, she has flashes of the aborted kiss and Zane's horrified expression. She vaguely remembers stumbling out of the pub to escape, but nothing after that. She lets the umbrella drop to her side. Bennet releases Rowdy, who leaps to the floor and runs to her side. "Don't be surprised when you go into the kitchen," Bennet says. "I did some dishes. It was a mess."

Natalie groans. She suddenly sees the house through Bennet's eyes. She thinks about the piles of pizza boxes by the back door and the collection of takeout containers that had filled the kitchen sink, and Bennet's own tidy apartment, where everything has its place. "What were you even doing here?" she asks.

Bennet folds the blanket he'd been using. "I wanted to talk. You never returned any of my calls and, you know, I wondered . . . I mean, wasn't it nice to see each other today?"

"I almost arrested you."

"I'll overlook it."

"And I was apparently drunk enough that I don't remember

what mortifying things I did or said. What exactly was the nice part?"

Bennet meets her eyes. He's earnest. She remembers that now. Earnest in a way that draws her in and makes her want to flee at the same time.

"I feel like hell," she says. "And I need to get to work. You should get going."

Bennet comes around the sofa. "You smell like a distillery. Won't you get fired if you show up to work like this? Tell them you can't come."

If Natalie were to take a Breathalyzer right now, she'd probably be at twice the legal limit, if not more. But she doesn't have the option of calling in sick, not for this, and to be honest, she's shown up to work in worse states than this one. "My niece needs me."

"My car's out front."

Bennet reaches for her keys, and she yanks them away. She meets his eyes, wanting to capture every subtlety of the next few seconds. Bennet is still a suspect. "Jake's dead," she says. "Someone shot him."

Bennet squints as though making sense of the words. He starts to speak and stops. He seems genuine. Or rehearsed. Finally, he asks, "What happened?"

"I'm not sure. The police are at the house. That's where I'm headed."

"Is this connected to . . . to whatever you came to my apartment about today?"

"What do you think?"

Natalie should be asking more questions herself. Why is Bennet really here, on this night of all nights? Why is he connected to another murder? Bennet is a viable suspect, and Natalie may need another viable suspect with Glenn at the station being interrogated. She gives in and hands him her keys.

"We'll take my car," he says.

"Fine," Natalie says.

She'll watch him to see how he handles what's to come. In the end, Natalie will put family first; she'll put Glenn first. She's also a good detective, one who knows how to build a case. She hopes the lieutenant remembers that.

Glenn sits alone in a small room. She wears a clean pair of yoga pants and a sweatshirt, but her hands are still covered with Jake's blood. It's in her nails, up her wrists. When she moves her face, she can feel where it's dried in a crusty layer. She can hear that same blood gurgling in Jake's lungs after she found him lying on the floor in the cottage and ran to his side as he tried to speak. She can feel the blood, warm and viscous as it pooled around them and the life drained from his body.

She focuses on the chair opposite her. This must be an interview room, she tells herself, though it isn't set up like the ones on TV. It's small, like a den, and the chairs are comfortable. A tiny table separates her from where the lieutenant will sit when the interrogation begins, and a camera lens pokes out from the wall. She sips the coffee they brought her. It, at least, is as terrible as she'd expected. She glances toward the two-way mirror. Who's standing on the other side right now, watching her and assessing her behavior? Natalie sometimes plays that role. Over the years, she's told Glenn of suspects who tore at their clothing or did headstands as the detectives narrowed in on the truth. Glenn wonders if she'll do anything strange, if she'll feel herself losing control. She remembers one story Natalie told of a suspect, one who'd killed an elderly aunt by slowly poisoning her. His feet had pointed toward the door throughout the interrogation, as though he'd hoped he might eventually leave. "He never did," Natalie said.

Glenn checks her own feet. One of them points toward the door. The other taps away. She plants them solidly in front of her and folds her hands on her lap.

They took her phone when she got here, and she wonders now what time it is, if Natalie had gotten to the house, if she's taken Mavis away. It seems as though she's been waiting here for hours, and she suspects they want her anxiety to grow as she tries to guess what they already know and what tricks they might play on her. They want her to imagine the worst, but, for Glenn, the worst has already happened. Her husband's dead, and her life will never be the same.

The door to the interrogation room opens. Charlotte Todd strides in, her curly hair bouncing, her face made up. She tosses a briefcase into one chair and takes the seat beside Glenn's, clutching her hands despite the dried blood. They sit in silence for a moment. Glenn hasn't felt anything since she came into this room, and now, here, she realizes that she's gone numb. She also remembers that Charlotte knew Jake first. They'd gone to college together, and he'd introduced the two women. Charlotte, in her own way, must be grieving too. The strangest thought flits through Glenn's mind, one that she voices without much forethought.

"Did you and Jake ever date?"

The question barely phases her friend. "A few times, before he met you. He wanted kids. I didn't. That ended it."

Suddenly, ferocious, embarrassing tears spill down Glenn's cheeks. Glenn hates crying, especially in front of others, but no matter how hard she tries to make the tears stop, they only flow stronger. Charlotte simply waits. When the tears do stop, Glenn rests her head on the back of the chair, all emotion spent. "How do you look so good? It's the middle of the night."

"Professional superpower." Charlotte hands her a tissue from her bag. "And remember, I'm not a criminal attorney. Not anymore. I'll handle tonight, but we'll need to bring in someone else tomorrow. Have you told them anything?"

Glenn blows her nose. "Not really."

"That means you told them something. Tell me too."

Glenn closes her eyes. Parts of the night are still a blur, but she remembers going down the back stairs to the kitchen, where she'd found a glass of whiskey on the counter. She'd known that Jake had been having trouble sleeping for months, that he would come to the kitchen and pour himself a drink, and that she would sometimes find him still sitting there in the morning when she got up. She'd tried more than once to get him to say what had him concerned, but he wouldn't tell her. And if she's being honest, truly honest, those walls that he put up are what made her turn away and turn toward Patrick Leary. But she can't share that, not even with Charlotte. Not now.

"I went outside to look for him," Glenn says. "I heard a noise. A popping sound coming from the cottage."

"As in a gunshot?" Charlotte asks.

Glenn nods.

"And you ran toward someone with a gun? They'll want to know why."

"Jake's been upset recently. I thought . . . I thought he might have tried to hurt himself."

Charlotte looks up. "We'll have to see if it's possible that this was self-inflicted. Tell me what happened next."

Glenn ran under the pergola. The door to the cottage was open, but the lights were out. Inside, it was too dark to see, but someone struggled to breathe near the fireplace. Glenn hurried toward the noise, and in the dark, she skidded through a slick of blood, losing her footing and sliding to where Jake lay. His eyes fluttered, and he tried to speak. The gun lay beside him. Glenn held his head and moved her ear to his lips. "Watch out," he whispered. "Still here."

"Who's still here?"

"Shot me," Jake said.

Glenn's first thought was of Patrick. Her senses kicked in. Behind her, someone moved. Even now, she doesn't remember picking up the gun, but she does remember the feeling of it in her hand, and the sound of it firing into the dark. She also remembers footsteps on gravel and a car engine starting, and wondering if Patrick had been here, if he and Jake had fought, if this was all because of her.

"I'm so sorry," she said to Jake as he took his last breath.

It was then that she heard the sirens approaching, followed by Mavis's scream.

"I don't know how much Mavis saw," Glenn says to Charlotte. "But she was standing in the doorway."

Glenn hurried to her daughter, but Mavis lifted her hands in defense. It was only then that Glenn felt the gun still in her hand. She let it drop to the floor as a police cruiser sped into the driveway and blue lights flashed across the yard. Mavis turned to run, her face a mask of terror, but Glenn clutched her, holding her close till she stopped struggling. Jake's blood was smeared across Mavis's pajamas.

"We need to be strong," Glenn said. "You and I, we need to watch out for each other."

Outside, the officers pounded on the kitchen door.

"Are you ready?" Glenn whispered, and Mavis nodded. "We're back here," Glenn shouted.

She stepped into the doorway and had the good sense to hold her hands out, if not up, as the officers approached. One of them aimed a flashlight at them and nearly dropped it as he reached for his firearm. "Don't move."

"On the ground," the other one said.

Mavis gripped Glenn around the waist.

"Do exactly what they tell you to," Glenn whispered, as she fell to her knees.

"Come to me, sweetie," one of the officers said.

"Go," Glenn said.

Mavis dashed around her to the cop, as if escaping a murderer. Glenn fell forward, her cheek resting on the damp ground as she imagined cuffs clicking into place.

Now Charlotte says, "What happened to your clothes? They must have been drenched with blood."

"They took them as evidence," Glenn says.

"Have they taken fingerprints? DNA? You don't have to give them anything."

Glenn shakes her head. She'd known how much trouble she was in almost from the moment she walked into the cottage. Now she realizes that she's reached the end of one phase of her life and is about to begin another, and she'll never be able to return to what was. She'll be a widow, like her mother. She wonders if she'll also be a murderer, if that label will follow her through life.

She turns to face Charlotte. "I didn't do this."

"Then we'll need to figure out who did."

CHAPTER 16

BENNET PARKS HIS ANCIENT HONDA CIVIC ON THE STREET IN FRONT of Glenn's house after driving the three miles from Jamaica Plain to West Roxbury. He pulls the hand brake into place. Natalie looks out the passenger's side window. By now, cars fill her sister's driveway, including three cruisers with flashing lights, and the yard has been cordoned off. A single news truck has set up camp, though Natalie imagines there'll be plenty more as soon as they connect this story to the Glenn Abbott who appears on TV and has a book due to publish next week. She wonders how long it will take them to connect it to the first murder, or to her father's death. She puts her hair into a hat and lifts the hood on her parka. Beside her, Bennet stares through the windshield. "This is real," he says. "It didn't feel that way, not till we got here. I can't believe Jake's gone."

Natalie turns in her seat. Rowdy leaps from the back of the car and settles on her lap. "Did Jake tell you that we found your wallet at a crime scene?" she asks. "It was another murder."

Bennet blanches. He runs his hand through Rowdy's fur and glances at the cruisers again. The blue lights flash across his face. "I thought you were going to arrest me in my apartment," he says. "And hadn't a clue why, but I've put most of it together since. And I saw a murder being covered on the news earlier. It was the same one, wasn't it?"

"Now there are two murders," Natalie says, "and that wallet connects you to both of them."

"You're connected too," Bennet says. "Through me, through your sister, through your niece. Seems to me you should step away from the whole thing."

"I already have, officially at least. But that doesn't mean I can't ask questions or stick my nose where it doesn't belong, including talking to you. And when I'm not a police officer, I don't need to play by the rules."

Bennet smiles. "I like it when you're tough. Are you planning to beat me up?"

Natalie shoots him a glare.

"Do you know how beautiful you are?" Bennet asks.

"I look like roadkill and smell like barf. There's nothing beautiful about me. And this really isn't a good time to flirt."

Bennet kisses the dog's snout. "I take what I can get."

"I've been doing this for a long time, and I'm pretty good at it, so let me lay the case out for you. Yesterday, my niece found a body. Later that same night, her father was shot dead. Somehow, I don't think those incidents are isolated. My bet is you know something that you didn't tell us yesterday, or maybe you thought it didn't matter because when we talked to you yesterday, Jake was still alive, and you planned on talking to him before you told us because you're loyal and he's a friend. And if he had something to hide—something worth killing over—you wanted to give him a chance to come clean." Natalie sits up and pokes Bennet's chest. "I have another guess for you: you didn't come to my house tonight because you missed me and wanted to snuggle; you either came to tell me that thing that you held back or to see what you could get me to tell you. I bet you even figured out that a part of me wishes I hadn't screwed things up with you. And you thought you could use that to get me to talk."

Bennet won't meet Natalie's eyes, which tells her that even if she didn't get it all, she got most of it right. Now she needs to figure out which parts to focus on.

"Do you wish that you hadn't screwed things up?" he asks.

"If I say yes, will you tell me whatever it is you've held back?"

"Maybe."

"Then yes. If you looked up 'commitment phobe' in the dictionary, it would say 'See Natalie Cavanaugh.' Good enough? Now it's your turn."

"I wish you hadn't screwed things up too."

"Not that. What didn't you tell me?"

"Jake and I work together," Bennet says with a shrug.

"Tell me the parts I don't already know."

"Six months ago, Jake told me he was in trouble, and it was something financial. He asked if he could borrow some money. I offered him ten thousand bucks."

"Did he take it?"

Bennet shakes his head. "He said it wasn't enough, and when I tried to get him to tell me more, he clammed up."

"He owed money, somewhere, but you're not sure where?"

Bennet scratches Rowdy behind the ears and doesn't answer.

"What do you know?"

"I run the IT department. People don't understand that there aren't many secrets at work."

"You go into people's systems and snoop. Let me guess. You found something Jake didn't want you to see."

"After he talked to me, I poked around his hard drive and went into his e-mail. I found some documents for Mavis's soccer club. He's the manager."

"I've given plenty of money to that club," Natalie says. "I still have a set of holiday spices Mavis talked me into buying. I don't even cook, though I bet you could have guessed that when you saw my kitchen."

"I've given the club plenty of money too. That was the problem. I found a second set of books. A second set of statements too. Jake had lost a lot of money, other people's money."

Natalie glances out the window, at the other houses on the street. The neighbors here, Jake and Glenn's friends, they all were part of that club. "How much did he take?"

"A couple hundred thousand dollars."

"What's a kids' soccer club doing with a couple hundred thousand dollars?" Natalie swears under her breath. "Do you know if any of these fine folks found out?"

"I'm not sure if the problem still exists," Bennet says. "Saturday's party was a fundraiser for the soccer club. I asked Jake about it that night, and he told me the problem was taken care of. When I pushed, he told me the less I knew, the better it was for me."

"You must have an idea, though?"

Bennet nods toward the house. "Things started changing as soon as that guy Patrick Leary showed up. The one who lives in the cottage. I've known Jake for fifteen years. He claimed Patrick was a friend from high school, but in all those years, he'd never mentioned the guy once. And Patrick came to the office on Monday. He and Jake got into it, loud enough that I could hear them through Jake's door. It had something to do with Glenn. And they were both pissed off."

"Is this why you sent me that text today? The one that told me to watch my back?"

Bennet waits a moment before answering. "Something happened between them. And it wasn't good. It was something I wouldn't want to get anywhere near."

"You know I'm a cop, right?" Natalie says. "You can't protect me. It's my job to get in other people's business."

She turns to face the house. Zane had told her that Glenn and Patrick were flirting on Saturday. She stops herself before asking Bennet the obvious question: what did Glenn know? "Would you keep this to yourself for now?" she asks.

"As long as it doesn't come back to me."

Natalie steps out of the car. "Wait here."

At the foot of the driveway, she waves over one of the uniforms. "There's a kid somewhere?" she asks.

"In the kitchen with the detective. She's pretty shell-shocked."

Natalie signs the log and heads to the kitchen, where Mavis and Zane play chess at the kitchen counter. As Natalie opens the door, Mavis says, "Check."

Zane glances up. Mavis turns, and her face crumples. She leaps from her stool, runs to Natalie, and sobs. Zane meets Natalie's eyes and makes a heart shape with his hands.

She mouths, "Thank you," though she doesn't know where to begin with Mavis or what she could possibly say to make her niece feel even the tiniest bit better. All she knows is that they all have a long night in front of them, followed by many long and difficult days.

"I'll give you some space," Zane says, but when he gets to the kitchen door, he adds, "What the hell is he doing here?"

Outside, in the driveway, Bennet lingers by the garage with Rowdy as the dog lifts a leg to pee.

"I told him to stay in the car," Natalie says.

"He clearly didn't listen. And why is he with you anyway? He's a suspect in this case, Cavanaugh."

Zane stops before saying anything else, though Natalie has no doubt he wants to ask if she slept with Bennet. He probably would have if Mavis weren't here.

"Not your business," Natalie says.

"But it is, and you know that. Everything is my business now."

Natalie crouches and lifts Mavis's chin to look her in the eye. "I'm taking you to my place tonight. Right now. What do you need to bring?"

"Nothing," Zane says. "We have a search warrant for the whole house." He catches himself. "Sorry," he says to Mavis, "but that means your room too."

"I have an algebra test tomorrow," Mavis says.

Natalie nearly tells her niece that she'll probably get all A's this year, no matter how she performs in school, but knowing Mavis, she also probably needs to focus on that test to survive. Natalie takes Mavis's schoolbag from where it hangs by the door. "Is everything you need in here?"

Mavis nods.

"Search this and we'll leave. I'll go talk to Bennet."

Natalie makes a move toward the kitchen door, but Zane stops her. "I need to talk to him," he says, "not you. And I'll search the bag when I get back. Don't touch anything."

"She'll need a set of clothing for tomorrow too," Natalie says.

"Fine," Zane says.

Natalie watches as he crosses the driveway and approaches Bennet with a hand extended. She could wonder what he asks, if Bennet mentions how drunk she was when he found her, if the two of them bond over what a hot mess she's become. Instead, she turns her attention to Mavis. Natalie's never forgotten finding her own father's body or the scrutiny of the ensuing investigation. Sometimes, late at night, something will rip Natalie from a deep sleep, and she'll swear she can smell the stink of rot in the air. Life can change in an instant, and Natalie wishes that Mavis hadn't had to learn that lesson tonight too.

"My pajamas were covered with blood," Mavis whispers now. "Detective Perez got me a new pair to wear." She pauses. "My mother had a gun."

Natalie puts her fingers to Mavis's lips. There are too many cops here, too many people to overhear. "Try not to think about it. And take your bag. We're leaving."

"But . . . Detective Perez said he needed to search it."

Natalie grabs it herself and waits as Mavis puts a coat on over her pajamas. "Have you said anything to Detective Perez?" she asks.

"We played chess."

"About what you saw tonight."

Even though Mavis shakes her head, Natalie isn't sure how much she should believe. "Don't speak to any police officers, not even Detective Perez, unless I'm there. Understand?"

"I know how this works."

Out in the driveway, Zane and Bennet still talk quietly with each other. As Natalie approaches, she holds the schoolbag out. Zane stares her down before taking it. He pulls on a pair of gloves and shines a light into it, taking longer than he really needs to. "You do all your schoolwork on that tablet?" he asks Mavis.

"Except what we do in class."

"You know you can't delete anything, not these days. If there's something on there that I should know about, you should tell me now."

Natalie steps between them and takes the bag.

"We'll need to talk to you in the morning," Zane says to Mavis. "There'll be lots more questions."

"Where's my mother?" Mavis asks.

"With the lieutenant," Zane says. "Answering questions. And I need to talk to your aunt and Mr. Jones for a sec."

Natalie hands Rowdy's leash to Mavis. "Take him for a little walk under the beech trees there. Don't go near the street, though. There's a reporter lurking."

Mavis leads the dog away, turning once to look back at them, but Natalie waits till her niece is out of earshot before asking, "What have you found so far?"

"The crime techs haven't arrived yet," Zane says. "We're securing the area and waiting for them. And you know I can't answer, so don't ask."

"Where did it happen?"

Zane sighs.

"I'll find out from my sister anyway."

"Fine," Zane says. "In the cottage."

"What about the tenant?" Natalie asks. "Patrick Leary. Where was he? You should be looking at him. He was at the party on Saturday too, you know. Have you done a background check?"

Zane takes a pad from his pocket and flips it open. "What do you know about Mr. Leary?"

Natalie shrugs and glances at Bennet. "He's Jake's friend from high school," she says.

"Have you dated him too?"

Natalie glares at Zane.

"We're looking into any and all suspects. So, back to the suspect *you* decided to bring to the scene of the crime."

"We were together tonight," Natalie says. "I met him . . ." The failed kiss flashes through her memory again. She needs to own this, or it will own her. "After my aborted mauling."

That at least earns a hint of a smile from Zane. "You were together the whole night?"

"The whole night," she says.

Zane flips the pad closed. "Noted." He puts his hands on his hips and speaks as though Bennet isn't there. "What are you doing with him?"

Natalie wishes she knew.

"You're a detective," Zane says. "Believe it or not, I like you. And I'm telling you that you're too close to this case, and if you can't see it, you're about to find out. You need to back off."

Natalie steps right up to him. "I'm taking my niece home. You know how to contact me. In fact, you know where I live, so come find us when you want to talk. In the meantime, go get her a change of clothes so that I can officially *back off,* Detective."

Zane meets her eyes before heading inside. Bennet waits till the door closes. "Remind me never to go toe-to-toe with you," he says.

CHAPTER 17

Mavis lies in the back seat of Bennet's Civic, watching the streetlights. Beside her, Rowdy sighs as he rests his head on her chest. In the front of the car, Bennet drives with Aunt Natalie beside him. They haven't spoken since they left Mavis's house. He shifts the gears, and the car sputters as he turns a corner.

"Still haven't mastered the clutch," Natalie says.

"I do just fine," Bennet says.

Mavis's whole body feels numb. She'd give anything to sleep, to bring a close to this terrible night, but as soon as she shuts her eyes, images flood her mind, ones that she can't pack away in boxes no matter how hard she tries. Rats tear at Patrick Leary's skin. A gun goes off. Her mother charges toward her. In the dark, the blood looks like chocolate syrup, but the metallic smell is unmistakable. A moonbeam shines across the cottage floor, lighting up her father's body and his empty eyes. She hears her own screams as she tries to escape her mother's clutches.

Mavis has kept that terror to herself, no matter what Zane had asked over the chessboard. She knows that what she tells the police will matter, and it will matter to her mother in particular, because the truth could send her to jail.

Mavis won't tell anyone about what she saw in the library on Saturday. She won't tell anyone about the fight her parents had last night, or that she recognized Patrick's body. Not even Aunt Natalie.

The car comes to a stop. Bennet yanks up the hand brake. "Is she asleep?" he asks, his voice soft.

Mavis squeezes her eyes shut.

"I think so," Natalie says. "Tell me more about what happened between Jake and Patrick on Monday. You said Patrick came by the office."

Bennet sighs. "I only heard part of the conversation. Jake wanted Patrick out of the cottage. He said something about not wanting him near his family anymore, and that he was through. Those were his exact words, *I'm through.*"

"And I take it you didn't hear Patrick's response."

"No," Bennet says.

"Do you know anything else about Patrick?"

"The only time I met him outside of the office was at the party on Saturday."

Natalie starts to say something and stops.

"Come on," Bennet says. "I shared. Now it's your turn."

The engine runs. Heat pours from the vents. But otherwise, a silence fills the car. Then a noise begins. It takes a moment for Mavis to put the noises in context, but when she does, she wants to be anywhere but trapped in the back of this car pretending to sleep. Bennet and Aunt Natalie are kissing.

"I can't," Natalie says, a moment later, but it's followed by more kissing sounds, and this time they're loud enough to make Mavis want to disappear.

"Stop," Natalie says, her voice firmer.

Bennet sighs.

"It doesn't matter what we want," Natalie says. "Not tonight."

"What about tomorrow?"

"Probably not anytime this week. And, besides, I don't know what I want."

"Tell me you liked seeing me today."

"I liked seeing you."

"That might get me through," Bennet says.

Another silence fills the car, and Mavis doesn't know if she can take another round. Thankfully, Rowdy barks, and Natalie turns toward the noise. Mavis sits up, exaggerating a yawn.

"And he's still jealous," Natalie says, smiling at Mavis. "We're home."

Cold air sweeps through the car and cools off whatever was about to happen in the front seat. Bennet gets out. Natalie follows, and they stand awkwardly on the sidewalk as Mavis gathers her schoolbag and untangles herself from Rowdy's leash.

"Can I call you tomorrow?" Bennet asks.

"We're sleeping in," Natalie says. "But, yes, you can call."

Bennet pushes his glasses up his nose, waiting, it seems, for Natalie to say something else. She glances toward Mavis and shrugs.

"That's that, then," Bennet says.

"Thanks for tonight," Natalie says.

"Bye, Uncle Bennet," Mavis says, and then is relieved to see him get into the car and drive off.

Natalie doesn't seem to know what to do next, so Mavis takes her hand and drags her toward the little house.

"Does Bennet come to your parents' house very often?" Natalie asks.

"He and my dad are friends."

It takes a moment for Mavis to realize what's wrong with the statement, that she'd used the present tense, and that everything she says now about her father will be in the past. Tears threaten to erupt, but she manages to hide the feelings away in time so that she can examine them later, when she's ready. A welcome numbness spreads through her body, but that doesn't keep Natalie from giving her Sad Eyes. With a sudden detached awareness, Mavis realizes she'll be facing Sad Eyes for days, if not years, to come.

Natalie says, "My dad died when I was a little older than you," and, as if reading Mavis's mind, adds: "I still don't talk about it. You can skip sharing your feelings tonight, but this kind of thing eats away at you, and most of the time you don't even know it's happening. I thought I'd outrun it. Look at me—I'm forty-two, running, running, only to find I'm standing still. Promise me you won't let the same thing happen to you."

Mavis can't imagine being forty-two. It seems so old. "I promise," she says. At least it will keep Natalie off her back for a little while longer.

"It's a mess inside. Sorry."

Mavis steps into the house, with its tiny front hall and narrow stairs that lead to the single bedroom on the second floor. A sour smell fills the air. "It's not so bad."

"You're a good liar."

Natalie leads Mavis through the living room and into the tiny kitchen at the back of the house, where she adds two ice cubes to a jam jar and tops it off with vodka. She scans the fridge, which holds a few takeout containers and a bottle of ketchup. She opens the equally bare cupboards. "Score," she says, taking out a two-liter bottle of Pepsi. "I don't even know where this came from, but at least it's not open."

When she unscrews the cap, there's a hiss and an eruption of foam as soda bubbles onto the counter. Natalie makes a half-hearted attempt to wipe it up. Mavis resists the temptation to finish the job. Her aunt seems to have her own rules, but if those rules involve drinking soda, Mavis doesn't plan to complain anytime soon. She listens to the soda bubbling around ice cubes in her own jam jar and drinks it down in two gulps before filling the jar again.

Natalie tops off her own glass. "You'll never get to sleep if you drink too much of that."

Mavis belches.

"Let me guess," Natalie says. "You aren't allowed to have soda at home. Do me a favor: you can finish the bottle, but don't tell your mother about it. She'll be pissed off."

"My mother says you drink too much."

Natalie raises her glass. "This is something else you don't need to tell her about."

Mavis glances at the clock. It's past 4:00 a.m. now, but she still can't imagine sleeping tonight, or ever again.

As if reading her mind, Natalie says, "It's almost morning. What do you do when you can't sleep?"

"Sometimes my dad can't sleep. We play chess."

Mavis had used present tense. Again. Those imaginary boxes, the ones she hides away, threaten to burst open. Natalie seems to sense the threat of emotion and welcome it even less than Mavis does. "I never graduated much beyond Candyland, and I saw you kicking Zane's ass back at the house." She grabs the bottle of vodka. "Let's watch TV."

Mavis takes the Pepsi. In the living room, Natalie clears empties from a coffee table as she digs around for the remote. Then she unfurls a knitted afghan and wraps it around them. "We can watch anything you want."

Mavis finds an episode of *CSI: Miami* that's already twenty minutes in, but she's seen this episode. It's about a model who gets electrocuted on a runway.

"Don't tell your mother I let you watch this," Natalie says. "I'll be in big trouble."

Mavis knows what to tell her mother, and what not to. She watches in silence, and when a commercial break begins, she closes her eyes and leans against Natalie. The ad is for an erectile dysfunction drug, and she can recite every line by heart.

"You were kissing Uncle Bennet in the car," Mavis says softly.

"And I take it you were pretending to sleep. You'd make a good cop."

"Are you dating?"

Natalie shrugs. "We went on a few dates a long time ago. Now I'm not sure what's going on, and we won't know, not till we figure out what happened with . . . your father."

The mention of her father catches Mavis off guard. An imaginary box bursts open, along with a sob from her chest. Natalie pulls her in even closer, and they sit in silence till the commercial break ends and the episode starts up. When the next commercial break starts, Natalie fumbles with something on the end table and hands Mavis a paper napkin that looks as though it came from a pizza shop. "It's all I have."

Mavis blows her nose. She could talk about her feelings, but right now, it's easier to look at the last few hours from a distance, like a cop would. "My dad got in a fight with Patrick," she says.

"Is that what you heard Bennet say? Or did you see it happen?"

"I just know," Mavis says. "And if I were a cop, I'd look at Patrick. And I'd want to know how all of this was connected to the body I found in the factory."

Natalie scrutinizes Mavis for a moment. "You have good instincts."

"Did they figure out who the first victim was?"

"If they have, they're not telling me. Do you know?"

Mavis isn't ready to confess what she knows, not yet at least.

Natalie says, "We found Bennet's wallet at yesterday's crime scene. And earlier today, when you were talking to the lieutenant, you held something back."

"That's not a question," Mavis says.

"No, it's a statement."

Mavis fills her glass again, but the Pepsi feels dry in her mouth.

"What were *you* doing in that building?" Natalie asks.

The commercial break ends. Mavis turns to the TV as the episode resumes, and Natalie's question sits between them. When the next commercial begins, Natalie takes the remote and turns the sound down. "I ghosted your uncle Bennet even though I really liked him. And I liked Rowdy even more." She sits quietly for a moment. "Aren't you going to ask me why?"

"Do I have to tell you something if I do?"

"Yep."

"Tell me why."

"I was scared of being happy and taking a chance. And I thought that if I let him like me too much, I might want to take a chance. And I didn't come to your mother's party on Saturday because I didn't want to face what I'd done and how much I'd hurt him, so I stayed home by myself instead." She waves a hand around the tiny living room. "Imagine giving all this up."

"I like this house," Mavis says. "It's efficient."

"But taking chances, that's what life's all about, right? And if there's something you should tell me, something I should know about your father or Patrick or your Uncle Bennet, or anything, why don't you tell me instead of waking up thirty years from now full of regret?"

Mavis watches the screen. She could turn up the volume and make Natalie wait. She could make her wait a lifetime, but what good would that do? "There's a boy at school that I like."

Natalie faces the screen, as though she knows that if she engages, if she makes one wrong move, Mavis might stop talking. But now that Mavis has given a voice to what happened, she can't stop. She finds the box with Kevin's name on it and rips off the bow.

"He dared me to go into the building."

"Where was he when I found you?"

"I don't know. He didn't wait for me."

"He sounds like an asshole."

Like with her mother, it surprises Mavis to hear an adult swear in front of her. She covers her mouth and squelches a laugh. She also thinks about Kevin Chandler and the way he doesn't leave her alone, even when she tells him to. She thinks about how much she wanted him to be there for her yesterday when she fled the factory, and how disappointed it had felt when he'd left.

Kevin *is* an asshole.

Natalie runs her fingers through Mavis's hair. "What's Kevin's last name?" she asks.

"Chandler. Kevin Chandler."

"Well, Kevin Chandler is a tool. Don't ever forget it."

Mavis lays her head against Natalie and closes her eyes. "The body I found," she whispers. "It's Patrick Leary. He's dead too."

Natalie puts her own glass aside. "And you didn't tell me because . . ."

"Because my parents got in a fight on Monday."

"And it was about your mother and Patrick."

Mavis nods.

Natalie shifts beside her. "Now that you've told me, I bet you can get some sleep."

* * *

Natalie listens as her niece's breathing finally grows steady. For the first time ever, Natalie wonders what it might be like to have a child or to love another human so deeply. She wonders if she and Mavis will be a team now while Glenn's fate is determined by others.

On the TV, the episode ends, but Natalie doesn't move, not even to take the remote from Mavis. She imagines Glenn at the station, in the box, being interrogated. Natalie hopes that her sister has the common sense to keep the secrets she can hide and share the ones she can't. She hopes Glenn understands that her only hope is self-preservation.

CHAPTER 18

Angela observes Glenn Abbott through the two-way glass as the woman talks to her lawyer and rubs her neck. Glenn is smart enough to know someone might be watching her, but even she relaxes occasionally. It's then that the emotion shows. Her face breaks, and the lawyer touches her arm, kind but reserved, the way lawyers are when they're rising above their clients' predicaments. When Glenn remembers the two-way glass, she straightens her spine and rubs her eyes with a fist. She folds her hands on her lap, and a hint of fear flashes across her face before she replaces it with a mask of composure. Glenn Abbott is imagining a future without freedom, and Angela's gut tells her that this woman is guilty, but suspecting and knowing are very different, and no matter what happens today, no matter what messages Angela receives from higher ups, she plans to take her time with this case. Angela tries not to give in to the pressure to close. Follow the evidence and ignore the outside voices. It's a motto she'd adopted long ago. Right now, Glenn Abbott is a witness. Sometime later, perhaps during this very interview, she might become a suspect.

Zane joins Angela at the mirror. "Find anything at the scene?" she asks.

"Nothing surprising," he says. "But they're just getting started. That's the lawyer. I met her at the party this weekend."

Angela takes in Charlotte Todd's strong features, her slick hair, her pale complexion and suit. The woman looks good for seven in the morning. Charlotte used to be a criminal lawyer. Now she works as a sort of fixer, one whom Angela's crossed before. She can handle a crisis. Glenn Abbott is lucky she can afford her.

"Where's the kid?" Angela asks.

"Cavanaugh came to get her," Zane says. "She brought Bennet Jones with her."

Angela tries not to react. "Like *with* her?"

"That would be my guess. They said they'd been together all night but . . . when I left Cavanaugh at the pub, she was three sheets to the wind."

"Okay, make sure I'm the one dealing with that piece. Did you get anything out of Mavis?"

"She killed me at chess. I lost four games in about a half hour."

"You didn't get her to talk in a half hour?"

"Like I said, she killed me at chess. She knows how to play the long game."

"Smart kid," Angela says. Smart kids know how to keep secrets. "She keeps popping up at the center of things. And I want to know what she was hiding from us earlier."

"I don't think Mavis is the key here," Zane says.

"That's not what I'm saying, but still, trends are good to note. And she must be a wreck."

"More in shock. But she seems okay physically. Mentally, I'm not sure."

Angela can't imagine relying on Natalie Cavanaugh in a crisis like this one. Glenn Abbott must be terrified for her daughter's future, a terror that Angela can use during the interview. She nods through the two-way glass. "Is she good for it?"

"She's the wife. She has the means and the opportunity, and we found her with the weapon."

"Go with the obvious, right? I'll take the lead. You? Be charming." Angela opens the door and strides into the small room. "I'm sorry for your loss, Mrs. Abbott. And for keeping you waiting so long."

Glenn tilts her head. Her gaze locks on Angela's. "Call me Glenn."

Zane leans in, smiling. "How are you holding up? You need coffee or anything?"

"If I have more coffee, I'll float away," Glenn says.

Charlotte Todd adjusts her chair. "They aren't your friends," she says, softly, but loud enough to be heard. "Neither of them."

"They aren't," Glenn says, "but we all want the same thing. To find who killed my husband. Ask me what you need to and let me know how I can help."

Angela takes the seat across from Glenn. She also takes in the woman's body language. It's open, defiant even. And it tells her that maybe she shouldn't go with the obvious, not yet at least. "Why don't we get some of the basics out of the way. Tell me about your husband. How long have you been married?"

"Six years," Glenn says.

"Mavis isn't his child?"

"She has been since we married. But, no, Jake wasn't her biological father. I had Mavis on my own." Glenn smiles as she seems to remember something. "Jake and I went out four times before I mentioned Mavis. He was younger than me. He wasn't even thirty when we met, and I thought he'd run the moment I told him that I had a five-year-old waiting at home, but he was better than that. He wanted to meet her right away. They've been inseparable ever since."

"And who is Mavis's biological father?"

"A turkey baster."

"You've never met him?"

"Only in his profile. Harvard business school. Played football. God knows if any of it was true. But Jake's the only father Mavis has ever known."

"He sounds like he was a good person," Angela says, letting the woman sit with her grief for a moment. "Tell me how you met."

"Through a friend. We went for drinks and hit it off."

"Who was the friend?"

Glenn misses a beat. "Bennet Jones," she says.

Angela catches Zane's eye. "And Jake grew up where?"

"In central Mass."

"And his parents? Have you let them know what happened tonight?"

Glenn shakes her head. "His parents died before we met, so I never knew them. They were in a car accident. He was an only child too. I think that was one of the reasons Jake was so ready for a family."

"Tell me about tonight. Let's start with the gun that you shot. Tell me what happened."

Glenn sits up. She must know that the interview has begun, that the softball questions have ended. She glances toward her lawyer, who says, "Go through what happened. You have nothing to hide."

Glenn takes a deep breath. "I entered the cottage and found my husband bleeding to death. The gun was beside him. He told me that someone was in the house. I heard noises, and I shot. In self-defense."

"Who did you think it might have been?"

"I didn't have any idea, but Jake indicated that it was the person who'd shot him."

"Did he say who it was? Or whether it was a man or a woman?"

Glenn shakes her head. "He could barely speak."

Angela takes a note and changes tack. "You have a tenant who lives in that cottage. Patrick Leary. Were you concerned it might be him? That you might shoot him by accident? Your daughter was in your house. Were you concerned it might be her?"

"I was acting on instinct," Glenn says. "I didn't think it through. If I had, I probably would have stopped myself."

"Do you know where the gun came from?"

"We don't own a gun. I've never shot one in my life," Glenn says.

"It's convenient, isn't it?" Angela says. "That the first time you've ever shot a gun in your life was right before we might test you for gunshot residue. Now, if we ran the test and it came back positive, you could claim that you shot the gun once, at an unknown intruder, but not twice."

"Did you agree to the test?" Charlotte asks Glenn.

"We don't need it, do we?" Angela says. "It's expensive, and your client told us that she fired the gun."

Charlotte grabs her bag. "Let's go. We've answered enough questions."

Angela can see that the lawyer is getting concerned, but Glenn shakes her head. "I want them to find who did this. I want them to find who killed my husband."

"Remember, Mrs. Abbott," Angela says. "We're here to help. It feels good to tell the truth. That anxiety you're carrying in your shoulders, it'll all go away when you tell us what happened."

Glenn leans forward. She drops her voice. "There's no anxiety, not about this, at least. The fact that my husband is dead and I'm sitting in a police station wondering if I'll ever leave again, that's anxiety-inducing. My husband was dying in front of me, and someone was in the house. That's the truth. And as for concocting an elaborate plan where I shot my husband once and shot the gun a second time in order to explain gunshot residue, you're giving me too much credit. I'm not that smart."

Angela flips through her notepad and pretends to read something from earlier. "What time was it when this all happened?"

"A few minutes past eleven. I looked at my bedside clock before I went downstairs."

"Tell me you have a security system. Video surveillance?"

Glenn shakes her head.

"That's either convenient or inconvenient, depending on what really went down." Angela glances toward Zane. "See what you can get from the neighbors. Mrs. Abbot, if you had to guess, why do you think your husband was in the cottage anyway?"

"I wish I knew," Glenn says.

Zane leans forward. "I talked to Patrick Leary at the party. Seems like a great guy. The two of you were friendly."

Charlotte touches Glenn's arm.

"I throw a good party," Glenn says. "I try to pay attention to all of my guests. You felt welcome, didn't you, Detective?"

"Let's talk about Mr. Leary," Angela says. "His car is parked on the street in front of the house, but he's not around. Where do you think he is?"

"The last time I saw him was on Monday night. I said hello. It was after dark, but not late. Maybe around seven o'clock. He seemed like he always did."

"How is he, *always*?"

"Confident," Glenn says.

"You went inside, where you and your husband spent the whole night together."

When Glenn nods, Angela can see that she told her first lie, or at least the first lie that she regrets. "And you don't have a clue where Patrick Leary is now?"

"I don't keep tabs on the comings and goings of my tenant. Maybe he has a girlfriend. Maybe he's on a business trip. I don't know anything about the man except that my husband said he needed a place to stay, and the cottage was empty, so I agreed."

Zane asks, "You don't know your husband's friends?"

"I have friends Jake doesn't know." Glenn seems to catch herself. "That he didn't know. We all have parts of our lives we keep to ourselves, our own secrets."

"Secrets can be dangerous," Angela says. "Are there any you want to tell me now? And I'll give you a hint on this one. It has to do with being home all night on Monday. Why don't you tell me what really happened? As soon as I see your husband's phone records, I'll know you're lying."

"I think this is over," Charlotte says, but Glenn overrules her lawyer again.

"I told you Jake and I were home on Monday night, but he left. I didn't hear him come in till late." She pauses. "And when I asked him about it yesterday, he wouldn't tell me where he went." Her back remains rigid, but her eyes shine with tears. "That was the last time we talked to each other."

Angela lets her sit with the thought for a moment.

"Could I get a glass of water?" Glenn asks.

Angela leans back and waits. "Where would you guess your husband went?"

Glenn flexes her fingers. "Jake has been upset about something . . . but I didn't know what. He's been spending a lot of time at work."

"At work? Or with someone else? An affair, maybe? Any guesses who?"

"I have a suspicion," Glenn says. "It's probably a long shot, but after last night . . ."

"The smallest leads sometimes get us answers," Zane says.

Glenn glances at her lawyer who shrugs. "Go ahead," she says.

"I had an event yesterday in my hometown. Elmhurst. It was for influencers, so that they could help promote the book before it publishes next week. This woman showed up. She wasn't an influencer, but she told me she knew my mother. It turned out she was a real estate agent. I thought she wanted me to list my mother's house."

Angela knows that Glenn's mother died earlier this year. Natalie had taken her first day off in years for the funeral. "But . . ." Angela says.

"Last night, she showed up at our house. She was standing in the dark, smoking."

"And you think this woman knew Jake. Maybe she was having an affair with him."

"I don't know what to think," Glenn says. "But Jake was dead two hours later. Her name is Olivia. Her card is on my kitchen counter, but I'm sure you can find her online."

Angela makes a note of the name. "That's the kind of information we need, Mrs. Abbott. It'll be easy enough to see if your husband has a connection to this woman. You can't hide much, not in this day and age. So Monday you see your tenant, you get in a fight with your husband, and your husband takes off and doesn't come back till late at night. The next day, you meet a stranger who shows up later the same day at your house. What else happened that day? Anything else out of the ordinary?"

"Not till I got home and found you at my house talking to my husband and daughter," Glenn says.

"Noted. But what did you do before that?"

"I met my sister in the morning." Glenn looks at Zane. "You were there. You're the one who told me you were in the neighborhood. Remember?"

Angela says, "What else was on your agenda for the day?"

"Not much. Charlotte and I met for coffee before the book event," Glenn says, adding quickly, "Charlotte helps me with PR."

"Expensive PR," Angela says.

When Glenn doesn't respond, Angela speaks softly so that Glenn needs to lean forward to hear her. "Your daughter found a dead body, and you met with your lawyer for coffee. That doesn't look good for you."

"I didn't know about the body till I got home," Glenn says. "You were there when I found out."

"You didn't answer your phone. For six hours."

"I was focused on the book event."

Angela opens the file folder with a printout of the autopsy report she'd received last night. She skims through the summary. "Did you think it was strange that two detectives showed up at your house so quickly last night?"

"My husband was murdered. Isn't that your job?"

Zane smiles. "We were already on our way."

Angela takes the top sheet from the report. "Here's the problem. The victim, the one your daughter found in that factory, was Patrick Leary. I'd just found out. We were halfway to your house when we got the call about your husband."

Glenn reaches for the sheet, but Angela slips it back into the folder and puts it away before Glenn can see it.

"Yesterday," Angela says, "what did you already know when you were meeting with your lawyer?"

Glenn bites her lip. "Do you have my phone records?"

"We will soon enough."

"I texted Patrick yesterday. I was hoping to meet him. I was planning to . . . I don't know what I was planning, but it doesn't matter now, because he never showed up and nothing ever happened. There'll be a lot to read between the lines when you see the texts."

"You were having an affair?" Angela asks.

"Not yet," Glenn says. "But the texts will make it look worse than it was."

"Not a sign of a strong marriage."

Glenn nods at Angela's wedding band. "Marriages have their ups and downs."

"Trust me on this, Mrs. Abbott. We know how to get to the truth, and there's nothing you can tell me that I haven't heard a hundred times before."

"Glenn," Zane says. "Were you having an affair with Patrick Leary?"

"An affair of the heart," Glenn says. "If you've been married, you'd know that there's a difference. A big difference."

Someone raps on the door. Zane steps into the hallway and returns with a red file folder that he hands to Angela. She scans a preliminary report from the crime scene. When Angela looks up again, Glenn has locked her with a stare. The report says that there were signs of a struggle, and that Jake Abbott had been shot at close range. When the police arrived, Glenn was covered in blood, which was consistent with her story of slipping on the floor. But she shows no apparent scratches or abrasions. Glenn Abbott may have been in the room when her husband was shot, but as of now there isn't enough evidence to charge her, and Charlotte Todd seems to sense this.

"We've given you enough," the lawyer says, standing. "If you need to speak to my client again, please let me know."

Glenn finally finds her feet, too, and turns them toward the door. "Find out who did this," she says.

"Don't worry," Angela says. "We will."

After they leave, Angela yawns. "It's been way too long of a night. Do we know anything about the gun?"

"Not yet," Zane says. "It's with the lab."

"Let's recharge for an hour or two. I want you to lean on Mavis Abbott this afternoon."

"Glenn Abbott won't like that. And Cavanaugh'll be in the way the whole time."

"I'll take care of Cavanaugh."

A moment later, Angela returns to her office and takes out the file she started on Natalie Cavanaugh. She makes a call and gets in her car to head to Elmhurst.

CHAPTER 19

When Natalie wakes on the sofa in her living room, her senses kick in one at a time. First, she feels the warmth of the sun streaming through her front window. Next, she hears the clatter of dishes in the kitchen. Finally, she smells bacon and coffee.

She sits up.

She can't remember buying bacon, ever, and it's only then that the events of the previous evening flood her memory. She groans and forces herself to stand.

In the kitchen, Mavis is already dressed. She looks showered too. She hands Natalie a cup of coffee and adds cream. "The way you like it," she says.

"Don't be so chipper," Natalie says.

The kitchen is spotless, even cleaner than Bennet had left it. Bacon sizzles on the stove, and Mavis adds a bowl of beaten eggs.

"This isn't leftover pad Thai," Natalie says. "Where did all this food come from?"

The toaster pops up. Mavis puts an English muffin on a plate and slides half the eggs onto it along with two strips of bacon. "I went to the corner store. I took money out of your wallet. I hope that's okay."

"You're like your mother," Natalie says.

Mavis eats her own breakfast right out of the skillet. "She says I'm like you."

"Do you mean rigid and unyielding?"

"Pretty much."

"Well, out of the skillet is how I eat most everything, so maybe she's right."

Natalie piles eggs onto half of the English muffin and takes a bite. Her hangover starts losing its grip almost at once.

"I don't mean to rush you, but I'm late," Mavis says. "Can you drive me to school? If I take the bus, I won't make it in time."

Natalie puts the plate down. Here's where Glenn is counting on her to play surrogate parent, though she doesn't really know where to begin. "Sweetie, you should take the day off."

For the first time in this brief exchange, Mavis looks as though she might break. "I want to go to school."

Natalie remembers when the news trucks packed the street on Starling Circle. Reporters ran alongside the Caprice Classic station wagon as her mother nosed the car through them. "Don't say a word," Ruth said, both hands on the steering wheel. "To anyone."

Now Natalie puts her plate aside. She understands the need for a distraction, even though she suspects her niece will crash sometime soon. "Here's the deal. I'll take you to school, but you have to promise me two things. First, call as soon as you want to leave, even if it's five minutes after I drop you off. And second, if anyone from the media shows up at school, go straight to the headmaster."

Mavis finishes the eggs in the skillet. "If we don't leave now, I'll be late."

"Is that a promise?"

"Fine, I promise."

Glenn, Natalie suspects, will be pissed off about this, and to be honest, Natalie doesn't have faith that she's making the right choice, but she has dealt with grief almost every day of her professional life, and she understands that people approach it in different ways. Mavis will keep moving till she hits a wall. "Get your bag," Natalie says, which earns her a smile.

Mavis dashes through the house. As much as the greasy breakfast helped with the hangover, Natalie can't quite muster the same energy. When she gets in the car and starts the engine, the radio is set to the news. It takes a moment too long for her to register the top story, the murder of "Jake Abbott, husband of local cookbook author Glenn Abbott." Natalie flips the radio off. Beside her, Mavis stares out the window, her breath fogging up the glass.

"Stay off the internet today too, okay?" Natalie says. "People say terrible things. But they'll be talking about something else soon enough, maybe even by tomorrow."

"I know," Mavis says.

The drive to West Roxbury takes ten minutes. When Natalie stops in front of the school, groups of students huddle outside one of the buildings before classes. Some of them stare at their phones, and Natalie wonders if the gossip channels have already begun. Mavis bites her lip and nods toward a girl with long black hair. "That's Stella," she says.

"She's your friend?"

"Best friend."

"That's a good thing to have. You sure you want to do this?" But even as Natalie asks the question, she knows she won't convince Mavis to lie low. "Which one is Kevin Chandler?"

Mavis points toward a gangling boy with red hair spilling from beneath a wool hat. His shirt is untucked, and a messenger bag hangs over his shoulder; he's like an annoying hipster in training, though Natalie can see her own seventh-grade self liking the boy. He hovers on the perimeter of a group of preppy boys who take turns shoving each other. "Two more promises," Natalie says. "One, call me after your test. I want to know how you do."

"Why would you care about an algebra test?"

"Why would you? And humor me, okay?"

"What else?" Mavis asks.

"Stay away from the Kevin Chandlers of this world. Boys should be nice to you."

"Can I go now?"

"I'll see you this afternoon," Natalie says. "Or before, if that's what you want."

Mavis gets out of the car and runs across the schoolyard to join Stella. Some of the kids look up from their phones to stare, and a decided hush falls over them all, but Stella steps out of the crowd as she leads Mavis inside.

Natalie lingers, watching as students return to their conversations or their phones, and soon it's as if Mavis had never been there. A few moments later, the students begin to filter inside, till only that cluster of boys remains, including Kevin Chandler. Natalie approaches them and flashes her badge for show. "I need a minute with you," she says to Kevin.

"Busted!" one of the boys says, punching Kevin in the arm as the others melt away and leave Kevin on his own.

"You heard about the body, right?" Natalie says. "The one they found in the factory. We're following up with anyone who's been inside that building recently, and your name came up."

Kevin kicks at the icy pavement. "I haven't been in there."

"You bragged about it. And you dared another student to go in too." Natalie steps close to him and lowers her voice. "This is a murder investigation. The truth is important."

"Maybe I went in earlier this week. But I never saw a body."

"What day?"

Kevin tries to step around Natalie and run to the school. She blocks him.

"I don't remember," he says.

Natalie waits. When Kevin doesn't add anything, she says, "You can go to jail for perjury."

"I don't think you're supposed to talk to me without my dad being here."

Natalie leans in and whispers. "I'll have him meet us at the station. You ready to go?"

"I don't know anything," Kevin says, his voice rising and his eyes shining with tears. "Mavis Abbott was the one dumb enough to go in there. Why don't you talk to her?"

Natalie stares him down till he looks away. "Mavis Abbott is dumb?" she says, her voice quivering with anger. "You know what I think? I think you already knew the body was there. In fact, I think you had something to do with what happened to that man. And I don't care how rich your dad is; he can't buy you out of a murder charge." Natalie mostly knows that she's already gone further than she should, but it doesn't stop her from continuing. "Don't be stupid enough to lie to me. I can arrest you for that too."

A voice behind her says, "Excuse me?"

Natalie whips around. A man charges across the schoolyard. Before Natalie can say anything, Kevin dashes away and disappears inside.

"I don't want any press on this campus," the man says. "Should I call the cops?"

Natalie almost pulls out her badge again but holds back. She's not supposed to be working this case, and it won't do her any good for the lieutenant to find out she's been harassing students at Mavis's school. She retreats and sits in her car till the man returns with a phone to take a photo of her license plate number. Natalie backs out and speeds away. She parks around the corner and calls Zane, who picks up on the first ring. "Give me an update," she says.

"Yeah, no," he says. "This is an open investigation. But give your sister a call. She left the station about fifteen minutes ago."

"Sounds like you didn't have enough to charge her," Natalie says. "That's good at least. What'd she tell you? Mavis said there was someone in the cottage last night."

"You have to stay out of this."

"Doesn't sound like they're safe at the house."

Zane sighs. "I've been up all night, so I'm not beating around the bush. Are you trying to tell me you actually believe someone besides your sister and your niece was in that cottage last night? You believe that your sister shot at a random intruder? Oh, and this'll be on the news soon too, so I might as well tell you—the guy in the factory? It was your sister's tenant, Patrick Leary. She told us they've been having an affair of the heart. And what do they say? Where there's smoke, there's fire? I feel for you, Cavanaugh, but we all know where this train is headed. The quicker we get there, the easier it'll be for everyone."

Natalie tries to make sense of every bit of information coming at her. "Here's what I think: there's no motive. Why would Glenn kill her husband?"

"Bad marriage."

"I don't know that they had a bad marriage. And that's something a divorce would solve."

"People make stupid choices, especially when it means admitting failure. And when kids are involved."

Natalie doesn't know what or whom to believe, not anymore, but if she knows one thing, it's that she can't imagine her sister killing Jake, not in a premeditated way and not in a fit of passion. Despite her biases, she's investigated enough homicides to trust her gut on this.

"Where's Mavis, anyway?" Zane asks.

"I dropped her off at school," Natalie says. "And before you say anything judgy, it wasn't my idea. I told her to take the day off, but she insisted. And I'll tell you who you should be talking to. A kid named Kevin Chandler here at the school. He's hiding something, though I'm not sure what. He's the one who dared Mavis to go into that building."

Zane sighs. "Stop poking the bear. If the lieutenant finds out you're snooping, she'll have your badge. And I do need to talk to Mavis, sooner rather than later. If you want to help, that'd be a better place to start."

Natalie hears something troubling in his voice. "You need to talk to her about what she saw last night," she says.

"Of course. She's a witness."

"Are you considering her as a potential suspect?"

Zane doesn't respond.

"Don't even try it," Natalie says. She hangs up and wishes for the days of slamming down the receiver.

Olivia Knowles stands under the showerhead and lets hot water stream over her body. She scrubs at her skin and hair. She tries to wash off last night, to forget the way Glenn had looked at her. Glenn has every right to hate her, of course, but not for the reasons she seemed to believe. Olivia's never met Jake Abbott, though she's seen photos of him on Glenn's blog and at Ruth's house. She's heard Ruth talk about the kind man who stepped in to help raise Mavis.

Olivia turns off the water and steps out of the shower. She towels off. She's not sure what she'd hoped to accomplish last night, but she wonders now what Glenn would have done if Olivia had simply said, "I knew your mother. We loved each other, in our own way. I'd like to know you too."

She wonders what Glenn would have done with the whole truth.

She swipes condensation from the bathroom mirror. Even now, the blond hair surprises her. She dries it and puts on her makeup, and when she looks in the mirror again, she only sees Olivia. She finishes getting ready, dresses to meet with a client, and descends the narrow stairs to her kitchen. She loves the uneven floors in the farmhouse, the low ceilings too, with their heavy oak beams. She loves the way the rooms run into each other, and how the memories of raising Jason infuse every square inch of the house. Now that Jason's moved and Ruth is gone, Olivia wonders if she'll stay in Elmhurst, or if she'll surprise her son in California. He wants his space these days, though. He wants to have his friends and smoke his pot and experiment without his mother hovering over him. He wants to reinvent himself, the way young people can. She'd called him again last night and left another voicemail. If he'd answered, she wonders what she might have told him, what she might have confessed, and if his anger would have traveled through the phone. She hopes he'll call back, eventually.

Olivia's led a quiet life in this town. She's talked about an ex-husband when she needed to. She's paid her bills and made sure her son stayed out of harm's way. As she grinds coffee and starts the pot, she remembers moving here. Jason had been in kindergarten, and on the last day of the school year, they celebrated with ice cream. Jason dropped his cone right outside the shop, and Olivia hadn't wanted the special moment to end in tears. "I'll get you another," she said, touching a woman's back. "Would you watch him?"

The woman turned. It was Ruth Cavanaugh.

"Hi?" Ruth said in that way you say to people you think you recognize but can't place. Back then, Ruth had dark hair barely touched by gray that fell to her shoulders.

It was bright out. Bright enough to justify sunglasses. Olivia lifted hers from her head and covered her eyes. "I'll be thirty seconds."

Ruth shivered despite the heat. "Take your time."

When Olivia returned with a new cone, she lifted Jason onto her hip. He was too heavy to carry for more than a few moments, but she wanted to imprint Olivia Knowles on Ruth's memory. Olivia was an adult, a divorcée, someone Ruth Cavanaugh could talk to without going to dark places. Olivia was the friend Ruth Cavanaugh needed, because in this town, this tiny town, this town with a long memory, some people would never stop seeing Ruth as the woman who might—just might—have killed her husband.

Now Olivia flips on the radio. She wonders if Glenn will come to find her and if she'll bring Natalie. Maybe, somehow, they can all find the truth together.

Something from the news registers in her subconscious. She turns up the sound and listens, realizing, suddenly, that it may be too late. They'll be coming for all of them soon enough.

CHAPTER 20

GLENN ABBOTT'S IMAGINATION HAS GONE TO THE WRONG PLACE. She sits on a wooden bench in the crowded precinct as people stare at her—police officers, detectives, other criminals—all striding by and looking at her in the way you look at a murderer. And why would they do anything else? Her husband is dead. Her non-lover, too, and everything, every action, points directly to her. Those detectives, her friend Zane, they've probably stopped considering other suspects. Glenn can't even think of someone else for them to consider. Jake didn't have enemies, at least not ones she knew about.

"Here," Charlotte says, standing over her and holding out Glenn's phone.

Glenn takes the phone. The clock is ticking toward eleven. She also takes note, again, of Charlotte's suit, of her hair, of the expensive bag that rests on her forearm. Yesterday Glenn and Charlotte had been the same, privileged, educated women with nothing to lose. Women who never imagined once that the world would turn against them. Now they couldn't be more different. Charlotte sits on one side of accusation, along with the rest of the world, and Glenn, in her yoga pants and ill-fitting sweatshirt, sits on the other, where she suspects she'll be from now on.

"And I wouldn't look at that phone," Charlotte adds. "We can deal with everything after we make our escape."

Glenn has over forty texts and voicemails. Those she can ignore. She scrolls right to Mavis and sends her a text: *Tell me you're okay.*

Mavis responds a moment later. *Fine.*

Where are you?

Busy.

Tell Aunt Natalie I'll give her a call.

Next, she scrolls to Patrick's name and pulls up the texts she'd sent him yesterday—*Meet me. I need to see you.*—reading them now through a new lens, as a detective building a case. They're salacious, or as salacious as Lieutenant Angela White will need to make them. Glenn had barely held it together in that room when the lieutenant told her that Patrick was dead, and Glenn wasn't upset because she'd miss him. She's terrified of what the police will assume when they read these messages.

"Don't delete anything," Charlotte says. "It'll only look worse."

"I need to call my sister," Glenn says. "She has Mavis."

"Let's get out of here first. You don't want to say anything that anyone might overhear." Charlotte offers a hand, and Glenn takes it, letting her friend haul her to her feet. Charlotte slips an arm through Glenn's. "And you need to prepare yourself. It's a zoo out there. And it's only going to get worse."

Glenn's legs feel like jelly. She's frightened, more frightened than she's allowed herself to admit.

"All we need to do is get to the car," Charlotte says.

They turn the corner.

Outside, on the sidewalk, a phalanx of reporters waits, microphones in hand, cameras ready.

"Keep your head up, your eyes forward, and think about something boring," Charlotte says.

As soon as the precinct door opens, the noise and the rush hit Glenn as two uniformed officers create a path for them to wade through a sea of humanity. They push forward ten yards to where the open door of an SUV waits. Charlotte shields her, arms extended as reporters shout questions.

"Glenn, do you have a statement?"

"Why did the police question you?"

"Did you kill your husband?"

Glenn stops. She looks at this last reporter, recognizing her. She's on the local news, Lisa something. Glenn talked to her a few months back at a fundraiser for the Boston Public Library. The reporter had been drunk and told Glenn that she was famous for her brunches, but, really, all the recipes came from the Happy Time blog. "I mean, like, all of them."

Now Glenn says, "Hi, Lisa."

The reporter's eyes go almost feral. "Were you having an affair?"

Even after Charlotte drags Glenn into the waiting car, the question lingers. How can they prove that something never happened?

Mavis is tired of Sad Eyes and stares. The stares come from her fellow seventh-graders, who shush each other as she passes through Fisk Hall. The Sad Eyes come from the teachers, even Mr. Sullivan, her algebra teacher, whose usual motto is "No crying over division." He gives her the Sad Eyes as she finishes her makeup test during her free period.

"You know you could have waited a few days," he says.

Mavis can't imagine what Mr. Sullivan would do with an emotion, though she considers pulling out tears if only to see him fumble with the offer. Instead, she says, "When can I get my grade?"

"I'll have it for you after lunch. But my guess is you aced the test."

Mavis would have aced the test, but she purposefully got the fourth problem wrong to see what Mr. Sullivan would do about it. She suspects she'll get an A no matter what.

"I'll be here all afternoon," he says. "Let me know if you want to talk. About anything."

Mavis conjures up a smile. She's already figured out that it's the only way to get Sad Eyes off her back. They want to believe that she's "moved on," and, honestly, she's happy to play their game.

"Good girl," Mr. Sullivan says.

Out in the hallway, Stella waits, even though the only class Mavis shares with her friend all week is English, and that's not even on the schedule today. They walk together down the hall, meeting anyone's eyes who dares to look at them, even as a wave of deafening silence follows. "Ignore it," Stella whispers as she deposits Mavis at her science class.

"You'd better go," Mavis says. "You'll be late for Spanish."

"Wait for me. We'll go to lunch together."

Mavis is already dreading walking into the dining hall, but she nods and watches as Stella hurries toward the other end of the building. Mavis takes a deep breath and opens the classroom door with what she hopes reads as confidence. The veneer melts away instantly. Mr. Geller has already begun his lesson, but he stops mid-sentence, Sad Eyes in place. The students stand behind Bunsen burners, goggles on, but it doesn't shield Mavis from their stares, especially the ones from Kevin Chandler, who, unfortunately, is her lab partner. She makes her way to her place beside him and opens the lesson on her tablet. And she smiles to help Mr. Geller relax. He nods and begins the lesson again.

"Mavis," Kevin whispers under his breath. "M-A-V-I-S."

"Shut up," she hisses.

"The police are after you."

Mavis tries to ignore him, but she can't focus on the properties of magnesium, and even with a second smile, Mr. Geller doesn't quite lose the Sad Eyes, except once when he snaps at Kevin. "Try harassing someone else, Mr. Chandler."

Mavis stares at the surface of the lab table. The class stares at her collectively, and she wonders if they'd prefer tears. She tries to muster some but can't deliver. At the end of class, she dashes into the hallway and manages to evade Stella and make it to the restroom. Two girls at the mirror turn in unison to stare. Mavis locks herself in a stall. One of the girls whispers, "Hold still, it's Happy Time," while the other laughs as they leave.

It's only now, in this moment of solitude, that Mavis allows herself to see the faces in the hallway and to hear the whispers. She perches on the edge of the toilet seat and takes out her phone. "Glenn Abbott" is trending everywhere, but so are "Hold still" and "Happy Time," and it doesn't take long for Mavis to find the meme of her mother holding a kitchen knife coated in raspberry sauce, her eyes wild. It was probably taken yesterday at that event she attended with the influencers, and there are probably hundreds of similar memes floating around.

A text from Stella beeps into her phone. *Where u go?*

Meet you at the dining hall, Mavis writes.

Not a chance. We'll go together.

Stella can be bossy, but Mavis won't lie: today she's grateful for it.

Someone comes into the restroom. Mavis steps out of the stall, washes her hands, and tries her best to ignore the feeling of being watched. She wonders how long it will be before she doesn't notice the stares anymore, because she suspects they aren't going away any time soon.

Out in the corridor, Stella leads them toward the dining hall. As they approach and the roar of conversation increases, Mavis stops. "I don't know if I can do this."

"I'll walk you home," Stella says. "Let's get our coats."

But no place is safe, not anymore. When Mavis goes home, her father will be gone, and her mother will be sitting with her grief and guilt, and the news trucks will be lurking outside, waiting to capture it all, to turn their lives into something to share. The only way to make the stares go away is to face them. "Let's have lunch," Mavis says.

Stella takes her arm, and when they get to the dining hall, the silence begins again. "Feels like a pizza day to me," Stella says.

She piles lunch onto a tray and leads them to their regular table with other kids from the soccer team, their friends, all of whom stare, mouths agape.

"What are you looking at?" Stella says.

A new emotion begins to take root in Mavis's core, and it's not the sadness she's been dreading. It's fear. A fear of being alone. How much longer will Stella stand by her? How many days does Mavis have before she'll need to face entering this dining hall on her own? When will she have to start sitting by herself?

She takes a bite of the pizza and barely tastes it. "I forgot something. It'll take me two minutes to get it."

Stella goes to follow, but Mavis says, "Really, I'll be right back. I swear."

Mavis makes it around the corner and out of sight before the sadness she's dreaded since last night erupts. She covers her face and slides to the floor as huge, wet sobs wrack her body, ones that she wants to stuff away forever. And she's not sure how long she's been sitting there when she senses someone standing over her. As if this day couldn't get worse, it's Kevin Chandler.

"Go away," she says.

Kevin slides down the wall and hands her a wad of paper napkins. Mavis blows her nose. He doesn't stare or give her Sad Eyes. Instead, he says, "My mom died when I was in fifth grade. Before I came to this school. It gets better, but it takes a while."

Mavis clutches the wad of soiled napkins and can't for the life of her think of what to do with them.

"It sucks, and people say terrible things," Kevin says, "even when they're trying to be nice."

"Do you have another dare for me?" Mavis asks.

"No dares."

"What do you want?"

"Nothing. I just . . . I wanted to tell you that." Kevin gets to his feet as someone calls his name. "I'll see you around."

He runs down the hall to catch up with his clique of boys. Mavis doesn't trust him, no matter how much he shares about his mother. She wonders if what he told her was true. She considers calling Aunt Natalie and asking her to come pick her up. Maybe she did come to school too early.

"I thought you were coming right back."

Stella stands over her, fists on her hips.

"What did they say about me after I left?" Mavis asks.

Stella takes the wad of snotty napkins from Mavis's fist and drops them in the trash. She offers a hand. "Who gives a shit?"

Mavis takes the offer. She smiles too.

"You don't have to smile," Stella says. "Not with me."

CHAPTER 21

Charlotte puts a hand on Glenn's arm as the SUV speeds through a red light. Glenn turns in her seat. Behind them, the mob of reporters outside the precinct grows smaller. "How did they know where to find me?"

"Someone at the station probably tipped them off," Charlotte says. "Every station has a source. We'll go to my apartment now. You need to lie low."

Charlotte's phone rings. She answers, and Glenn lets her head fall against the back of the seat and closes her eyes. The driver speeds through another light and turns toward downtown.

"I need to get home," Glenn says. "I need to see Mavis."

Charlotte cups a hand over the phone. "Call your sister and find out where they are. The police are still at your house, and so is another army of reporters. You'll want to steer clear for the next few days. We'll probably put you up in a hotel."

"A hotel?"

Glenn thinks about Charlotte's hourly rate. Glenn has her own bank account. She manages her own finances, but Jake had paid Charlotte's bills, telling Glenn that it was easier to bundle her expenses in with the firm's. It was probably unethical, but Glenn had been happy to have the costs sit on someone else's books. She'd been happy to meet Charlotte for coffee and not worry if she was being billed for the time. Now Glenn wonders how long they'd talked to those detectives? How much time has Charlotte already billed today? How much did this car cost?

Glenn takes out her phone. The ringer is off, but the voicemails are coming in one after another. So are the texts. She doesn't dare read any of them. She clicks on Natalie's name, and her sister picks up on the first ring. "Let me talk to Mavis," Glenn says.

"She's fine," Natalie says.

"But where is she?"

Natalie pauses. "She's at school." And before Glenn can protest, she adds, "She insisted."

Glenn almost snaps at her sister. The last thing in the world Mavis needs is to be surrounded by twelve-year-old vipers, ones who are finding out about this mess in real time.

"I know about Patrick, too," Natalie says. "Tell me you weren't sleeping with him."

Natalie will believe Glenn no matter what she says, but the truth is good for now. "I didn't, but it doesn't mean I didn't want to."

"And what did he want?"

"What any man wants," Glenn says—at least that's what she'd assumed. She'd thought she was in control with Patrick, but now she wonders if either of them had been pulling the strings.

"What do you know about him?" Natalie asks.

"Nothing. Jake told me he was a friend from high school, but I'd never heard of him before."

"Any chance you have Patrick's birth date?"

"I don't even have a middle name."

Glenn had almost thrown her whole life away for a complete stranger.

"I'll see what I can dig up," Natalie says. "What will they find in your phone records?"

Glenn sighs. "I sent two, maybe three texts to him yesterday."

"Nothing else? You didn't call him obsessively or leave any embarrassing voicemails?"

"Yesterday was the only time I ever contacted him electronically, and yes, I wish I hadn't, and I wouldn't have if I'd known the guy was dead." Glenn hears the detachment in her own voice. "I don't mean to sound heartless, but I didn't know the stakes were so high."

"What did the texts say?"

Glenn reads through the brief texts. Natalie is quiet for a moment. Finally, she says, "They won't look great, but if they had anything on you, you'd still be at the precinct. You'd probably be in cuffs. The lieutenant's fair, I'll give her that much. What else did you tell them at the station? Even something small."

Glenn glances at Charlotte. "This woman came by the house last night. She was at my event yesterday too. She's a real estate agent. She says she was friends with Mom. Her business card's in a bowl in the kitchen."

"I'll see what I can find out about her too. Where are you?"

"We're headed to my lawyer's apartment," Glenn says.

"I'll pick up Mavis after school and bring her to my place."

"She has soccer. They finish at five."

Glenn ends the call. She listens to Charlotte banging texts into her phone and watches out the window as the car maneuvers through the narrow streets of Boston. A few moments later, the driver stops in front of a tall, modern building in the South End. Charlotte steps onto the sidewalk and holds the door. Glenn feels like a fugitive as she scurries along the sidewalk and past the doorman. They take the elevator and step right into Charlotte's loft-style apartment, with its reclaimed wood and mid-century-modern furniture and views of Beacon Hill. Glenn's been to this apartment before. She stood in the kitchen and took glasses of champagne from a caterer and helped herself to canapés and believed that these views and this opulence would always be hers to take. Now she can see are the cost of a life she'll never be part of again.

"Take a shower," Charlotte says. "Try to get an hour or two of sleep."

"I won't be able to sleep."

"Try. You've been up all night, and you look like hell. We have a very long few days in front of us."

In the bathroom, Glenn turns on the water and catches a glimpse of herself in the mirror. She'd forgotten about the blood. Jake's blood. It's still splattered across her face. She gets in the shower and watches the blood flake off and swirl down the drain. She wonders if she'll ever feel clean again.

CHAPTER 22

THE ELMHURST POLICE STATION SITS IN A MODERN COMPLEX NEAR a small downtown. Angela parks and turns off the news, where coverage of Jake Abbott's murder has run almost nonstop since she left the city. Following this hunch could be a waste of time, especially as the case spirals out of control, but now that she's here, she'll see what she can learn.

She reviews her file on Natalie Cavanaugh one more time, including the newspaper clipping and accompanying note. She's stored the handwritten note in a paper sleeve so that she can request testing at some point if it comes to that, but for now, she rereads the message, WATCH THOSE WHO WORK FOR YOU, with its block print. She also reviews the envelope the whole package came in, particularly the postmark.

It had been mailed from the Elmhurst post office.

She sends a text to Cary. *At work all day. Sorry. Will you pick up Isaiah from swimming?* And then a second text to Zane. *Following up on a lead in Elmhurst. Probably nothing. Will call later. Get the party guest list from Glenn Abbott. If she won't give it to you, get a subpoena. And send me an update on any video from the neighbors.*

Inside the station, a middle-aged woman at the front desk eyes Angela warily, even after Angela identifies herself. "Boston Police Department," the woman says, her accent heavy with a missing R. "We don't see city police here too often."

"Chief O'Neil's expecting me," Angela says. When the woman doesn't move, Angela pulls off her knit cap and runs a hand through her natural hair. "Maybe you could point me in the right direction?" She glances at the woman's name tag and adds, "Marjory."

Marjory takes her time lifting herself out of the chair. "I'll see if he's around." When she returns, she takes her time sitting down again. "Second office on your left," she says.

As Angela strides away with the confidence of a lieutenant, she can feel Marjory's stare. She has no doubt her visit will make it into the town's gossip channels, if it hasn't already.

She stops at an open office door. The chief sits at his desk, typing on a laptop. He's five or six years older than the headshot on the town's website, likely approaching fifty, with a thatch of hair that's gone from dark to white in those ensuing years. His most prominent feature is a bulbous nose, rosy with burst capillaries. When Angela knocks lightly, he glances up with eyes the color of the sky and waves her toward a chair as he finishes typing. "Paperwork is endless," he says.

"Especially when you're the chief," Angela says.

"Or a lieutenant." He takes a moment to assess her, the way good cops do. "Not sure what a lieutenant wants in this little town. I'm happy to help you in any way I can, and I'll let you know if I can't. But you didn't tell me much on the phone, Lieutenant White."

"Call me Angela."

"Tom."

"There was a homicide last night in Boston, the second one in two days. I'm following up on a long-shot lead." Angela glances toward the hallway. "And I bet folks are wondering why a Black lieutenant from Boston came to the station this morning. This story is getting enough coverage that they might put two and two together on their own."

Tom crosses to the door and closes it. "Marjory's not the only one with big ears and a big mouth around here. And we don't get too many homicides either. When we do, we hand them off to the state cops. We don't have the resources for major crimes."

"It's a beautiful town," Angela says.

"One where people can still be really, really terrible. You'd be surprised. Or maybe you wouldn't."

Angela has seen the worst of the worst, but most cops have, even in towns like this one.

"Tell me about your case," Tom says.

"Jake Abbott. He was shot to death last night."

"Heard about it on the news this morning."

Angela nods. "He was married to a woman who grew up here. Maiden name is Glenn Cavanaugh." Angela watches for Tom's reaction. He recognizes the name, but she suspects he already knows the connection and why she came here. He rests his elbows on the desk and waits for her to continue.

"There was a homicide here in the nineties," Angela says. "Glenn Abbott and her sister, Natalie, found the body. It was their father, Alan Cavanaugh. Do you remember it?"

"You know that I do."

He's right. Angela does know. Tom O'Neil had been the responding officer when the homicide was reported.

"But I'd start with the state cops," he says. "They're the ones who closed the case."

But the state cops don't know the players. They don't know what runs beneath the surface in this small town. That's why Angela came to the source. She says, "Humor me. And let's consider the whole conversation off the record. I don't want this turning into something it isn't."

"Neither do I. That case was all over the media, local and national, and I'd like to retire before something similar ever happens again. And from what I see, your whole theory comes from a woman having two people in her life die unexpectedly twenty-five years apart. No offense, but that seems like a pretty flimsy connection to me."

"I'm working on little sleep and a lot of intuition here, so bear with me. Glenn Abbott visited Elmhurst yesterday. She says she had a book event. I'm curious if something else happened while she was here."

"Nothing that came to this department," Tom says. "Full disclosure, I know Glenn. I knew her as a kid, obviously, but I had to work with her recently, too, as her mother's condition got worse."

"Tell me about her mother."

"Ruth Cavanaugh? Quiet woman. She mostly kept to herself after her husband died. I think she worked for a textbook publisher from her home. She never really shook the label of possible murderer, you know? Murders in small towns, they're more like scars than bruises. They fade but never go away."

"What about Glenn?"

"Nice. Driven. I was happy to see her having some success. She works hard. I can't imagine she'll come out of this situation with anything she was dreaming of. I doubt we'll be seeing her at the bookstore next week." Tom leans back in his chair. "I did my own research too. Natalie works for you."

Angela would expect nothing less. "It won't be good for me or the department if that part of the story keeps getting bigger."

"One of my officers got caught fixing tickets last month, and it was the only thing I worked on for about three weeks."

"Nothing like a PR nightmare," Angela says. "And there's nothing like talking to a cop involved from the start with a case. Can you tell me what you remember from Alan Cavanaugh's death?"

"Who doesn't love a cul-de-sac love triangle that ends in a murder-suicide, right?"

The chief opens a file drawer and takes out a faded folder. Angela has plenty of files like this one herself, cases that didn't turn out the way she suspected they might, cold cases that keep her up at night, the closes that she still believes targeted the wrong person.

"I joined the department in ninety-three," Tom says, "right out of college, so I'd been in uniform for a couple of years when the murder happened. The Cavanaughs lived in a new development on the other side of town where most of the houses hadn't been completed yet. It was in the middle of nowhere back then, two houses side by side surrounded by cellar holes. The Cavanaughs in one house. Their neighbor was a woman named Diane Sykes. She lived in the other house with her two kids, Tonya and Lindsey. Alan and Ruth both grew up here, but Diane was new. She moved to town from Connecticut in the winter of ninety-five. She told me she wanted a new start after her husband died."

"Lots of death," Angela says. "Anything to follow up on there?"

Tom shakes his head. "Her husband had leukemia, and all reports were that it was a long, sad death and that his wife was devoted to him the entire time. I didn't know Diane Sykes that well, but that's the kind of person she was—friendly, open, funny, selfless. She served on committees in the PTA and at the Unitarian Church. People liked her. And they didn't even have much time to get to know her. She only lived here for five or six months. And she was kind to Ruth Cavanaugh, too. They were friends for a while, and Diane seemed to want to watch out for Ruth."

"Did Ruth need someone watching out for her?"

Tom plucks a sheet from the file. It's a photocopy of a police report for a domestic disturbance. "This is from the night of Alan's murder. I responded to the call. Alan had a superficial wound on his upper arm from a paring knife. There was blood everywhere. Ruth Cavanaugh claimed that she slipped while doing dishes."

"Did you believe her?"

"Not at all. But that's not what stands out to me. I see domestic disputes nearly every week in this job. Most neighbors know what's going on and don't want to get involved, but Diane Sykes called this one in. She didn't think twice about getting involved."

"No love lost between Alan Cavanaugh and Diane Sykes," Angela says. "But the narrative says there was a love triangle, that Alan and Diane had an affair."

Tom nods. "The whispers started a week or so after the murder and took on a life of their own. See the problem? Diane hated Alan. Why would she sleep with him?"

"Did the state cops know this?"

"Yep. Rumors are one thing, but evidence is another. They came up with evidence to back up the theory," Tom says. He takes another sheet from the folder and slides it across the desk. Angela scans it and sees the DNA matches to Alan Cavanaugh on a piece of fabric found in the Sykeses' fireplace. "Blood?" she asks.

Tom nods.

"And you just said there was blood everywhere in the Cavanaughs' house."

"There was."

"And you were also called out to the house when the body was found?"

"Natalie and Glenn found the body in an old hunting blind. I was on duty that afternoon. It was the middle of the summer, and the body had been there all day. I can still smell it."

"What happened next?"

"I called it in to headquarters and secured the scene. Exactly what I was supposed to do. The chief at the time handed it off to the state cops."

Angela's never known a cop, a good one a least, who hands over a case that easily. "What else?"

"I took the girls home. And I talked to their mother, Ruth. Diane was there, too, running interference. She was a legal secretary, probably could have been a lawyer herself. She knew the cops would home in on Ruth as soon as the investigation got underway."

The obvious suspect, Angela thinks. Like with her current case. "Did you think Ruth was good for it?"

Tom pauses for a moment. "Everyone thought she did it. Alan and Ruth both grew up here. A lot of us knew them. Alan Cavanaugh was handsome and charming, but he was a jerk. A drunk. He taught at the community college and had a reputation for sleeping with students. If you'd taken a poll of the department here, I bet most of us would have said Alan deserved what he got, but we weren't in charge. The state cops were. They narrowed in on Ruth but didn't have evidence to make an arrest, and she didn't buckle when they interviewed her either. What turned the focus was when one of the Sykes kids claimed to have seen Diane and Alan in the woods together."

Angela checks her notes. "Which one? Tonya or Lindsey?"

"The little one, Lindsey."

"Age?"

"Six, maybe seven."

"Coerced?" Angela asks.

"I've watched the tapes of the interview maybe a dozen times," Tom says. "I don't know if I can watch it objectively anymore, but let's say I wouldn't have conducted the interview the way it was conducted."

"Any chance you have a copy lying around?"

Tom opens the file drawer again. "I hope you have a VCR," he says, laying a VHS tape on the desk. "I'm sure the state cops have a copy in a vault somewhere. Still, I'll need that back."

Angela doesn't have a VCR, but she knows someone who almost certainly does. She adds the tape to her bag. "Eyewitness testimony and DNA evidence," she says. "I'd have closed the case too. What was wrong?"

Tom shrugs. "Diane Sykes wasn't someone who'd settle for second best."

"What about the original suspect, Ruth Cavanaugh? Could she have done it?"

"She could have. I wouldn't rule out Glenn or Natalie either. And there was Tonya Sykes too. Diane's daughter. She was fifteen, maybe sixteen, and ran with the wrong crowd at school. She disappeared a few months later when she ran away from her foster parents."

Angela puts a hand on the file folder. "Can I take a copy of this?" she asks.

"A favor first," Tom says. "This is one that's stayed with me. Let me know if you find anything."

"Professional courtesy," Angela says.

Tom nods, and Angela opens the file. Inside are a few handwritten notes, a police report, and copies of black-and-white photos taken at the Alan Cavanaugh crime scene, a clearing in a forest. "Cause of death?"

"Blunt force trauma. Probably a rock, but they didn't recover the murder weapon."

"Self-defense?"

"Maybe the first few strikes," Tom says. "But the guy's head was crushed. He'd been hit at least a dozen times. Whoever killed him was pissed off."

Angela flips through the photos. They're standard for a crime scene, taken from various angles to capture as much detail as possible. Evidence tags appear in some of them. A close-up of the wound catches Angela's attention.

"What happened here?" she asks, holding up the photo and pointing to Alan Cavanaugh's face.

"I told you it wasn't pretty," Tom says.

"But what happened?"

"The woods out there are filled with animals, racoons, possums, foxes. They ate his eyes out."

A few moments later, Angela gets into her car and makes a call to the Harvard librarian she'd shown the *Boston Globe* article to when it was first delivered, Hester Thursby. Hester's a friend. She's also good at working databases and research. She's even better at synthesizing information on crime. Most importantly, she knows how to be inquisitive and discreet. Angela relies on Hester for research when she needs off-the-record information, and Angela isn't ready to let anyone else know about her suspicions. "You working this murder in the news?" Hester asks when she answers the phone.

"Don't be nosy," Angela says.

"His wife's one of the girls in that newspaper clipping you showed me. What are the odds?"

Hester has an annoying and useful habit of being five steps ahead.

"I'm in Elmhurst following a lead," Angela says. "But answer a question for me. When I gave you that article, any chance you kept digging?"

"What do you need?"

"Tell me what happened to the Sykes girls. Lindsey and Tonya. Lindsey would be thirty-three or thirty-four now. Tonya would be forty-two or forty-three. They both went into foster care."

"On it," Hester says.

"One more thing," Angela says.

"I know. Don't tell anyone you asked."

"That goes without saying. What I really need is a VCR."

CHAPTER 23

Natalie parks a block from Glenn's house and cuts the engine. Usually, this neighborhood is quiet. Now news trucks line the street, while lights flash on police cruisers parked in the driveway.

Natalie's spent the last few hours trying to learn more about Patrick Leary, starting with the high school Jake graduated from in central Massachusetts, and while she hasn't discovered much about who Patrick was, she has figured out who he wasn't. He hadn't gone to school with Jake. Now she's beginning to wonder if Patrick existed at all. She punches Zane's number into her phone. The call goes straight to voicemail. He's probably blocking her calls at this point.

Natalie gets out of the car. She shouldn't be here. It won't do anyone any good to have her name or face connected to the case or to Glenn, but thankfully it's cold, and she's never been one to stand out in a crowd anyway. She yanks a hat over her hair and joins a small group of neighbors huddled outside the cordon. "What's going on here?" she asks one of them, a man who looks as if he might crown himself mayor of the neighborhood.

"Owner of the house got shot last night," he says.

Natalie mumbles under her breath and waits for him to continue.

"The wife's been arrested," he says. "Or that's what they're saying. They took her in last night. She's on TV sometimes. Glenn Abbott."

"Did you know her?" Natalie asks.

"Our kids play soccer together. Jake managed the team. He did everything. I'm not sure how we'll do it without him."

What other rumors have taken hold? And who was the first to declare Glenn guilty? Natalie slips away and strides toward the cordon like a cop. The reporters barely seem to notice her as she steps under the tape. At the house, the investigation is underway. Crime techs move in and out of the cottage, taking samples and marking evidence. Zane stands beneath the pergola. Natalie catches his eye, and he crosses the driveway to join her.

"You haven't returned my calls," she says.

"Last time we spoke, you hung up on me."

"The last time we spoke, you told me you considered my twelve-year-old niece a suspect in a murder."

"You know how this works," Zane says. "You consider every possibility."

"*Every* possibility? How about paying attention to what my sister told you? She says there was someone else there."

Out on the street, the reporters seem to sense something brewing. They move toward the property line, microphones out.

"We should avoid the cameras," Zane says.

Natalie leads him around the house and into the kitchen, where drawers have been emptied and cabinets searched. "Is the whole house like this?" she asks.

"You know what a search looks like, Cavanaugh. Don't act like this is a surprise."

"What have you found?"

Zane shakes his head. "The only person who can relay information here is you, and my guess is you haven't been sitting on your hands all day. Why don't you tell me what you found and why you're here? You've probably thought of something we haven't."

"Same thing I mentioned last night. Patrick Leary. What do you know about him?"

"I put in for a background check," Zane says, "but nothing's come back."

"See, that wasn't hard. You tell me a little, and I'll tell you a little. It's like a game."

"Fine. It's your turn."

"I bet you pulled up Glenn's phone records, too. And you've found the texts she sent to Patrick. What do they tell you?"

Zane makes a zipping motion over his mouth, and Natalie says, "This is what they tell me as a detective: Glenn thought the guy was still alive yesterday."

"Or," Zane says, "that's what she wants us to believe. It's pretty convenient that the first documented communication between the two of them happened yesterday, and that it supports Glenn's narrative."

Natalie would have made the same argument in Zane's place. That won't keep her from pushing, though. "Patrick is the key to this case. Jake told Glenn that they went to high school together out in Southborough, but I checked, and there's no record of a Patrick Leary graduating in any of the years when Jake was there." Natalie pauses. She doesn't know if she should continue, but in the end, she has to trust Zane to do the right thing. "Bennet Jones told me that Jake was in trouble with money a few months ago. Bennet followed up with him recently, and he said it was all taken care of."

"Let me guess, the money problems went away when Patrick Leary moved into the cottage," Zane says. "And by Bennet Jones, you mean one of our other suspects in this case. Was this pillow talk?"

"There is no pillow talk."

Zane jots something down on his pad. "I'll follow up with Jones, but if you talk to him again, make sure he understands we need to know anything and everything regarding this case. Maybe if he'd told us this yesterday, we wouldn't have another dead body on our hands. Here's a question for you: does Bennet Jones know Patrick Leary? What's the connection there? Or are you too into him to see it?"

Natalie almost answers but stops herself. Sure, she might consider giving Bennet a second chance once this is over. Right now, she's more interested in spreading suspicion beyond her sister, and Bennet's still the best bet. Letting Zane drive that focus is in her best interest. She asks, "Do you have a Social Security number for Patrick Leary? A passport? Anything?"

Zane sighs. "Leave this alone."

"What did you find in the cottage? What's the evidence trail?"

One of the crime techs calls Zane's name. "Don't move," he says. "And don't touch anything, either. You are not a detective here."

He steps into the other room. Natalie's eyes sweep across the kitchen till she finds the bowl Glenn mentioned. She plucks out a business card for Olivia Knowles, Elmhurst Realty.

"What is that?" Zane asks as he returns.

"It's a business card."

Zane stares at her, hand extended, till she gives him the card.

"I don't know who she is," Natalie says. "But she showed up at my sister's event yesterday afternoon claiming to be a friend of our mother's. Later, she showed up here a few hours before Jake was shot. Glenn says she hadn't met her before."

Zane lays the card on the counter and snaps a photo of it. "I'll look into this. You won't."

"Tell me who Patrick Leary is and I'll leave," Natalie says.

"Listen to me," Zane says. "I have to go meet with the medical examiner. You need to go home, and then later today I need to talk to your niece and find out what the hell she's been keeping to herself, because we both know there's something, and I'm sorry to say this, but I bet it has to do with your sister or her father or Patrick Leary or your fucking boyfriend. I know this is hard, and I know you're worried about Glenn, but guess what you don't want?" He points through the window at the reporters gathered on the sidewalk. "To get dragged into this case in a way that you can't get out of it. You could easily wind up fired or on desk duty for the rest of your career."

"I'll stay out of it," Natalie says.

"Somehow I don't believe that, but at the very least, stay away from the crime scene." Once outside, Zane holds her arm. Natalie abhors being touched. She shakes him off.

"Do you know that I like you?" Zane says. "And that everything I said to you in there is because we're friends and I want to see you make it through this and out the other side? You're probably one of the best detectives I'll ever have a chance to partner with. No matter what your sister did, please don't mess up your life for her."

Natalie matches his stare. "Mavis is in school," she says. "We'll be at my house tonight. Come by when you want to talk."

She walks down the driveway as the cameras point right at her. In her car, she sits with her heart racing till she sees Zane drive away. She could go back. She could try to get information from the techs working the case, but it's a few minutes after 2:00 p.m. She'll need to be at the school to get Mavis at 5:00. That gives her enough time to get to Elmhurst and back. It's enough time to find out who Olivia Knowles is and why she showed up at Glenn's house last night.

CHAPTER 24

After a fitful hour of trying to sleep, only to wake in a cold sweat, Glenn surrenders to her anxiety and gets up. Charlotte must have snuck into the room at some point, though, because Glenn finds a fresh set of clothing at the foot of the bed—simple pants and a sweater, both in the appropriate black for mourning. She changes. In the bathroom, she splashes water on her face and prepares herself for the next steps, whatever those may be. Out in the main living space, her lawyer stands at the loft's floor-to-ceiling windows, listening to someone speaking on the other end of the phone. When she notices Glenn, she says, "Let me call you back," and clicks off the call. She crosses to the kitchen and holds up a French press. "Coffee? I just made it."

Glenn nods, and Charlotte hands her an oversized mug. The coffee is delicious. Rich and satisfying, so much better than the coffee at the station this morning. Glenn cups the mug in her cold hands and feels the warmth spread through her body. Outside, the sun has begun to set over the city. "It's so beautiful here," she says.

Charlotte smiles, but the sides of her mouth are strained. Her whole face is strained, and Glenn wants one more minute before learning what's happened in the last hour. "Where'd you get this outfit?" she asks.

"My assistant picked it up."

Add it to the tab. "Mavis'll be done with school soon. I'll need to go be with her. And we won't need a hotel. We'll squeeze in at my sister's." Glenn closes her eyes. "Who was that on the phone?"

Charlotte answers quickly, her words clipped, like someone used to delivering bad news. "Producer at *Good Morning Boston*. We canceled Friday's appearance. Better optics that way."

Glenn puts the mug down. "Who's *we*?"

Charlotte doesn't answer.

"Who else has canceled?" Glenn asks.

"Come." Charlotte puts an arm over Glenn's shoulders and leads her to a sofa. "Let's talk about optics. Your husband died. *Fact.* You're in mourning. *Expectation.* You can't go on *Good Morning Boston* to bake a cake when you should be planning a funeral. *Perception.* But you also can't go on *Good Morning* when you're a suspect in your husband's murder. *Fact.* Like it or not, it's a live show, and anything could happen. *Reality.* They could ask you questions that you don't want to answer. Like I said, optics. I'll release a statement saying you're postponing all public appearances for the time being. It'll be carefully managed."

"*Spending time with family*," Glenn says.

"Something like that." Charlotte meets Glenn's eyes.

"What?" Glenn asks. "There's something else, isn't there?"

"We need to take the blog down, or at least disable the commenting feature."

Glenn's heart begins to race. She opens the app for the blog and accesses the dashboard. The site usually gets a few dozen comments a day, more when she has a new recipe posted. Now she sees comments posting one after the other. She clicks into one where HumorlessPat writes, *I don't believe it. Not for one second.*

The next post is less kind. *They arrested her. The police are at her house. Bitch is guilty.*

Finally, Glenn sees readers have already dug up her past.

AdamsAunt posts, *Not the first time*, with a link to a *Dateline* clip about her father's murder.

"We can't do anything about social media," Charlotte says, "but you can control the site."

"Won't that make me look worse?"

Charlotte's silence speaks volumes. Glenn couldn't look much worse than she already does. She clicks into the dashboard and turns off the discussion-board feature. She doesn't dare switch over to any of the social media sites to see how she's trending.

Charlotte says, "My job here is to save you at any cost, and to do that, I need to know what the police will find. They'll go through your e-mail and your texts. I know about Patrick. That's a start. But what did you know about Jake? Did he tell you something last night? Something that surprised you?"

"We barely spoke," Glenn says. She'd been so angry with her husband she hadn't been able to listen, but now as she remembers, it feels as if Jake had wanted to tell her something, and she only wishes she'd asked what it was.

Glenn stands and crosses to the windows. The winter sun hovers beyond the rows of brownstones that make up the neighborhood. Below, on the sidewalk, people hurry through the cold on their way home. What Glenn would give to go home right now, to return to what was and will never be again. How could she have been naïve enough to believe she'd get through these weeks of publicity without someone dredging up her story?

Behind her, Charlotte says, "Your father was murdered, but tell me the rest. The things that didn't make the news."

"My father was an asshole," Glenn says. "He drank and slept around. I only learned that later, but I sensed it from reading between the lines, from the way my parents acted toward each other. The hardest part was when my mother was the prime suspect."

Glenn had wondered what it was like for her mother to take on the state police, to maintain her innocence in the face of so much doubt and scrutiny. Now she knows.

"Your mother died in a nursing home," Charlotte says, "not in jail. What happened?"

"A rumor took root that our neighbor was having an affair with my father before he was killed. It was enough to justify a search warrant, and the state police must have found more evidence, because they came back with the intention of arresting the neighbor."

Glenn stops. The rest of the story is hard to relive, let alone recount, but Charlotte fills the silence. "When the police arrived, Diane Sykes confessed to killing your father. Then she used an unregistered gun to shoot herself."

"You've done your research. You even know her name."

"Part of my job. What happened next?"

"Social services kicked in. Diane's kids, Tonya and Lindsey, went into foster care."

"Did you hear from them again?"

Glenn shakes her head.

"You never tried to look them up? Never tried to apologize?"

"I doubt they'd want to hear from me," Glenn says, just as Charlotte's phone rings.

Charlotte answers and crosses to the kitchen, where she speaks softly enough that Glenn can't overhear the conversation. Glenn turns toward the window again. She thinks about Mavis at school, wandering the halls, working her way through those algebra problems. She wonders whether one of her daughter's classmates has called her mother a whore.

Charlotte ends the call. Glenn, in her heart, can already see the end to this story. She should have seen it from the moment she found Jake bleeding to death. Still, it doesn't hurt any less when Charlotte says, "That was your agent. The publisher is pulling the book."

Glenn starts to speak, but there's really nothing to say. She finds her coat and puts it on over her new black clothes. She wants nothing more than to be outside, to feel cold air against her skin, to watch the last of the day's sunlight. God knows how many more days she'll have these freedoms, because the noose is tightening. She can feel it digging into her flesh. It must be what Diane Sykes felt that night the detectives knocked on her door, when lights flashed in her driveway and reporters huddled to record her final descent.

"What aren't you telling me?" Charlotte asks.

"Nothing," Glenn says.

"You can trust me. With anything. I'm your lawyer. We'll share the burden."

Glenn doesn't look at her friend. She doesn't want to see herself lose another ally when she says, "I killed Diane Sykes."

CHAPTER 25

ANGELA HASN'T EATEN SINCE LAST NIGHT. STILL IN ELMHURST, SHE leaves her car in the station's parking lot and walks to a pizza shop in downtown, where she hears Cary scolding her in the back of her mind as she orders two slices and a Coke. "Don't bother heating them," she says, suddenly too hungry to wait.

Standing at a high top and inhaling her lunch, she dares a peek at her e-mail, where her inbox has exploded with messages from the communications team, and her boss, and Angela assumes they're all about Jake Abbott's murder and when she'll be ready to either close the case or give the media an update. Angela learned a long time ago that the best way to get to a close is to shut out the noise, and that includes ignoring these e-mails, at least for now. Instead, she calls Zane. "What's the latest?" she asks.

"Cavanaugh came by the house. She's been looking into Patrick Leary and trying to find a connection to Jake Abbott."

Angela sighs. A defense attorney will have a field day with any evidence Natalie Cavanaugh digs up, especially if they peg these murders to someone besides Natalie's sister. But Cavanaugh isn't the type to fade away, and chances are her instincts are good. They usually are.

Zane says, "She might be looking in the right place. I got some information on Leary."

"Let me guess: he's not who he claims to be."

"In a way," Zane says. "According to Glenn, Jake Abbott told her that Patrick Leary was a friend from high school who needed a place to stay. That looks like it wasn't true. But Patrick Leary is exactly who he says he is. Name, date of birth. We finally found a Social Security number, too, not that he's paid much in taxes. He has a record about a mile long, everything from auto theft to larceny to extortion. He's been in and out of jail for most of his adult life."

"How much of this do we think Jake knew?"

"That's the question, right? Apparently, Bennet Jones told Cavanaugh that Jake had been having financial troubles a few months back. Bennet asked him about it on Saturday, and Jake told him he'd found a solution, and the solution seems to have showed up along with Patrick Leary. We're looking at financial records to see what we can find."

"Here's another question for you," Angela says. "How did Jake even know Patrick? Who introduced them? See if you can find out. The answer is important."

"Let's see if Glenn knew," Zane says. "Speaking of which, we searched her office. We found a balance sheet, printed out. And it doesn't seem to have anything to do with her business. It's for a soccer club. Mavis's soccer club. The party on Saturday was a fundraiser for the club, and most of the people who attended had kids who play together."

"What kind of entries on the balance sheet?" Angela asks.

"Big ones," Zane says. "Much bigger than you'd expect for a kids' team."

"So if there were some financial shenanigans, Glenn might have known about them. We'll need to get this report to a forensic accountant and see what they can make of it."

Angela clicks off the call, puts the phone aside, and finishes eating. None of what Zane told her looks good for Glenn Abbott. When Angela's phone rings a moment later, she's relieved to see it's Hester Thursby and not her boss.

"I have something for you," Hester says.

"Record time," Angela says.

"I'm still digging around on Lindsey Sykes, who seems to have disappeared off the face of the earth, but didn't you tell me you were in Elmhurst?"

"Why?"

"Because I found the older girl, Tonya Sykes. She's a real estate agent. She goes by Olivia Knowles."

A block away, Olivia Knowles leaves the office.

To Olivia, using the name Tonya feels like speaking a foreign language. She left Tonya behind decades ago and doesn't see any part of her anymore, not even when she looks in the mirror. She'd grown her dark hair out of its jagged bob and died it blond. She'd let the nose piercing close. Her features had hardened with adulthood, while her body had softened. Now, even if the whole world learns her secret, Olivia doesn't believe she could ever return to being Tonya again.

Across the street, the poster for Glenn's event at the bookstore is gone. Olivia pops into the store. "What happened to the signing next week?" she asks the manager.

"Canceled."

"I saw on the news that her husband died. Tragic. Let's hope she can reschedule."

"The book is canceled too," the manager says, turning to the next customer. "We have hundreds of copies in the storeroom. Now we have to send them back to the publisher. There goes Glenn Abbott's career."

Olivia has her phone out. She searches Glenn's name. She scrolls through the headlines, carefully worded to avoid libel, but anyone can see that the media is gunning for Glenn's guilt. In a way, it feels redemptive, even though the little piece of Tonya left in Olivia knows that's not fair.

Outside, she hurries to her car and drives toward the farmhouse, turning off the winding road and into the conservation land that surrounds it. It had been a risk returning to Elmhurst only a few years after leaving. At the time, she had wondered if people would recognize her behind the changes she'd made to her appearance. But while Tonya Sykes may have been a twenty-one-year-old, Olivia Knowles claimed to be thirty, a divorcée starting over, with a kindergartener, Jason, in tow. It was easier for people to believe her story than it was to face the alternative.

The biggest chance Olivia took, of course, was befriending Ruth Cavanaugh. Olivia wanted to ferret out what really happened on Starling Circle. She'd wanted to blame Ruth. She wanted to know why the woman hadn't simply walked away from her husband. If Ruth had left, all their lives could have been different, and maybe Olivia's own mother would still be alive.

Ruth chose to take Olivia on as a new friend without question. A few years later, they became lovers, which seemed to surprise them both. By the time Ruth confessed her history one night as the couple lay in bed, it had felt like a betrayal when Olivia asked the one question she'd wanted to ask for so long, "Why didn't you just leave?"

Ruth snuggled in close and closed her eyes. "It seemed like the harder path to choose. Being alone. Leaving my husband. Raising children without help. I wished I'd known it was actually the easier path. Look at you with Jason. You haven't needed a husband. If I could go back in time and do one thing different, it would be to whisper that truth in my own ear."

Now Olivia pulls up the long driveway, through the trees, and parks by the barn. She chose this remote house with its stone walls and apple orchards to be her retreat. Of all her own mistakes, she wonders which she'd choose to undo if she had that option. For the first time since she saw the initial hints of Ruth's dementia, for the first time since Ruth died, Olivia is grateful that she's no longer here and Olivia doesn't have to confess her own lies. But she still needs to call Jason. Her son will want to hear the truth from her before the world tells him his story.

The last time she'd seen him, he'd been sitting at the kitchen table reading on his phone in the last hour before he had to leave for the airport.

"Do you remember my friend Ruth?" Olivia asked.

His eyes creased in a smile. "Your friend?"

"She died," Olivia said.

At first, it seemed as if he might have misunderstood. He laughed and shook his head. "What do you mean?"

"It was sudden."

"Why didn't you tell me?"

Olivia turned to the sink. Warm water ran over her hands. "I'm telling you now."

In the driveway, a car sounded its horn. Behind her, she heard Jason lift his bag. And he punched the wall. "Why can't you be honest about one fucking thing?" he said.

It had been the last time they'd talked to each other.

Now Olivia hurries inside. Photos of her and Ruth, of a life together, line the kitchen walls.

They'd been happy, despite everything unspoken.

Olivia's biggest secret, something she almost can't admit to herself, is that even after all these years, she can still feel Alan Cavanaugh's touch. She can hear his voice in her ear. "You know I love you," he'd told her.

"Tell me again," she'd said.

And he did.

She was the one who'd had an affair with Alan the summer he was killed. Not her mother. The only person who'd known was Lindsey, who'd crept up on them in the woods. But Diane Sykes had been the one to take the blame, the one who paid the ultimate price, and she'd done it to protect Olivia, like Olivia would do anything to protect her own child.

Now, as Olivia takes out her phone to call Jason, to call Alan Cavanaugh's son, she hears footsteps approach across the gravel. She glances out the window, where the light has begun to fade. She lays the phone on the kitchen counter and crosses to the door. When she opens it, it's as if she's traveled back in time.

"You came," she says.

CHAPTER 26

I STEP INSIDE THE HOUSE. THE FLOORBOARDS CREAK BENEATH MY FEET. The ceilings are low, but it feels like home. Coming here, I'd wondered what her instincts would tell her to do, if she'd hug me or if she'd turn and run. More than that, though, I'd wondered what I *would do.*

For once, I don't have a plan.

My shoes are wet from the trek through the woods and across the field. I should be careful. I wipe the soles off carefully before following her into the kitchen. It's warm here. Bright, and not too modern. Potted asters spill from a rusted-out watering can. A woodpile sits beside a deep hearth.

She seems wary as she crosses to the stove and puts a kettle on. "Why are you here?" she asks again.

I turn to her. She stands against a wall of photos. I focus on the smiles. And the joy.

Now, suddenly, I have a plan. Rage boils inside me.

I want her to pay.

CHAPTER 27

NATALIE GETS LOST TWICE, EVEN AS SHE FOLLOWS DIRECTIONS ON the GPS through subdivisions and into a densely wooded section of Elmhurst. She grew up here, but she's rarely seen this part of town. A winding road leads to a blind driveway that wends up a hill to a farmhouse perched in a clearing that feels more like Vermont than ten miles outside of Boston. By now, the sun hovers at the horizon.

Natalie eases alongside a car parked in front of the barn. Chickens scratch at the ground in a coop. She should call her location in to headquarters, but she's not on the clock. She's not a police officer today. As she gets out of the car, she calls Olivia's name. When no one answers, she takes out her phone, half-expecting to have lost service, but she has plenty of bars. She punches in 9-1-1 to have it at the ready. The front door is ajar.

"Ms. Knowles?" Natalie shouts.

She toes the door open, wishing she'd taken her firearm from the safe when she left this morning. Inside the front hallway, a narrow staircase leads to the second floor. Two doorways offer options to the left and right, one leading to a living room, the other to the kitchen.

"Boston Police. Anyone home?"

She edges inside, her senses finely tuned. As she scans the living room, a groan emanates from the kitchen. Natalie rushes forward. A splash of red arcs across a wooden floor. A woman lies facedown, her blond hair caked in blood. Toward the back of the house, a door crashes open.

At the window, Natalie scans a darkened field only to see a figure disappearing into the trees. She hits 9-1-1. As she waits for the operator to answer, she glances up. The wall on the opposite side of the kitchen is covered with photos. Dozens of them. At first, Natalie thinks most of them feature Diane Sykes, but as she focuses, she recognizes her own mother. With this woman.

Olivia Knowles groans again. Her lips move.

The operator answers. As Natalie reads off the address, she leans over and puts her ear close to the woman's mouth as she struggles to say something Natalie can't quite make out.

A voice behind her catches her off guard.

"Don't move."

Natalie spins around. Angela White stands in the doorway with her firearm out. Natalie raises her hands in the air.

When Angela reaches for her phone, Natalie drops her hands and runs toward the back of the house.

"Cavanaugh!" Angela shouts.

But Natalie's out the door and headed toward the woods.

The boys play soccer on one field and the girls on the other. This, being outside, translating anger into energy, is what Mavis has both looked forward to and dreaded all day. In the before time, her father would be here, coaching from the sidelines, cheering her on. He came to every practice, every game. Mavis tries to imagine him now, as she dribbles the soccer ball up the line. He'd have run alongside her and known to let her focus. But now, when she tries to pass the ball to Stella, a defender from the other team intercepts and sends the ball down the field.

"Fuck!" Mavis screams, and for the briefest moment, it's as though the last twenty-four hours never happened. Girls near her on the field grin at the swear word, and one of the coaches calls from the sidelines.

"Watch the language, Abbott," he says, and then—she can see

it—he remembers what happened and who she is, and he gives her the Sad Eyes and says, "Don't worry about it," with a wave of his hand.

With that, the girls stare again. Mavis takes off up the field. As the afternoon light fades, she tries to focus on the ball, on moving it down the field, but she can't keep the posts that have taken over the internet from her mind, the ones calling her mother a murderer. Even as the game continues, Mavis swears she sees the other girls gathering in pairs and trios; she swears she can hear them whispering about her.

The ball arcs across the field. Mavis manages to catch it with her toe. Out of the corner of her eye, she sees a flash of the opposite team's blue. Her foot catches something. She hurtles forward, her chin skidding across the grass as the taste of copper floods her mouth. Behind her, the coach blows the whistle. Mavis lies on her back. When she opens her eyes, she's surrounded by girls staring down at her. She searches for Stella but can't find her. One of the other girls says, "My bad," and offers a hand.

Mavis considers the hand. All day, she's been waiting for someone to confront her, to say something cruel, but this kindness is almost harder to bear. The coach joins them, dropping the ball to the grass. "Everything okay?"

Mavis stands and kicks the ball as hard as she can. Stella jogs in from the other side of the field. Right then, the coach's phone beeps. All around, phones are beeping. Including Mavis's.

She glances at the screen. There's a text from the soccer club group account with a link to a news article. She opens it, and the headline reads: MURDERED HUSBAND OF COOKBOOK AUTHOR SUSPECTED OF EMBEZZLING HUNDREDS OF THOUSANDS FROM KIDS' SOCCER TEAM.

"Damn," the coach says.

Mavis backs away. It feels as though everyone on the team, Stella and the coach included, is glaring at her. She trips and falls. And then she's on her feet, running toward the athletic center.

She keeps running till she reaches the locker room. It's time for this day to be over. She thinks about the rest of her week, and every bit of it seems long and beyond challenging. She'll have to face going home, being with her mother, sitting with their sadness even as the world tries to tell their story. She'll have to face learning whether the headline she'd read is true. She doubts she'll be able to make it through two more days at school or to face her friends ever again.

It's 4:50, with ten minutes before the end of the day. She changes out of her uniform. This afternoon, Kevin had mentioned that coming to a new school had been challenging because no one had known about his mother. To Mavis, the idea of a new start sounds amazing. Aunt Natalie had been right last night when she'd called Kevin a jerk, but he'd been nice today when he'd talked about his mother, and talking to someone, anyone, who understands what Mavis is feeling might be nice right now. Maybe he can help make all of this hurt less. For a moment, Mavis allows herself to remember being in the kitchen yesterday, listening to Taylor Swift and beating her father at chess. She allows herself to remember being happy.

She hears voices approaching.

She grabs her bag and runs.

She reaches the outer hallway just as the other girls enter the locker room from the field. She hurries down the hall and out the athletic center's main entrance. The air feels cool and crisp and smells of falling leaves. She skirts the school and heads to the empty playing fields. As she watches, the overhead lights go out. If she cuts across the darkened fields and around the cabana by the tennis courts, she'll avoid bumping into anyone, and be closer to home. She dashes across the grass, half-expecting to find Kevin smoking pot or drinking. He's that kind of boy. But no one's there.

A gust of wind whips leaves along the asphalt and into Mavis's face. A street runs alongside the campus, separated by a stone wall. On it, a single car drives slowly as someone peers through the window.

Mavis suddenly shouts into the evening air as the anger and despair she's held onto all day erupts. It feels so good to let go that she shouts again. She kicks at the cabana's foundation till her foot throbs. She presses her back against the brick and lowers herself to the cold asphalt.

Her phone beeps with a text from Stella. *Where RU?*

I want to be alone, Mavis responds.

No you don't. And I don't want you to be either. Frig whatever that article says.

Stella is right. Like usual. Mavis doesn't want to be alone. She'll sit here for five minutes before finding her friend. She can get through tonight. She can get through tomorrow. She'll take it step by step, like she does with math and chess and everything else in her life. And her first step is to go home. It's time to be sad. It's time to understand how much she lost last night in that cottage and how much life has changed.

As she pulls herself to her feet, she hears footsteps approaching.

"Stella, is that you?"

The footsteps stop.

"Who's there?"

Mavis backs away.

A shadowy figure approaches and steps into the light from a streetlamp.

"Uncle Bennet?"

Bennet smiles. "I'm here with your Aunt Natalie. We were looking for you."

1995

FOR YEARS, IT WASN'T ALAN CAVANAUGH'S MURDER THAT STAYED with Tonya, or even her mother's suicide. Instead, it was those final, angry words she'd said to Lindsey when the social workers arrived to take them away while the Cavanaughs next door watched in horror.

"This is your fault," she whispered to Lindsey when no one else could hear. "If you remember one thing, remember that I hate your fucking guts."

Lindsey sobbed in the back of one car, while Tonya went in another.

"This is temporary," a social worker said in calm, gentle tones. "A week. Maybe two. We'll get a placement where both of you can be together as soon as we can."

Tonya knew to smile. It was the easiest way to get them to believe that you cared. "That would be wonderful!"

He drove her to the next town and dropped her off at a house on another cul-de-sac, as if she were going to stay with an aunt and uncle. The couple was nice, kind even. Older. Stan and Yvette Robbins. They'd had a parade of foster children come through over the years, enough so that they had a Christmas tree covered with names. "We'll make you your own ornament come December," Yvette said a few nights later over dinner.

"That would be wonderful!" Tonya said.

"Our children can always come home."

Tonya smiled to put Yvette at ease, and to get her to stop watching. Once she did, Tonya ran away. At that time, she was sixteen and tougher than even she realized. She moved to Hartford and got a job waiting tables and lived in a shared apartment till her stomach grew too big to hide anymore. She kept working, even after Jason was born. With a baby, it was easy enough to tell people she was eighteen or twenty-one. Who'd want to believe the truth? Olivia was her middle name, so she used that to help hide in plain sight. And when Jason was two years old, a few days past Tonya's actual eighteenth birthday, she married a twenty-seven-year-old plumber named Daryl Knowles who believed she was twenty-five and that she loved him. She stayed with him long enough to finish changing her name, earn an associate's degree, and get Jason to kindergarten. And when she left, Daryl seemed as relieved to lose his ready-made family as she was to lose him.

She returned to Elmhurst, to where it all began and where it all ended. More than five years had passed since she'd left, and she was unrecognizable, not so much because she'd changed the color of her hair, but because no one wanted to see the girl they'd failed return as a success. Tonya met with Jason's teachers, but unlike her own mother, she eschewed the PTA and committees. Those people hadn't done her mother any good, not in the end. She led a quiet life. She talked about an ex-husband when she needed to; she made sure her bills were paid and her son was safe. She met Ruth. And she hoped that Lindsey would seek her out, that she could find a way to atone.

Now, all these years later, memories flit through her mind as she goes in and out of consciousness, as lights shine in her eyes, and she feels herself rising on a gurney.

"You'll be fine, sweetie."

An EMT smiles down at her.

"Can you tell us who did this?"

A woman leans close. And Tonya would tell her, if she could find the words, if she could talk around the oxygen mask, if she could move her lips. "This is my fault," she wants to say. "I got what I deserved."

CHAPTER 28

MIST RISES FROM THE WET GROUND AS NATALIE'S FEET POUND across the field. The moon slides behind a cloud, making it dark enough so that she nearly collides with a stone wall. She stops in time and swings over it. At the tree line, she crashes forward and lets darkness swallow her. She remembers running through a similar forest on the other end of town as she tugged Glenn after her. She remembers her father's bloated body. "Did Mom kill him?" Glenn asked.

"Don't say that," Natalie had said. "To anyone."

Now, tonight, a thick canopy of pine and oak blocks any lingering light. Natalie's foot catches on a root, and she flies forward, her palms skidding across leaves and pine needles.

And she stops.

She rolls onto her back. Dampness seeps through her coat. She listens, first to the blood pounding in her ears, and then to her own breathing. When her heart rate slows, she tunes into the forest. It's quiet, but beneath that quiet, she hears the creaking of branches in the wind, the rustling of leaves yet to fall, the flapping of wings. Somewhere, a coyote howls.

And not fifty yards away, footsteps make a quiet retreat.

She rises. Her eyes have adjusted to the dark. She searches among the shadows for a human silhouette. A twig snaps. Natalie moves toward the noise, steady and quiet this time, stepping carefully to avoid stones and roots. Off in the distance, a siren screams as a cruiser approaches the farmhouse. She imagines the lieutenant, flashing her badge to the local cops. She tries not to imagine what the lieutenant will have to say if Natalie makes it back to the farmhouse herself.

Ahead, light from a cell phone flashes briefly. Again, footsteps retreat across the forest floor. Natalie follows till she stumbles through another tree line and onto an access road. Above her, the moon, out from behind its cloud, shines bright on ghostly tree trunks rising around her.

A car door slams. An engine roars to life. A radio set to Magic 106.7 shatters the quiet. Tires bounce off rocks. Natalie spins to see headlights speeding toward her. She throws herself off the road and into the trees. The car flies by and skids to a stop. It reverses and Natalie freezes, her back pressed to a tree trunk. She feels around on the ground, for anything to defend herself with. She'd made a rookie mistake, a mistake even Zane wouldn't make—pursuing an assailant, unarmed and without backup.

But the driver is making a mistake, too, by allowing her a second look.

The sedan glides along the road. The driver aims a flashlight out the window. Natalie blocks the light with an outstretched palm, trying to see beyond it, to take in critical details. She realizes just how pissed off she'll be if this winds up being her last moment on planet Earth.

"What do you want?" she asks.

The Cranberries sing that there's no need to argue.

Natalie takes a step forward and throws a Hail Mary. "Boston Police. You're under arrest."

The flashlight goes out. The car speeds away.

Natalie runs to the road, phone out, trying to capture the license plate, but the car disappears around a corner before she can snap an image.

She takes in the cool autumn air, breathing for what feels like the first time since she entered the woods. She should move. She should get back to the farmhouse before whoever was driving that car has second thoughts and returns. But she can't move, not yet. She goes over what she knows. Whoever was in the farmhouse came here purposefully and knew about an access road that led to the property. That someone also drove a dark-colored sedan, one that will hopefully have left tire treads in the deep mud from yesterday's storm. Olivia Knowles has photos of her mother on her walls. Olivia also bears a striking resemblance to Diane Sykes in a blond wig—too striking of a resemblance for it to be a coincidence.

Off in the distance, another siren approaches.

Battered and bruised, Natalie makes her way through the trees toward the farmhouse. Now it's time for her to tell the lieutenant what she knows, and to face the consequences.

Glenn's been walking through the South End for over an hour, ever since she left Charlotte Todd's apartment, ever since her confession.

I killed Diane Sykes.

She's held those words close for years. There were days, weeks even, when she managed to forget her role in what happened. Earlier, the lieutenant had said it would feel good to tell the truth. But now Glenn doesn't feel anything. Not even regret.

Back at the loft, Charlotte had blocked Glenn's escape. "You can't leave me with that kind of cliffhanger. What happened?"

"I started the rumors about Diane Sykes and my father having an affair. It wasn't true. Or at least I don't think it was, but I told a girl at school, Kimberly Green, and she told someone, and the rumor spread until it was out of control, and I could have spoken up, but it was so much easier to have the whispers be about someone besides me. Without those rumors, the police never would have considered Diane a suspect and she wouldn't have killed herself. It's my fault she's dead."

Charlotte had looked at her, her face impassive. "Anything else?"

Glenn had shaken her head. When Charlotte had finally stepped out of her way, Glenn had fled to the elevator.

Now she calls a car and waits on the sidewalk till it pulls up beside her. As the driver heads away from downtown Boston, she dares a glance at her phone, only to learn the latest, that Jake had embezzled money. From the soccer club. From their neighbors and friends. From practically everyone Glenn knows.

"You having a good day?" the driver asks.

"The best," Glenn says.

When he turns onto her street, she sees the wall of news trucks parked along the sidewalk.

"That the house?" the driver asks.

Glenn nearly tells him to keep going. But she needs to face this new reality at some point, no matter what it brings. "Pull into the driveway."

He maneuvers around the trucks. Reporters press their faces to the windows, trying to get a shot of Glenn in her shame. She keeps her face neutral and her eyes straight ahead. And when the driver stops at the garage, she leans forward. "If anyone asks about me, tell them I was nice and gave you a big tip."

"You got it," the driver says. "Want me to walk you to the door?"

"That earned you a five-star rating. But I can do it on my own."

As she exits the car, automatic lights shine off her copper-colored hair. She can almost hear the camera lenses focusing. Someone calls her name. Someone else shouts that Jake got what he deserved.

"Thanks for the ride," she says to the driver.

"Good luck."

Glenn watches him back the car through the reporters. She stops herself from retreating, from covering her face, from admitting that Charlotte was right and that she shouldn't have dared to return home. She forces herself to pause, to pose even. She imagines Jackie Kennedy, as shutters click and record her public grief. She takes a few steps toward the kitchen, but the cottage tugs at her till she crosses beneath the pergola and stands facing the site of her husband's death. She touches the doorknob, where crime tape still hangs. The crime techs have installed a padlock too. She feels as if this should be a moment, one where grief finally breaks through numbness. Maybe one of the photographers will capture it with a telephoto lens. But as much as she hopes, no tears come.

Inside the house, every drawer is open, every cupboard emptied. The contents of the entire house seem to have been piled into the center of the floor. She wades through the mess. She can't stay here. Mavis should be at Natalie's house by now. Glenn will pack a bag and join them. She sends a text to Natalie. *I'm at home. Will stay here for a bit to straighten up, then I'll head to your place.*

She lets the phone fall to her side. How can she possibly begin to put her life back together? One room at a time. One pile at a time. One item at a time.

She starts in the front hallway, slowly returning the contents of a dresser to its drawers. She sorts through what she finds, weeding out items she should have gotten rid of years ago. When she finishes with the dresser, she moves on to the front sitting room. Decks of cards are strewn across the floor. She remembers playing gin rummy with Jake when they first met, huddling in one room of her old apartment while Mavis slept in the other. They'd played a century, day after day tallying their scores as they tried to reach a thousand points. She'd kept the pad with their scores. She swore it had been in one of these drawers. She searches but can't find it. She wonders if the cops took it as evidence, if they thought it was some secret code that might solve the case. What else did the cops find? Glenn has a little bag of pot upstairs in her dresser. It's not illegal anymore, though it still feels dangerous, like something she wouldn't want the police to know about. So does the vibrator that sits next to it.

Glenn tosses handfuls of playing cards into a trash bag without bothering to sort them. She and Jake haven't played cards in years, and who would she play with now anyway? She won't have friends, not after Jake betrayed their trust. Glenn hadn't known anything about the soccer team's finances, but who will believe that? Who could possibly forgive her for her own willful blindness?

This is when the tears should come. Still, they don't.

She moves to the kitchen.

The cabinets are open. Spices and cans and fruit litter the counter. On her blog, Glenn shames people for using spices that are more than three months old, but really, how often can any of us replace the bottle of mace in our cabinets? She suddenly feels frozen as she looks around, at the lights in the ceiling, at the counters she so carefully designed, at all her dreams, gone. Soon enough, Glenn's hair will have grown out, the luster gone, and she'll face paparazzi trying to capture her shame in a grocery store parking lot.

She hurls whatever's in her hand at the wall, realizing too late that it's a canister of confectioners' sugar. It explodes into a cloud of white that contaminates everything and fills the air with sweetness.

Someone taps at the door.

Lisa, the reporter Glenn recognized from the local news, presses her face to the glass. A cameraman stands behind her. "Can I get a statement?" Lisa shouts.

Glenn wrenches the door open. "You want a mimosa? I hear they're good at brunch."

The cameraman focuses in on Glenn's face.

"How much did you know about your husband's finances?" Lisa asks.

Glenn slams the door. She can feel her shoulders slouching as she turns off the kitchen lights and trudges up the back stairs. Mavis's bedroom is empty, but in disarray. So is her own bedroom, with clothing strewn everywhere. The vanity in her bathroom has been dismantled. The stash of pot is gone, but the vibrator is still there. Glenn sits on the edge of the bed. She imagines staying at Natalie's house, all three of them existing alongside each other, and a laugh starts at her core and makes its way through her body. Would she and Natalie have to cram into that bedroom with its slanted ceiling and tiny closet? Would she have to ignore the bottles of liquor hidden in every alcove?

She checks her phone. Natalie hasn't returned her text.

Tell me you're alive, she taps into her phone to Mavis.

She hesitates before hitting SEND. Is she being too trite, too flip? The girl's father died less than twenty-four hours ago, after all, but Glenn doesn't have the energy to revise or retype. She hits SEND. A moment later, Mavis responds. *At Stella's!*

Where's your aunt?

Three dots appear, but it takes a few moments before a single question mark appears on the screen.

Didn't she pick you up? Glenn types and then deletes. Natalie was supposed to pick Mavis up after school. This whole time, Glenn had thought Mavis was safe with her sister.

She texts Natalie again. *Tell me you're not dead because I want to be the one to kill you if you're alive,* she writes, and this time she doesn't hesitate before hitting SEND, but regrets it as soon as she does. There have been two murders in the last two days. The last thing in the world Glenn needs is to be linked to a third. Natalie still doesn't respond. When five minutes have gone by, she calls Natalie and listens to her voicemail message. Next she dials Zane, who doesn't pick up either.

I'm coming to get you, she writes to Mavis.

Can't I stay here?

Why wouldn't Mavis want to stay at her friend's house, somewhere she could feel safe? But Glenn gives in to selfishness. She wants to be with her daughter. *I'll be there in a half hour. We'll head to Aunt Natalie's for the night.*

Glenn pushes herself to her feet and makes it to the bathroom. She remembers Jake standing here on Saturday, telling her that she didn't know what she was getting into with Patrick. She remembers wishing he would shut up and let her be. It's another moment she'd redo if she could.

She flips on the light in the walk-in closet. Suddenly, a deep, silent sob wracks her body. She tries to ignore it as she takes her suitcase down and opens it. She stuffs jeans and T-shirts into the bag, but the tears won't stop, even after she snatches a white Oxford from the hamper and buries her face in it. Finally, she gives in, presses her back to the wall, and lowers herself to the floor with her legs splayed in front of her.

She rubs at her eyes. She blows her nose in the Oxford. It's

Jake's, he'd worn it on Monday, but wouldn't need it anymore. As she wipes the snot away, she stares at the shirt as a thought tickles the back of her mind. She holds it to her face and inhales. The scent of citrus thrusts her back in time, to standing in a kitchen, to watching her mother lay an orange tube of lip gloss that Glenn had stolen from the A&P on the counter like evidence. She remembers a hot summer morning, the slick of tangerine on her lips. She remembers the simple joy of leaping into chlorinated water and feeling the heat wash away. She wishes her mother were here to help her face these coming weeks.

She sniffs the shirt again. But this time, she catches the floral notes, the sophisticated expense. The tears stop like a faucet.

You can trust me. With anything.

Why does Jake's shirt smell like Charlotte's perfume? And who has Glenn trusted with her darkest secrets?

CHAPTER 29

*T*HE DRIVE BETWEEN BOSTON AND ELMHURST DOESN'T TAKE LONG. *I stay just below the speed limit. It won't do to be stopped, not here where I shouldn't be.*

At a self-service car wash, I spray off the mud that's splashed onto the fenders. Afterward, I drive through puddles to be sure the car won't appear too clean. I swap the burner for my real phone and stop forwarding calls.

I can see Natalie Cavanaugh's expression out in the woods as she faced off with me, no weapon, no backup. I could have shot her, but that would have been too easy to trace back to me.

And I'd rather her suffer along with her sister.

Finding the source of the rumors had been easy. Glenn was still popular before her father died, and yearbooks are archived. One girl, Kimberly Green, seemed to show up next to Glenn in nearly every photo. Kimberly still lived in Elmhurst. And she liked to drink. One night over cocktails, she told me about the murders and the gossip that followed. "Glenn said she didn't know if it was true or not," Kimberly said, her words slurred, "but it was too good not to repeat. What was that woman's name who shot herself?"

"It's your story," I said. "You'd have to tell me."

Kimberly touched my hand. "You're so pretty. I could eat you."

"Diane," I said. "You said her name was Diane."

"Diane Sykes," Kimberly had said. "Poor thing. You don't get away with something so obvious."

But maybe you do.

CHAPTER 30

BLUE AND RED LIGHTS FLASH ACROSS THE BARN AND OAK TREES IN the farmhouse's front yard as Natalie trudges through the field. She dreads the scrutiny that will come from the lieutenant as soon as she returns to Olivia Knowles's house. In the front yard, two EMTs wheel a gurney out the front door. Natalie's grateful to see an oxygen mask instead of a body bag. Two state deputies hover, awaiting the arrival of their team.

"Cavanaugh."

Natalie turns to face the lieutenant, who stands beside a man with white hair. As she approaches, he holds out a hand. His blue eyes seem familiar. "You've grown up," he says.

"It happens," Natalie says.

"Tom O'Neil."

"He's the chief of police here in town," Angela says. "You've met before."

And Natalie remembers. The flashing lights. Leading a young officer through the woods. Showing him her father's body. She remembers that he was kind, especially to her mother. She remembers him as being so old, too, but he can't even be fifty now, less than ten years older than she is.

"Why were you here?" Natalie asks Angela.

Angela leads Natalie away from O'Neil. "You can skip the interrogation of me, because I found you with a woman who'd been assaulted, and you bolted for the back door. I should be arresting you. So you answer my questions, no equivocating, no obfuscating. Is that understood? And whatever you've been keeping from me, now's the time to come clean, not only about the what but the why, the who, the how, all of it. The assault is going to the state cops anyway, so I can only protect you so much."

Natalie tries to gather her thoughts in a way that will make sense to both her and the lieutenant, but no matter how she slices it, nothing makes sense. She starts with the easiest to explain. "There was someone in the house when I got here." She gives a summary of the chase into the woods but leaves out that she was nearly run down. "There was a car on an access road in the woods."

"You chased down a perp without backup?" Angela says.

And without a weapon, but Natalie keeps that detail to herself too.

"Why did *you* come here?" Angela asks.

"My sister had an event yesterday. Olivia Knowles showed up. She also came to my sister's house last night, a few hours before Jake was killed. Glenn thought Jake might be having an affair, but I don't think that's it. Did you see the photos in the kitchen? They're all over the wall. They're of my mother. Olivia Knowles and my mother knew each other, but my mother never mentioned her."

Angela waves Tom O'Neil over. "What do you know about the woman who was assaulted?"

He shakes his head. "Not much. Keeps to herself. Moved to town fifteen or twenty years ago. She's a real estate agent. Has a son who went off to college a while back. If I remember correctly, he was a handful in high school, but nothing the administration couldn't take care of. In this job, you don't get to know the quiet ones."

Right then, a sedan pulls up the road. An older man steps out and strides toward them. "What happened?"

Tom pauses. "This is Paul. He works with Olivia."

"We're not sure," Angela says. "She's unconscious but stable. They took her to Brigham and Women's."

"I heard police cruisers had come to the farm," Paul says. "Let's hope she's okay in the morning."

"Let's hope," Tom says. "And the state cops'll want the crime site cleared, so let's get you home."

He moves the man toward his sedan, where they chat quietly for a few moments.

"Here's the thing, Cavanaugh," Angela says. "You're holding out on me."

Natalie turns to her. "Why did you come here?"

"Follow me," Angela says. In her car, she hands Natalie a file folder. "Take a look inside."

One glance at the newspaper clipping is all Natalie needs. "I assumed you already knew about this. It's on the internet for the world to find."

"Someone sent that to me a few weeks ago. It was mailed here in Elmhurst."

Natalie glances toward the farmhouse. "You think Olivia sent the letter."

"I don't think Olivia sent it. I think Tonya Sykes did."

Natalie turns to face her.

Angela continues, "How long did you know Tonya Sykes was living here under an assumed name? And why does she have photos of your mother all over her walls?"

"I didn't know till tonight," Natalie says. "If I'd met Olivia Knowles on her own, if I'd bumped into her on the street like Glenn did, I don't know if I'd have seen Tonya either. She's changed. She doesn't look anything like the Tonya who lived next door." Natalie sighs. "There's the posting too," she says, telling Angela about the discussion-board post to Glenn's site.

"Cavanaugh, we have two bodies, a stalker, and a twenty-five-year-old murder, and they're all pointing toward you and your sister. It's not a matter of if they're connected, it's how. You should have told me about the discussion-board posts hours ago. We could have had a tech team tracing them."

Another car speeds into the yard, and two state detectives get out. Natalie takes a moment to glance at her phone. There are about ten texts from Glenn. With everything happening here, Natalie forgot to pick up Mavis at school. Now there would be hell to pay.

"I don't have any jurisdiction here," Angela says, "so any information I get from them will be through mutual interest. And if there's a connection to what happened at your sister's house, I wouldn't be surprised if I lose that case too. Let me help you while I still can. Please be honest with me."

"I chased someone into the woods. I didn't see who it was. I'm sure there are tire tracks in the mud, and unless this guy is really good, there must be other evidence in the house. We should try to figure out what that might be."

"Anything else?"

Only that when Natalie put her ear to Tonya's lips, she swears the woman whispered, "Lindsey." But she'll keep that to herself, at least for now.

Glenn hasn't moved from the floor in her closet when her phone rings and Charlotte's name flashes across the screen. She doesn't answer. She doesn't trust herself to keep her cool. Part of her wants to burn Jake's shirt. And she would if it wouldn't make her look like someone hiding evidence. Instead, she folds the shirt, puts it in a bag, and takes it downstairs to the darkened kitchen. Outside, the news trucks wait. So do the neighbors. She pours some wine in a glass and drinks it down in a single gulp that leaves her coughing.

For her whole life, no matter what, Glenn has had a plan. When she'd wanted a child and didn't have a husband, she'd found a donor. And when she'd wanted to start a new career, she'd created Happy Time and worked her ass off till it turned into something. She's known how to keep moving and when to pivot. But the only thing she knows right now is that she's never felt more alone in her entire life.

She creeps through the dark house. She tucks her hair into a knitted hat and slips out of the side door, past the cottage, to the six-foot-tall fence at the back. She scales the wrought iron, her coat tearing as it catches on a spike, and she rolls into the neighbor's rhododendron. After extracting herself from the branches, she runs through the yard. Automatic lights flash on. A dog barks at the window. She imagines one of those news cameras capturing this, Glenn Abbott, on the precipice of success, reduced to running through a neighbor's backyard in a desperate attempt to escape the press.

When she gets to the street, she slows her pace and keeps her head down as cars drive by. It takes her ten minutes to crisscross West Roxbury, where she comes to Stella Klein's house, a mock Tudor, all brick and roses set back from the street. Glenn will pick up Mavis, take a car to Natalie's, and regroup there. Maybe she'll give in to gluten and order pizza, and Natalie can tell her what she knows, and what she guesses about the investigation. Maybe they'll stay up all night drinking. Maybe they'll wind up having fun.

Her phone rings. It's Zane Perez.

"You called me." His words are clipped. "What do you need?"

Glenn lifts the latch on the Kleins' front gate. "The press. They're surrounding my house."

"That's the First Amendment at work."

"One of them came to the door."

"If it happens again, call nine-one-one. Or you can hire security, which might not be a bad idea with everything going on."

Glenn hears the cash register again. "My husband was having an affair," she says, in one long gasp. It embarrasses her to admit it.

"You're represented by counsel," Zane says. "I really can't talk to you."

But Glenn can't seem to stop herself from spilling everything she knows. "I thought I was being paranoid. Even now, I'm not one hundred percent sure, but you should talk to Charlotte Todd. She has something to hide. She's the one who was having the affair."

"Your lawyer was having an affair with your husband?"

"I think so."

"Find a new lawyer," Zane says. "And I'm ending this call. You might be recording me."

He clicks off.

Glenn steps into the garden, latches the gate behind her, and looks up. Stella's mother, Josie, stands at the front door, glaring. It's in that moment that Glenn remembers having the Kleins over to dinner last year, the way they lingered over dessert and listened to the girls playing in the other room. "We're thrilled to have you managing the team," Josie had said to Jake. "I'm lost when I look at a balance sheet."

"What do you want?" Josie asks.

Shame takes over Glenn's body. "I'm here to pick up Mavis. We'll get out of your way."

"Mavis isn't here. She's not welcome anymore, and neither are you."

Angela's phone rings. Zane's name flashes on the display. "Don't move," she says to Natalie, leaving the detective by her car. "What have you got?"

"Bad news," Zane says.

A moment later, Angela clicks off the call and returns to where Natalie waits. She tries to speak but can't find the words.

"What is it?" Natalie asks.

"It's your niece," Angela says. "She's missing."

CHAPTER 31

It's cold. Frigid, really. It's the kind of cold that seeps into your bones.

But Mavis runs.

She leaps and flies through the air, landing on her sled, and hurtles down an icy chute. She zips up a steep bank and down the other side. She looks over her shoulder. Her father follows on his own sled. "I'm coming for you," he shouts, and his voice fills her with joy.

Mavis has been so sad. She's grateful to know that she can release that sadness, that she can take her father's hand and they can run together to the top of the hill and sled down again. But when she speeds up an icy bank and hurtles into the air—high, high, higher, till the world below looks tiny, the trees like models in a train set—she understands that she's dreaming.

She also understands that it's time to wake up.

She needs to face the terrible truth.

Still, her father is here. And she doesn't want to leave him even as he shouts, "Keep going! Don't think about looking back." She turns on her sled and watches as he waves into the sky.

"You can do this," he shouts. "Be strong. Fight!"

She wants to hug him. To say goodbye. But there isn't time.

She forces herself toward consciousness. The first thing she feels is the cold, but this time it's real cold, not the cold of a dream. It makes her want to pee. She fights to open her eyes. She tries to move her hands, and that's when she feels plastic digging into her flesh, and she's watched enough *CSI: Miami* to know that her hands are bound with zip ties. Her eyes open to complete darkness. Something covers her head, and a drawstring digs into the flesh around her neck. She takes a deep breath of stuffy air and can feel her heart racing. She closes her eyes. She takes another deep breath, willing herself toward calm.

She remembers being behind the tennis courts and seeing Uncle Bennet approach. "I'm here with your Aunt Natalie," he said. "We're parked over there, on the street."

"Where is she?" Mavis asked.

"In the car. With Rowdy."

Mavis almost went with him. But something that had sat at the back of her mind came forward, something that had seemed like nothing at the time, but now, after the last few days, seemed like something. "Why were you in my mother's office on Saturday?"

Bennet didn't answer, and Mavis went to pass him, but he blocked the way. He had a hat pulled down over his hair. Mavis could have been a good girl and done what he told her.

Instead, she turned and sprinted. She could see the street getting closer. Twenty yards. Then ten. Behind her, Bennet's feet pounded on the pavement. She crashed to the ground, curling into a ball. He plowed into her and sprawled forward. And she was on her feet again, sprinting toward the school. A hand latched onto her ankle. She swung her bag. The edge of her tablet slammed into his head. And her mother's words came to her, "If you're ever in trouble, scream your fucking head off. Your father, me, Aunt Natalie, one of us will find you wherever you are."

Mavis's screams echoed against the school. She wanted her mother to hear. She'd settle for having Kevin Chandler hear. She scrambled forward, across the ground, but this time Bennet hurled himself on top of her and covered her mouth with his hand. She couldn't breathe. He felt in her pockets till he yanked out her phone. "Give me the code," he whispered. "And don't scream again. Understand?"

She nodded.

He lifted his hand, and she mumbled the code.

"I'm sorry," he said.

And the world went black.

Now Mavis forces herself to breathe till her heart rate slows. She also forces herself to forget the bag over her head and the dark and the desperate loneliness. She opens her imaginary boxes, packs away anything that isn't about escaping, ties those boxes with the tightest bows possible, and shoves them into the darkest recesses of her imaginary closet.

The box that she shoves farthest away is the one holding her future, because if Mavis opens it, if she examines it too closely, it will tell her that if she doesn't save herself, she won't survive this night.

CHAPTER 32

NATALIE PARKS ALONG THE CURB BEHIND ANGELA'S CAR. ZANE already waits in front of the Tudor-style house. "What's she doing here?" he asks as Natalie approaches.

"Later," Angela says. "Get me up to speed."

"Not much beyond what I already told you on the phone," Zane says. "We have officers canvassing the neighborhood around the Abbotts' house and around the school. Mavis texted her mother at about 5:30 and said she was here at her friend's house." Zane looks at Natalie. "You were supposed to pick her up at school."

"This is my fault?" Natalie asks.

"I'm saying the same thing your sister's going to say to you when you see her inside."

Natalie steps toward him, but Angela manages to get between them. "Not worth it," she says. "For either of you. We're working on this together, all hands on deck. There'll be an Amber Alert out soon, which means this goes way beyond the department."

"Where were you?" Zane asks.

"I was following up on something," Natalie says.

"That real estate agent?" Zane says. "Why can't you stay out of this?"

Angela puts a hand to his arm. "Let's cool it. What's going on with video surveillance at the Abbotts' house?"

"A few of the neighbors have security systems in place," Zane says. "We accessed what we could and are reviewing it, but there's a lot to go through. This is what we have so far."

A video plays on his phone. The camera isn't focused on Glenn's house or her driveway, but on a neighbor's instead. It shows a sedan stopped along the sidewalk. Someone steps out and lights a cigarette.

"That confirms someone was there," Angela says. "Hard to tell if it was Olivia Knowles or not."

"Who?" Zane asks.

"The real estate agent in Elmhurst. She has an unnatural interest in Glenn Abbott. She was attacked in her home earlier, so unless she has an accomplice, she's not a good candidate for Mavis Abbott's disappearance, which is our number one priority at this point. And if we find Mavis Abbott, my guess is we'll find her father's killer."

At the front door, a blond woman glares at them, her arms folded as tight as her face. "Let's get this over with," the woman says, showing them into the house, which is modern and decorated in every shade of beige. From this morning, Natalie recognizes Stella, who sits beside Glenn on a sofa.

"How are you holding up?" Natalie asks her sister.

"I've had better days."

"Could we have a moment alone?"

The lieutenant nods. The blond woman leads them to a small room lined with bookshelves. "Don't steal anything," she says.

"Thanks for your support, Josie," Glenn says with a sigh.

"Can you excuse us?" Natalie waits for the woman to leave and enfolds her sister in an embrace, something she rarely initiates. "I went to meet with Olivia Knowles."

"Did you get anything out of her?"

Natalie can't help it. The detective side of her wants to gauge her sister's reaction when she says, "She's Tonya Sykes."

Glenn steps away. "Wait, what?"

"Are you sure you didn't recognize her?"

Glenn shakes her head. "She seemed familiar, but I didn't know why. When I got to Elmhurst yesterday, she was across the street in the doorway to the real estate office. Later, she came up to talk to me. I thought I recognized her, but from seeing her earlier. All I remember about Tonya is her nose ring and black hair and that we shared a bottle of Zima."

They hadn't had social media or digital cameras in 1995. If Tonya had disappeared a few years later, her image would have been burned into both their memories. Back then, Tonya had been sixteen to Glenn's twelve. She must have seemed impossibly old and sophisticated to Glenn, and certainly a different person than Natalie saw in Elmhurst today.

"She has photos of Mom all over her kitchen wall," Natalie says. "They knew each other. But Mom never mentioned her, not to me at least. Are you sure she didn't come to your party on Saturday? Maybe she posted that comment to your blog?"

Glenn shakes her head. "I'd have noticed her, that hair, her clothes. She'd have stood out. Could she have had something to do with what happened to Mavis?"

Natalie was at Olivia's house when Mavis was last seen. "We'll find out soon enough. And every agency in the state will be looking for Mavis. Whoever took her won't get far. I promise. But the next few hours are going to be difficult. The questioning will be relentless."

"All I want is to have Mavis back," Glenn says. "And if I go to jail, so be it. I should get out there and let them start the inquisition."

"One more question," Natalie says. "Have you heard from Lindsey Sykes?"

"Lindsey? Why would I have?"

"Because Tonya whispered Lindsey's name in my ear when I found her."

"Then it sounds like you need to find Lindsey Sykes."

Glenn and Natalie return to the living room.

"A state detective is on his way here," Angela says. "And the local office of the FBI will be involved soon, too. Before this gets out of control, think carefully. Is there anywhere Mavis may have gone tonight to get away?"

"She'd usually come here," Stella says, from where she hovers on the edge of the room. Her black hair is tied in a ponytail, and her eyes are red with tears.

"Anywhere else we should check?" Angela asks.

Glenn looks to Natalie. "She's like you. Where would you be?"

"Here," Natalie says. "I'd be trying to help."

"Do you have a photo?" Angela asks, rattling off a phone number. "A recent one."

As Natalie steps away from the interview, she hears her sister say, "This is from the party over the weekend. If you need more, I have dozens."

Natalie slips into the den and waves Stella after her. "The lieutenant will have questions for you, and anything you say to me, you'll need to say to her, too. Okay? But tell me anything you can think of, even if it's uncomfortable or boring or seems as though it doesn't mean anything. Can you do that?"

"I think so," Stella says.

"Tell me about today. Start to finish."

Stella considers the question before answering. "There was a lot of staring and whispering, especially as the story got bigger as the day went on. Teachers were trying to control how much we were on our phones, but they can only do so much, you know?"

"How did Mavis react to it all?"

"She seemed okay at first. I know she wanted to take her algebra test, but after that . . . I think she wanted everything to go back to normal, you know, the way it was two days ago."

"I'd have wanted the same thing."

"Me too. It's hard to know what to say when . . ." Stella stops herself.

"It's hard to know what to say when your friend's father dies," Natalie says. "Believe me, I know. But you and I can talk about it, and you don't have to feel uncomfortable because it's all about finding your friend. Did you spend the whole day with her?"

"As much as I could. We don't have the same schedule, but I met her between classes. And we had lunch together. And soccer practice. Sometimes I forgot that anything had happened, but it would hit me, like really quickly. When we were playing soccer . . ."

When a long enough silence has passed, Natalie says, "This is my cue that you might have some important information."

"We were practicing, and a bunch of us got a text telling us . . . telling us what Mr. Abbott did, that he stole the money from the soccer club. I think Mavis got it too, because the next thing I knew she was running toward the locker room. I thought I would catch up with her there, but when we finished practice, she was gone."

"Did you look for her?"

Stella nods. "Everywhere. And I texted, too. Then I went to the Abbotts' house to see if I could find her, but there were vans jamming the road. After that, I went to the Starbucks where we sometimes hang out. She wasn't there either."

"You did part of our job for us." Natalie would have liked to have had this girl as a friend when her own father died. "You were at the party on Saturday, too, right?"

Stella nods.

"Did you see anything there?"

"Maybe."

"Tell me."

"You can't tell my mother."

"I can't promise that, but I can give you a maybe. And if what you tell me helps us out, no one will care anyway."

"We saw Mrs. Abbott and that dead guy. Mr. Leary? They were in the dark, in the library. I don't know what they were doing. But they could have been kissing. Maybe."

Thankfully, Natalie already knows about most of this. And so do the cops. "Good to know. Anything else?"

Stella looks as though she'd rather be anywhere but here right about now.

"You'll feel better if you tell me."

"We snuck a glass of eggnog," Stella says, the words spilling out in a tidal wave. "Or I snuck it, and Mavis had some too, but Mr. Jones came out of Mrs. Abbott's office and caught us."

Zane comes to the door. "Cavanaugh, the lieutenant wants to talk to Stella."

"One minute," Natalie says, turning her back to him. "Mr. Jones came out of my sister's office? Was anyone with him?"

"I don't think so."

"Did he say why he was there?"

"We didn't ask."

Natalie puts her hands on Stella's shoulders. Bennet Jones has just gone right back up to the top of Natalie's list of suspects. "That was awesome," she says. "And it's the exact kind of information we need to find Mavis. Now think through your day. Was there anything else at all that happened? Anything that bothered you or stood out?"

"There were memes going around of Mrs. Abbott holding a knife."

"I've seen them," Natalie says. "And I bet she has too. I've known Mrs. Abbott since the day she was born. She has a thick skin."

"Everyone was awful," Stella says. "Especially in the locker room after practice when the news about Mr. Abbott and the money was out. Even the nice girls were mean. Except . . ."

Stella stops mid-sentence again.

"What comes after 'except'?"

"Mavis left during lunch and kind of disappeared. When it was time to go to class, I found her sitting on the floor in the hallway. She'd been crying. Almost everyone was ignoring her, but the weird part was that she'd been talking to Kevin Chandler. Honestly, it looked like he was being nice, and he's kind of a jerk."

Kevin Chandler. Again.

"Do they usually talk to each other?" Natalie asks.

Stella turns red.

"She likes him," Natalie says. "She told me last night. Does he like her back?"

"He's always teasing her."

"That sounds like a yes. Any chance you have his address?"

Stella flips through her phone and forwards the address to Natalie.

"Good job," Natalie says to Stella. "Tell everything you told me to the lieutenant, okay?"

Stella dashes into the other room. When Zane turns to follow, Natalie holds him back. "Did you find evidence in my sister's office?"

"You know I can't say."

"What did you find?" Natalie asks, and when Zane still doesn't answer, she says, "Bennet Jones was in my sister's office on Saturday night. And remember the lead I gave you at the beginning of the day? Kevin Chandler. You never followed up with him, did you? We need to talk to him. Now."

"*We* don't need to do anything," Zane says.

Angela joins them from the other room. "The Amber Alert is active, and a state detective arrived. The feds will be here soon, too. We'll finish up interviewing Stella and then move this show down the road to your sister's house." She glances from one of them to the other. "What?" she asks.

Natalie tells her about the conversation with Stella, finishing with Kevin Chandler.

"Sounds like a lead to me," Angela says. "Get to this kid's house and see what you can learn."

"On it," Zane says.

"I mean both of you," Angela says. "Like I said outside, all hands on deck. I'll deal with the state cops and the feds."

Natalie says, "Someone needs to stay with Tonya, or Olivia. Whatever her name is. Someone needs to be there when she wakes up."

"We have a uniform at the hospital," Angela says.

Natalie follows the lieutenant through the house, where a man with a crew cut and a nicely tailored suit is talking to Stella in the living room, while Glenn listens.

"I'll be out in a second," Natalie says to the lieutenant.

"Don't be too long," Angela says.

Natalie takes her sister's hand and squeezes. "We'll find Mavis, and we'll find out who did this to you. Understand me? After that, we can deal with the rest."

Out on the sidewalk, Angela watches her breath freeze in the cold air. Right now, all she wants is to go home and spend time with Isaiah, to tell him that she loves him more than anyone in the world. "What're you thinking?" she asks Zane.

"I don't want to say it."

"Then I will. You're thinking about all those awful stories you've read in the news, about desperate parents making decisions you can't dream of ever making. You're thinking Glenn Abbott killed Patrick Leary and then killed her husband. You're thinking Mavis saw something she shouldn't have, and Mrs. Abbott made one of those choices that no parent should make, ever."

"I didn't know you could read minds," Zane says.

"I'm not reading minds. Those state cops, the feds, they don't know Cavanaugh. They don't know anyone involved with this case, and that scenario I laid out is the first place they'll go, and they'll stay there unless they find somewhere else to look." Sometimes Angela gave in to being a softie. Today might be one of those days. "Let's see if we can prove them wrong."

The front door to the Kleins' house opens. Natalie steps outside, stopping as she sees the two of them talking. "She knows you'll be watching her," Angela says to Zane. "Make sure you do."

"I'm driving," Zane says, getting into the car.

Natalie puts a hand on the passenger's-side door.

"Be careful," Angela says.

Natalie won't meet Angela's eyes. "I don't know if I can be anymore."

"Try harder. One false step, and we're both done."

As her detectives drive away, Angela hopes she doesn't regret sending Natalie into the night.

The Kleins' front door opens again, and the state detective leads Glenn to his car. Angela follows as they make their way to the Abbotts' house. In the driveway, she calls the officers canvassing the neighborhood. So far, no sightings of Mavis Abbott. When she clicks off, her phone rings with a number she doesn't recognize. A moment later, she's headed toward Cambridgeport.

CHAPTER 33

GLENN ABBOTT HAS EXACTLY ONE THING TO BE THANKFUL FOR right now: she's left Josie Klein's house and no longer needs to put up with the woman's glares. She wonders, though, what she'd do in Josie's shoes. Glenn herself would certainly strangle Jake right about now if she had the chance. Instead, she asks the cops that have taken over her house if they want coffee. "Tea, maybe?"

There are about a hundred of them. Actually, less than ten, but she can't keep any of them straight with their tailored suits and strong jawlines and clipped speech. She focuses in on the state detective.

Brock London.

You can't make names like that up.

He has blue eyes and a buzz cut that highlights his bone structure, and he catches her watching him.

"Care to share?" he asks.

"I'm having a bad day," Glenn says.

"I can't imagine a worse one," Brock says.

If this were a romance novel, Glenn would choose Brock London in a second. She wonders if he'd choose her, in her prison stripes.

"We'll need your daughter's devices," he says. "Yours, too."

Glenn leads him to Mavis's room. "She mostly uses her tablet from school and her phone."

"Where are those?"

"With her, would be my guess."

Glenn crosses to the bed and lays a hand on the pillow, where Mavis had been last night.

"We'll contact the provider and get a location," Brock London says. "What about yours?"

Glenn hands him her phone and tells him the password. So much for secrets. She tells him everything else, too, about the non-affair with Patrick, about her fight with Jake. "I told the police that he was here with me on Monday night," she says. "But I lied. He wasn't. He left. And now his shirt smells like my lawyer's perfume."

She retrieves the shirt from where she'd stashed it. She tells him about the strange posts on her blog and the visit from Olivia Knowles. "My sister went to see Olivia tonight, and it turned out we'd known her growing up. She's been living under an assumed name. But someone attacked her before Natalie could talk to her."

To Glenn, things feel different now, and it's not because her before and after keeps shifting as her losses mount. It's because the game has changed, and she knows now that she's in this for Mavis, and only Mavis. Everyone, from Angela White to Josie Klein to this impossibly handsome state detective staring her down—they all assume she's guilty. And she isn't.

Glenn imagines the TV shows she's seen about missing children, the crying mothers and the reel-to-reel tapes awaiting calls from kidnappers with muffled voices. "Aren't we supposed to set up a call center? You'll want to trace the call, right, if she's kidnapped?"

"We're working on that," Brock says. "Do you have a landline?"

"Not that anyone uses."

"If there's a kidnapper, let's assume they'll call this phone." He holds up hers. "And we'll be here to answer it."

Glenn's heart sinks. They're not even looking for another suspect. And unless they find a way to believe her, unless they start looking for the person who actually is guilty, something unimaginable will happen to her daughter.

Angela parks alongside Bennet Jones's apartment building in Cambridgeport, where Officer Aldrich waits for her by the front door.

"When we were here yesterday," he says, "you asked me to call if anything suspicious happened. This may be nothing."

"Or it may be something."

"The neighbor called in. The dog's been barking."

"Have you been inside?"

He shakes his head.

Angela steps into the street and surveys the apartment on the second floor. One light is on, but the rest of the apartment is dark. Even from here, she can hear Rowdy. She'd tried calling Bennet Jones on the drive here, but he didn't answer. "Let's check it out," she says, ringing the neighbor's bell and leading the way to the second floor.

The neighbor waits outside her apartment, her hair tied in a messy knot, a wineglass in hand. "That dog's been barking for hours."

Behind her, a lug of a man hovers, also with a glass of wine in hand.

Angela shows her badge. "When was the last time you saw Mr. Jones?"

"Why is a Boston cop responding to a noise complaint?" the neighbor asks.

"Answer the question," Angela says.

"Not since yesterday." The neighbor nods at Aldrich. "When he was here."

"Does the dog bark like this a lot?" Angela asks.

"Not continuously and not for this long."

"We'll see what we can do. Why don't you go back into your apartment? We'll let you know if we need anything."

After the neighbor closes the door, Angela stands in the hallway for a moment. She can hear Rowdy pawing and whimpering behind the newly repaired door. It's not a sound that she likes.

"What do we do?" Aldrich asks.

They don't have a warrant or probable cause, not for a hungry dog, though an Amber Alert provides some elasticity. "We could force our way in again," Angela says.

Aldrich checks under the door mat first, and then runs his hand over the door trim. He holds up a shiny new key. "Voila."

Angela takes it from him. "I wish my detectives had thought of that yesterday. And I'll take the blame for entering without a warrant." She turns the key.

Rowdy rushes into the hallway. He paws at Angela's knees. She lifts him up and holds him under her arm. "Mr. Jones," she shouts. "Are you home?"

When no one answers, Angela edges forward. Aldrich follows. After the last thirty-six hours, Angela almost expects to find Bennet Jones lying in a pool of his own blood, but as she makes her way down the hallway and into the kitchen, all she finds is an empty apartment. She toes open each of the bedrooms, and the bathroom, but those are empty too. "No one's here," she says, putting Rowdy down.

Aldrich retrieves the dog's water bowl from the kitchen floor and fills it from the tap. Rowdy laps up the entire bowl, as if he hasn't had anything to drink for hours. There was nothing out of the ordinary here, but, to Angela, it doesn't feel right. "I wish he was answering his phone."

"Maybe he's at the movies?" Aldrich says.

If Angela wasn't working on a double homicide and a missing child, she might think that too. "Did you come into the apartment yesterday?" she asks.

Aldrich shakes his head. "I was out in the hallway."

Angela pulls up the photos from the scene yesterday and scans through them. "Give me your number," she says, and forwards the photos to the Cambridge officer. "What do you notice?"

Aldrich walks through the apartment, comparing the photos

Zane had taken yesterday to what he sees today. Angela follows him, doing the same thing.

"Here," he says, a moment later in the bedroom. "What's missing?"

Angela looks at the photo and sees it. There had been a framed print on the wall yesterday, a blue and red abstract. "Good eye."

Out in the kitchen, she scoops Rowdy from the floor. "Outside or dinner?" she asks him.

Probably both.

She fills his bowl with food and waits for him to finish, while jotting a note for Bennet asking him to call when he gets home. She puts Rowdy on a leash and leads Aldrich outside, where he gets into his car. "What are you doing with the dog?" he asks, through the open window.

"I'll take him with me. Don't report me, okay?"

"I have you covered."

"Good job tonight," Angela says. "You'd make a great detective, and you have my number. Call me if you ever want to come work in Boston."

"Will do."

After Aldrich drives away, Angela walks the dog around the block and ponders her next step. When she gets in her car, she holds Rowdy on her lap and calls Zane. "Have you talked to the Chandler kid yet?"

"We're just getting to the house," Zane says.

"I'm at Bennet Jones's apartment." Angela gives him the rundown of the call. "Ask Cavanaugh if she's talked to him since this morning."

Angela hears a muffled conversation in the background, and when Zane comes on the phone, he says, "She's trying to call him now."

"So that's a no," Angela says. "Do you believe her?"

"I'd be fifty-fifty on that."

Angela would give her better odds. Natalie won't compromise Mavis's safety. "When you were here yesterday, what did you notice?"

"A guy who was pissed off that we kicked in his door."

"What else? What surprised you?"

Zane takes a moment to answer. "He had good taste. Expensive taste for such a small apartment. How old do you think he is? Early thirties? If I had enough money to buy a Philip Guston, I'd be living in a fancier apartment."

"That's the painting? The one in the bedroom? You don't think it was a print or a reproduction?"

"I'm not an art appraiser, but it looked pretty genuine to me."

"Well, it's missing."

"Just a second."

Angela hears Zane get out of the car and shut the door. When he comes back on the phone, he says, "What do we know about Jake Abbott's money problems? Bennet Jones told Cavanaugh that Jake had stolen money from the soccer club, but the problem evaporated."

"Maybe he stole money from someone else. Or maybe he took out a mortgage without telling his wife. That house has to be worth some bank."

"Or he could have laundered money for someone."

Angela glances at the photo again. "And what's one of the best ways to launder money?"

"Artwork," Zane says. "Expensive artwork. I'll get Bennet's phone records. We can see where he's been today."

Angela clicks off the call. She has a bad feeling about two things. The first is her getting a good night's sleep or seeing her family again in the next few days. The second is about Bennet Jones. She should have paid more attention to that wallet. It was with Patrick Leary's body for a reason. Now she suspects Bennet Jones won't be coming home any sooner than Patrick Leary . . . or Jake Abbott.

CHAPTER 34

EVEN WITH HER HANDS BOUND BEHIND HER BACK, MAVIS FORCES herself into a sitting position. Her mouth is dry and pasty, and her stomach rumbles. She hasn't had anything to eat since that single bite of pizza at noon. She wonders what time it is, whether anyone has noticed that she's gone. She takes a moment to break down what needs to be done and comes up with three steps: cut through the bindings, get out of this room, and then out of the building.

All she needs to do right now is focus on Step One.

She squeezes her knees to her chest and slowly shimmies her bound wrists under her hips. For a moment, it feels as if her arms might get stuck, and for another moment the bones in her wrists feel close to snapping, but she dismisses any thought of panic. At last, her hands slip under her feet and in front of her. She yanks at the cord tied at her neck, but her fingers are numb, and she can't get the knot undone, and suddenly the air in the bag feels heavy, and her body deprived of oxygen. She wishes she hadn't seen Bennet's face, that he didn't know that she knew he'd kidnapped her; if watching every single episode of *CSI: Miami* has taught her anything, it's that she's in deep shit. Victims like her don't make it to the end of that show.

Don't freak out.

Back to the plan.

Cut through these bindings.

And keep moving, no matter what.

With her ankles and wrists bound, she rolls to a carpeted floor, wriggles till she reaches a wall, and moves along the perimeter of the room, bumping objects along the way. There's an old chair and a moldy cardboard box and something that feels like a stuffed bear. She comes to heavy drapes. She manages to wriggle into a standing position, push the cloth aside, and touch the cool windowpanes.

Glass.

That's what she needs.

She hops along the wall till her knee hits a piece of furniture. She feels the flat surface of a dresser, a lamp, a stack of books. Finally, she comes to what feels like a framed photo. She smashes it into the corner of the dresser. The glass shatters. And the sound is loud, louder than anything Mavis has ever heard in her life. She could be alone. But Bennet could be here, waiting. Bennet probably killed her father and Patrick, and if he killed them, he won't hesitate to kill her.

She hops to the bed and lies down, waiting for the sound of footfalls outside the door. She waits for what seems like hours. When no one comes, she slides off the bed, returns to the smashed frame, and finds the largest piece of glass among the shards. She thinks of Patrick, with his rat-gnawed face, and her father lying on the floor of the cottage. She thinks of her mother, covered in blood.

She angles the glass to slash at the plastic tie. She winces as she cuts herself and warm blood drips down her wrists. Tears sting her eyes, but they're more from sadness than from pain.

Be strong. Fight!

She can do this for her father.

She can do it for herself.

She angles the glass, and she slashes again.

CHAPTER 35

NATALIE LOOKS OUT THE CAR WINDOW AT A BUNGALOW ON A STREET of identical bungalows located just over the city line in Dedham. Kevin Chandler lives here.

"What's our strategy?" Zane asks from the driver's seat.

"I'm taking lead," Natalie says.

Zane starts to respond, but Natalie holds up a hand. "My niece, my sister, my brother-in-law."

"Your voice gives you away," Zane says. "You're emotionally involved."

Natalie gets out of the car and slams the door. She walks half a block away, her heart pounding. It was only yesterday that she was the senior detective and held the upper hand. When she returns, Zane stands beside the car. "I called in to dispatch," he says. "You take the lead. If you make one misstep, though, I'll pull you out, and it won't be good for your ego."

"Am I supposed to thank you?"

Natalie holds his stare as she lets herself in through the chain-link gate and up a cracked cement walkway. A moment later, a man in his late thirties or early forties answers. He has an apron tied around his waist with lettering that reads HOT MAMA and a spatula in hand. Smells of roasting spices spill out into the cold night air. Natalie's stomach growls. She's forgotten to eat again today. "Whatever you're cooking, I'll have some."

The man cocks his head and waits expectantly.

"Detective Cavanaugh," Natalie says, "this is Detective Perez. Can we have a few minutes?"

The man's friendly expression hardens. Unconsciously or not, he steps into the doorway, blocking their path.

"We need to talk to your son, Kevin," Zane says, which doesn't help the situation. Natalie sees the protective walls going up, right in front of her. Now the man is outside, the door closed behind him.

"Your son goes to West Roxbury Prep," Natalie says.

"So do about a thousand other kids," the man says.

Natalie shows him a photo of Mavis. "This girl went missing this afternoon. We're following up with students in her classes."

"I saw the Amber Alert," the man says. "I didn't know she was Kevin's friend."

"That's one of the things we'll want to ask about," Zane says, stepping into the man's space. "May we come inside?"

Natalie pulls Zane back a step. "We'll only take a few minutes. But it's important."

The man eyes both detectives. "I'm Jeff." He holds the door open. "You can tell we're in the middle of dinner."

The house is chaotic. To the left, a small dining room opens onto a kitchen, where Kevin sits beside a younger girl at the counter, working through homework. On the stove, something smokes. Jeff Chandler jogs over and turns the gas down. "You told me you'd keep an eye on this."

"I'm working on my homework," Kevin says.

"It's burning," the girl says with an exaggerated shrug.

"That's helpful," Natalie says.

Kevin glances up from his tablet, and she can see his mind working. It takes a moment for him to connect her to their conversation from earlier today.

"These detectives want to ask about your classmate," Jeff says. "The one who's missing."

"I'm Natalie. This is Zane. It's good to see you again, Kevin."

Jeff picks up on the "again" right away, while Kevin tries to disappear into his homework.

"What's your name?" Zane asks the girl.

"Emma. I'm in second grade."

"One of my favorite grades," Zane says.

"Why don't you go watch TV," Jeff says to his daughter. "I'll come join you in a minute."

Emma jumps from her stool and dashes into the other room.

"Is your wife around?" Natalie asks.

Jeff shakes his head, while Kevin answers. "She's dead."

Natalie takes off her coat, hands it to Zane, and slides onto the stool that Emma vacated. "Things have changed since we talked this morning. Mavis Abbott, you know her, right?"

"Whatever," Kevin says.

"Hey," Jeff says. "Respect, okay?"

"She's lame, okay?"

Jeff starts to say something else, but Natalie catches his eye. She can feel her temper rising. "Mavis Abbott is missing, so whatever you didn't tell me this morning, you're going to tell me now."

Smoke starts spewing from the pot on the stove again, and this time the fire alarm goes off. Jeff ignores it. "Why were you talking to my son?"

Zane steps around him, turns off the flame under the pot, and wrenches open a window. "You might be ordering takeout tonight."

"What's going on?" Jeff asks.

Natalie stands and faces him. "I'm a detective with the Boston Police Department. My niece is missing, and your son knows something he isn't telling us. I need him to tell me right now what that thing is."

Jeff stares Natalie down. She's dealt with frightened, harried parents for her entire career, and there are a thousand different paths this man might take, and she prays that he'll choose the right one. The smoke alarm stops. "Please," Natalie says. "I need his help."

"I didn't do anything," Kevin says.

"You dared Mavis to go into a building where a body was found," Natalie says.

"What is she talking about?" Jeff asks. Now Natalie sees fear in the man's eyes. If she's not careful, he'll shut this conversation down. "You didn't tell me you had something to do with that."

Kevin kicks at his stool.

Zane comes around and crouches in front of him. "I'm going to level with you. We don't think you had anything to do with the murder. But if something happens to Mavis and you didn't help when you could, it'll stay with you. Forever."

"Whatever it is, spill," Jeff says. "We're not playing games here."

Kevin stares at the kitchen counter. "Some guy paid me twenty bucks to dare her to go into that building."

Jeff puts his hands to his face. Natalie touches his arm. "That is exactly what we need," she says. "You are doing a great job. Both of you. Just a few more questions and we'll get going. Had you ever seen this man before?"

Kevin won't look at her.

"Answer her," Jeff says.

"Never seen him," Kevin mumbles.

"What were you doing talking to some man you don't know?"

"Please, Mr. Chandler," Natalie says. "We really need to get to the heart of what happened here. Kevin, what did this man look like?"

Kevin shrugs. "I don't know. Old?"

"Old like me and your dad? Or old like your grandparents?"

"Like you," Kevin says. "Or maybe not so old."

"Black? White? Hair color?"

"He was white. Dark hair. Like a million other people."

There are two prime suspects in this case. Glenn is one of them. The other is a white man with dark hair. Natalie finds a photo of Bennet on her phone. Kevin barely glances at the image before shaking his head.

"Look again," Kevin's father says.

This time, Kevin takes the phone in hand and scrutinizes the image. "He was wearing a hat when I talked to him," he says. "And sunglasses."

"But is it him?" Zane asks. "Yes or no."

"It could be."

Zane catches Natalie's eye. "I'm calling this in. We'll put out a BOLO."

He dashes to the car.

"You were awesome," Natalie says, even though she could strangle this kid. If he'd said something this morning, maybe she wouldn't be standing here right now. Maybe Mavis would be safe at home.

"If you are holding back on anything else," Jeff says, "you better tell us."

"I'm not, okay?" Kevin says. "Can I go to my room?"

Jeff stares him down and finally nods. Kevin leaps from the stool and dashes away, and Natalie hears a bedroom door slam shut.

"Their mother died two years ago," Jeff says, rubbing the bridge of his nose. "We're all trying our best."

"You are doing fine," Natalie says, handing him a card. "Call me if anything else comes up. And we may need him to come to the station for an ID. You'll come too."

"I'm sorry about your niece," Jeff says, walking with her to the door.

"I am too. Tell your kids you love them."

As Natalie gets to the car, Zane clicks off the phone and hands Natalie her coat. He scrolls through his e-mail. "We got the report from Bennet Jones's service provider. Here's where there's been activity."

He opens a graphic and enlarges a section of a map. Natalie looks at the map and recognizes the street names. "I know exactly where he is," she says.

The front door opens, and Jeff Chandler runs out. He still wears the HOT MAMA apron and hasn't bothered with a coat. He shivers in the cold. "There's more. Kevin just told me that the same guy showed up at school today. He offered Kevin a hundred bucks to ask your niece to meet him later, but Kevin said he wouldn't do it."

Natalie reaches for her phone, but Zane tosses her the keys. "I'll call this in," he says. "You, drive like the wind."

Lights from news trucks shine in the kitchen window, where Glenn stands, watching them watch her. A dark sedan noses through the throngs and into the driveway. Charlotte Todd gets out and strides toward the house, her heels sinking into the wet ground. She doesn't bother to knock as she comes in through the kitchen door, arms extended for an embrace. A cloud of citrusy perfume trails her.

Glenn steps away. "What are you doing here?"

Charlotte glances at the men in suits who fill the house. "You haven't talked to them, have you?"

Charlotte can't be trusted, not anymore. An affair seems so insignificant now, but it's something Glenn can get her head around. It's something where she can assign roles. She can be one hundred percent good, and Charlotte can be one hundred percent bad.

"My daughter is missing," Glenn says. "I'll tell them anything they need to know."

Brock London enters the kitchen. "One of the cops canvassing by the school has a lead," he says. "A neighbor heard screaming at about five this afternoon."

"But she texted me after five," Glenn says.

Brock nods. "We should assume that whoever has her phone has her code. Do you have her code?"

Glenn doesn't answer, but of course she does because she's a good mother, but she can hear the implication in the question. Charlotte steps forward. "I'm taking my client out. I need to speak with her in private."

"Don't go too far," Brock says.

Charlotte leads Glenn outside to her sedan. "Get in," she says.

"I don't want to go with you," Glenn says.

Charlotte slides into the driver's seat, tosses her bag into the back, and leans over and opens the passenger's-side door. When Glenn still won't get into the car, Charlotte speaks, her voice barely a whisper. "They're already hinting on the news that you did it. That puts pressure on the cops to close soon. That kind of pressure won't be good for you."

Images flash through Glenn's mind, of Susan Smith drowning her boys because a man didn't love her, of Chris Watts strangling his family because he wanted to escape his life. The world sees her that way now, coming at Mavis with a raspberry-coated knife.

"Think clearly," Charlotte says. "If there's anyone you can trust, it's me. Not that sister of yours. And certainly not that detective you tried to set me up with."

Glenn looks back toward the house, toward the men in suits invading every room. Against her better judgment, she gets into the car. Charlotte backs out through the throngs of reporters and speeds away. "Want to tell me why you're giving me the cold shoulder?"

"I know about Jake. I know he came to see you Monday night. His clothes reeked of your perfume. You were sleeping with him."

Charlotte glances at her. Lights from the console shine on her face.

"Who are you?" Glenn asks. "Where did you come from? Why are you even in my life?"

CHAPTER 36

Angela parks on the familiar street in Somerville. Rowdy has fallen asleep across her lap. She runs her fingers through his fur, and he opens a sleepy eye as she checks the time. It's almost seven, which means Cary and Isaiah have probably given up on her coming home. She calls them anyway. "This case is turning into something bigger than I expected," Angela says.

"Brenda has Isaiah for the night," Cary says.

Angela had managed to forget Isaiah's schedule, too. This would have been a date night for her and Cary. They might have gone to their local pub, or they might have curled in front of the TV and watched a movie. "There's a missing child," she says.

"I saw. It's all over the news."

"I'm worried about her. Too many bad things have happened already. I can't let something happen to her, too."

"That child needs you way more than I do," Cary says. "I have George, a bowl of popcorn, and nothing to worry about except you."

Angela closes her eyes. Her wife's voice is soothing, peaceful. It makes her want to curl up in their bed and fall asleep for a week. "If I were with you, I'd be snoring on the sofa."

"Sounds sexy," Cary says. "Now go save this kid, okay?"

Angela clicks off the call and sends Zane a text. *Update me on the Kevin Chandler call.*

She lifts Rowdy onto her shoulder and steps onto the sidewalk.

At the front door of the multi-family house, she rings the second bell from the top. A chorus of dog barks erupts, which Rowdy promptly joins. A basset hound, a greyhound, and a tiny white dog charge down the stairs, followed by slippered feet attached to a tiny woman with a black ponytail and glasses.

"I need that VCR," Angela says when the woman opens the door.

"At your service," Hester Thursby says.

"Only three dogs?" Angela adds Rowdy to the pack.

"Looks like four, now."

"Do you mind?" Angela asks, as the greyhound sniffs her hand. "It may just be for the night."

"The more the merrier."

Hester waves Angela up the stairs and into the second-floor apartment. Hester's husband, Morgan, is a veterinarian, and Angela is never quite sure what creatures, great or small, she might find when she visits this house. She has Morgan to thank for George, even though Angela doesn't like to admit how much she enjoys having the dog in her life.

"You want a beer?" Hester asks, opening the refrigerator.

"I'm on duty, but I wouldn't mind some coffee. I've been working for thirty-six hours straight."

"You look it," Hester says, taking a beer out for herself. She moves a six-foot-long iguana from one counter to another and puts some coffee on to brew. "Have a seat. I'll be over in a minute."

To Angela, this apartment feels like a second home. She, Cary, and Isaiah visit nearly every weekend, usually to watch a game or spend the evening with a small group of friends. Now she settles into the sofa only to have all four dogs form a pile on her lap. "Doesn't look like you're going anywhere," Hester calls from the kitchen.

"I don't mind," Angela says.

Hester brings her a cup of coffee and a peanut butter sandwich.

"Where are Kate and Morgan?" Angela asks.

"Kate has a gymnastics class. They'll be home in a bit. Morgan's picking up Thai if you want to stay for dinner."

Angela holds up the sandwich. "This may need to tide me over."

Hester sips her beer, then plucks Rowdy from the pile, holding him over her head and kissing his nose. "Is this about our call earlier today? The cul-de-sac love triangle?"

"That's the one."

"Juicy. Sad. Like most true crime. Did you find Tonya Sykes?"

"I did. Have you been able to find her sister, Lindsey?"

"Not yet. I had to do some real work this afternoon, but I can give it a try this evening if you need me to."

"I'm working a case that's messy," Angela says. "And there's a connection to the Elmhurst case, and I can't decide if there's an actual connection or if I'm seeing things because whoever decided to send me that crappy article has gotten into my head."

"Tell me about the case first, or watch the video?"

Angela sips her coffee. She also closes her eyes and jerks awake when she feels the mug slipping from her hand. Hester takes the coffee from her and puts it aside. Angela sits up as one of the dogs licks her hand. "I'll tell you about the case," she says, walking Hester through the high points, beginning with Patrick's body and ending with Jake Abbott, though she leaves Bennet Jones's name out of it, for now. As much as she trusts Hester, she can't risk having the media get hold of Bennet's name just yet.

"I heard about this on the radio," Hester says. "Glenn Abbott, née Cavanaugh, the baker. Her publisher canceled her book earlier today. And it sounds as if she'd be your prime suspect."

"You know all of this is off the record, right?"

Hester rolls her eyes. She doesn't need to be reminded of the power of a secret. She also seems to be mulling over something in her head.

"What?" Angela asks.

"You first since I'm not there yet," Hester says. "Keep going and tell me what else happened."

"One of my detectives is Glenn Abbott's sister."

"I remember. She's the one in the article you had me research."

"And here's the part you really can't tell anyone. The missing child, the one on the news, she's the same kid who found Patrick Leary's body yesterday, the one in the abandoned factory. And she's Glenn Abbott's daughter and Natalie Cavanaugh's niece. And I think she's really missing, as in someone kidnapped her. And it can't be a coincidence that the whole mess started with her going into that building, but I can't figure out the connection either."

Hester seems to consider the whole case for a moment. "Where's the tape?" she asks.

Angela's eyes begin to close again. "My bag."

"Don't get up." Hester slides off the sofa.

Angela settles in. It's warm here under these dogs. Comfortable. She rests her eyes, and it seems as though only a moment has passed before she feels Hester beside her. "How long have I been out?"

"Twenty minutes," Hester says. "I thought it would do you some good. And it gave me a chance to ponder. You can keep sleeping if you want."

Angela forces herself to sit up. She swallows a mouthful of cold coffee. "I need to get back to the Abbott house soon."

"You said that Glenn Abbott was having an affair with Patrick Leary," Hester says. "Who knew about it?"

"Not an affair, more like flirting. Or so Glenn claims. We have some texts she sent to him. They are flirty, but nothing more than that. She says he came on to her at a party on Saturday night."

"What else happened at the party? Have you talked to the other guests?"

"We asked the Abbotts for the guest list earlier, but they said no. My guess is that Glenn will give it up now." Angela sighs. "I'll add it to my follow up. The only person I know who was there is Zane Perez, one of my detectives. Have you met him?"

Hester shakes her head. "The name sounds familiar."

"He used to be in my squad when I was a sergeant. He got shot last year."

"I remember now," Hester says. "And in a sea of coincidences, shouldn't you look at all the coincidences? Why was he there?"

"He's friends with Natalie's sister."

"It wouldn't hurt to ask some follow-up questions there."

"Point taken," Angela says. "Let's look at the tape."

Hester slides the VHS tape into the VCR, flips on the TV, and hits PLAY on an ancient-looking remote. The tape runs for a moment with nothing but static and a time stamp for September 6, 1995. When the image appears, it's grainy, with muffled sound, but Angela recognizes the scene. There's a state detective sitting in a room filled with toys, and Lindsey Sykes, a tow-headed tomboy, is sprawled in front of him playing with a truck. The detective asks about the truck to start establishing a rapport. Lindsey seems happy, content. The detective hands her a car, and she smashes the car into the truck. The detective asks a few questions here and there for the first ten minutes of the tape, but mostly he watches Lindsey moving around the room.

"Where do you like to play?" the detective asks.

"In the yard, by the pool."

"Where else?"

"At school, I like the swings," Lindsey says. "And the monkey bars."

"Can you make it all the way across?"

"Yes," she says. "And back."

"Nice," the cop says. "I don't know if I could make it halfway. Do you ever play in the woods around your house? Maybe out by the hunter's blind?"

"Mommy says not to go there."

"But have you? You can tell me if you've been there."

Lindsey turns her attention back to the car.

"You've been there, right?"

"I don't know," Lindsey says.

"You don't know, or you don't want to tell me?"

"I can swing high enough to touch the clouds."

The detective watches her play for a few more minutes. "You're friends with Mr. Cavanaugh, right?" he says. "Tell me about him."

"Mr. Cavanaugh passed away." Lindsey's voice skips over the

words in a way that makes Angela question whether the girl understands their meaning.

"That's sad, right?" the detective says.

Lindsey shrugs again, but this time she jumps to her feet and runs across the room. She pulls out another car and zooms it over the floor.

"You don't like to talk about Mr. Cavanaugh?" the detective asks.

"I can do a cartwheel." Lindsey puts her hands over her head and cartwheels through the room, crashing into a pile of stuffed animals. She laughs as the plush toys fall around her. "You do one!"

"I'm even worse at cartwheels than I am at monkey bars. Did Mr. Cavanaugh do cartwheels with you?"

"He's Mommy's friend," Lindsey says. "Sometimes they play."

The cop takes the car from Lindsey. "Sometimes they play? In the woods?"

"I don't know."

"But if you saw them in the woods, you'd tell me."

"In the woods around the house. I've seen them."

"What do they play?"

Lindsey shrugs.

"Was it tag or hide and seek? Wrestling?"

"Wrestling!" Lindsey says.

"Tell me anything you remember. Like, what were they wearing? Were they wearing anything? Maybe they weren't wearing anything?"

Angela pauses the tape. "I don't like where this is going."

She wonders what the cops told Diane Sykes before this line of questioning began. She wonders if they convinced her that she was being a good citizen. She hits PLAY just as Lindsey giggles. The detective laughs too. "You have a funny story," he says. "I can tell."

Lindsey covers her mouth and shakes her head.

"Sometimes we see things that we think are really funny, but make us feel as though they should be secret, too. But then it feels good to tell. Like maybe you saw your mommy, and there was something about what you saw that made you feel nervous or afraid or uncomfortable."

Lindsey stands and runs around the room, her arms flying behind her. "They were naked!" she shouts. "Naked, naked, naked!"

"Who?" the detective asks, just as the door to the playroom opens. Diane Sykes walks in. For Angela, it's strange to see the woman alive. She's fit, with dark, shoulder-length hair, and wears jeans and a T-shirt. She looks like someone who doesn't put up with much. "We're done," she says.

The detective stands. Diane glances right toward the camera, her expression a mixture of rage and fear. "Stop taping. Now."

The detective walks toward the camera. The screen goes black. Angela sits with the silence for a moment. She feels as though she got a glimpse of something going very wrong, something she would never allow in her own interrogation rooms. "That tape never would have been admitted in court. But they used it to get a search warrant. And imagine if Lindsey is out there. Imagine if she knows what she did."

Hester rewinds the tape a few frames to where Lindsey sits on the floor with her truck. "You've been up too long," she says, nodding at the screen. "You're missing something really important."

Angela glances at the screen as Rowdy barks. The other dogs join in. All four of them leap from the sofa as the apartment door bursts open, and Hester's husband, Morgan, lets himself in, animal crate in hand. Even through bleary eyes, Angela can see the kittens piled on top of each other behind the wire caging. Kate runs into the apartment after him, seemingly six inches taller than the last time Angela saw her. She's in first grade now. She throws her bag by the door and shouts, "Kittens!"

Morgan opens the crate, and a flood of kittens spills to the floor, at least a half a dozen of them. Two head upstairs with one of the dogs in pursuit. Another pair leap into some curtains, tearing them down in a wave of fabric.

"Does George need a friend?" Morgan asks, running a hand through his red hair.

Angela extricates herself from the sofa. The twenty-minute catnap has done her good. So has her conversation with Hester. "Hit me up another time," she says, giving Kate a high five and fist-bumping with Morgan.

"You staying for dinner?" Morgan asks.

"She needs to get back to work," Hester says. "We'll see you this weekend?"

"Always," Angela says. "And I can't play any more guessing games. What am I missing?"

Hester points to the screen, where Lindsey sits cross-legged on the floor. "It should be easier for me to find Lindsey Sykes now."

"I still don't get it," Angela says.

"Lindsey Sykes isn't a girl. He's a boy."

Angela looks at the screen and groans. She'd been so convinced of what she saw that she'd transformed the child sitting in that room into a tomboy. "Lindsey Sykes would be thirty-three now. Maybe thirty-four." Something in Angela's tired brain clicks. "Jake Abbott told his wife that his parents died in a car crash. She never met them. Jake was the same age as Lindsey Sykes. Patrick Leary was, too." And Bennet Jones, though Angela holds that back for now.

"I'm on it," Hester says.

Out in the car, Angela checks her phone. Zane hasn't responded to her text. She calls him. The phone rings, but he doesn't answer. She calls Natalie next. Her phone goes right to voicemail.

CHAPTER 37

CHARLOTTE TODD DRIVES INTO DOWNTOWN WEST ROXBURY AND parks alongside a row of small restaurants. "What do you want?" she asks Glenn, waving toward the storefronts. "My treat."

"Is it?" Glenn asks. "Or will it show up on my next invoice?"

"I could use a burrito," Charlotte says, striding across the sidewalk to wait in the short line. When she returns a moment later, she hands Glenn a paper bag. "I got you the works. Chips. Churros. Everything. A wad of napkins too. You'll need them."

She opens her own bag, peels the foil off the top, and takes a bite. The smell of guacamole and spices and grilled meat is strong enough to overpower even the scent of Charlotte's perfume.

"You'll need to do a week of yoga to make up for eating that," Glenn says.

"Then I'll do a week of yoga." Charlotte takes another bite. "And it's not going to do you any good to turn on me. Not now. I know it was hard to confess to starting those rumors about Diane Sykes, but starting a rumor isn't the same thing as killing someone."

"The cops wouldn't have searched Diane Sykes's house if I hadn't spread those lies."

Charlotte takes another bite. "Were they lies? It sounds as though you did the cops a favor. They found a blood-stained piece of cloth in the Sykeses' fireplace that linked Diane Sykes to the crime. That could have been enough to convict her."

"I'm almost certain my mother killed my father. I've always believed that."

"The evidence says otherwise. And even if your mother did kill your father, no one's going to open a thirty-year-old case, not without a living suspect and a compelling reason."

Glenn looks out her window. Charlotte touches her arm, and she shrugs it away. "What were you doing with my husband on Monday night?"

"I was meeting with a client," Charlotte says. "Are you going to eat those chips?"

Glenn tosses the greasy bag at her. Charlotte catches it and crunches on a tortilla chip. "Jake hired me. He needed help. He knew this day would come and that you'd need someone to watch your back. There's nothing quite as powerful as a friend with an hourly rate. That's who I am. If you remember one thing from this conversation, remember that."

"I don't have any money," Glenn shouts, loud enough so that a couple passing by on the sidewalk turn to stare. "My book was canceled. The publisher is probably going after the advance, and my husband stole money from a kids' soccer team. Who the fuck steals money from a kids' soccer team?"

Charlotte takes another chip from the bag. "I'm a fixer. You wouldn't believe the messed-up things people do. But there's money waiting. Jake set it up offshore. He made sure that it would be impossible to trace."

At first, Glenn can't process what Charlotte says. "He knew this was going to happen," she says at last.

"He was planning to leave," Charlotte says. "That's why he came to see me. I had a passport for him. Money too. He was going to start a new life under a new name. He didn't say this outright, and I'll deny having ever said any of this, but I think he planned to kill Patrick Leary too."

"Because I flirted with the man?"

"Because Patrick Leary was dangerous. He had ties to organized crime. Jake had been laundering money for him, and it was one of those things that he couldn't stop saying yes to once he said yes for the first time."

Glenn feels a little part of her soul die. No matter what, she'd believed that she could trust Jake. Now it feels as if he's died for a second time.

"Jake called the whole thing off," Charlotte says.

Glenn turns to her. "Why?"

"Because he was a mostly good guy who made a bad choice," Charlotte says. "He didn't want to betray you. He didn't want to leave Mavis. He called me last night and told me he wanted to turn himself in to the feds. And he knew that if he left, you'd be stuck having to clean up a mess you didn't even know about."

"I'm still stuck with the mess."

"But now you know what caused it, or at least part of it, and we can start fixing things."

"What happened to the passport?" Glenn asks. "And the money?"

"I wish I knew," Charlotte says. "And they're the last things in the world we need the police to find right now."

With one last slash, the plastic tie on Mavis's wrists snaps apart. Mavis drops the shard of glass. The imaginary bow on one of her imaginary boxes bursts open, and claustrophobia spills out. She yanks at the hood over her head. It's tied too tight and won't come loose. She tears at the seams holding the cloth together, but then forces herself to move inward, to center. In the darkness, she rubs at her wrists till the feeling returns to her fingertips. Her skin is slick with blood. She feels around the base of the bag till she comes to a nylon cord tied tight enough that her fingers won't be able to work it apart, not quickly, at least.

She counts to ten. She finds the shard of glass she dropped, and with one slit, the cord rips in two. She yanks the hood off and gasps for air.

Focus.

Step one: Nearly complete. She's freed herself.

Step two: Get out of this room.

Step three: Get the fuck out of here.

She slashes apart the tie on her ankles and tests her legs. They're like liquid, but she feels her way around the room till she comes to a door. It's locked. Beside the door, she flips a switch, but the lights don't work. She closes her eyes and listens again. This time, she hears wind and leaves rustling. But she also hears the distant sound of traffic.

She can make her way to that traffic.

By now, her eyes have adjusted to the dark, if only a bit, as the room fills with the gray contours of furniture and the outline of a window. She pulls the drapes aside, only to see that the shutters have been closed and locked shut. She screams and bangs on the glass. She calls out her own name. Surely someone might hear. She listens again. This time, the silence is deafening. She pictures the chessboard, the algebra problem, the question she got wrong for Mr. Sullivan. She can work her way through those numbers, multiplying Y, working through the factorials. She can solve any problem that comes her way. Including this one.

Outside, a car approaches the house.

The sound yanks Mavis into the present. She considers what to do next, whether to scream again. One step at a time.

Listen.

What does she know? What doesn't she know? What can't she know?

The car stops outside the house. She listens for sirens or a radio, any hint that the police are here. Instead, the driver engages the hand brake. She remembers the drive last night from her house to Aunt Natalie's, the way Rowdy had snuggled against her as if the dog knew she needed the comfort of another being. She remembers the way Aunt Natalie had kissed Uncle Bennet. Bennet is the only person she knows with a manual transmission.

He's back.

He's here for her. That's something she can't solve for. It's something she can't know. What she does know is that Bennet is strong and fast. He's already proven that at the school. He'll be desperate, too. But what Mavis has is the element of surprise. She moves as quietly as she can. She searches for a weapon.

Downstairs, a door opens.

She palms a pen. She gets in bed. She pulls the hood back on and lies on her side, facing the wall, her hands behind her back.

Footsteps approach. A chain clanks. The door creaks open.

"Mavis?"

She recognizes Bennet's voice.

Stay still, she tells herself.

"I'm so sorry," Bennet says. "This got out of hand. You saw me. You and your friend saw me."

He creeps into the room, crouches, and shakes her shoulder. She moves as though waking from a drugged sleep and rolls toward him.

He touches her again.

She sits up. And she thrusts the pen forward. He swears. She rips the bag off her head. A flashlight rolls on the floor. Bennet's face is contorted in pain. He holds a kitchen knife in one hand. Mavis drives the pen into his right bicep and twists. "Fuck," he says, as the knife clatters to the carpet.

She leaps up. He hooks a hand around her ankle. She skids across the floor. But this time she's prepared. She kicks. Cartilage crunches beneath her sneaker. She kicks again, right where the pen juts from his arm. She scrambles away. And she's on her feet.

Step two: Get out of this room.

And she runs.

CHAPTER 38

Natalie barely hears what Zane says into the phone. She drives, siren blaring, through the streets of Elmhurst. As she swerves into Starling Circle, she turns off the siren and the lights. At the house, she glides down the driveway. No need to alert anyone that they're here. Bennet's Civic is parked by the garage, like she knew it would be.

This house. The neighborhood. The hunting blind. They've been calling her this whole time.

She leaps from the car.

"Wait!"

Zane grabs her from behind.

"You aren't armed," he says.

Natalie reaches for the doorknob. He steps in her way.

"That's Bennet Jones's car," Natalie whispers. "God knows what he's doing. Right now. God knows what he wanted with her."

She pictures every crime she's ever worked, every broken child. She thinks of Tonya and Lindsey, of the disappeared.

"We've got this," Zane says. "But you need to let me take the lead. You'll get all of us killed, your niece included, if you don't."

He's right. And on a normal day, Natalie would trust Zane Perez with her life. Today isn't a normal day, but she needs to treat it like one. Zane hands her the flashlight. It's heavy and feels good in her hand. She could use it to crush Bennet's skull. "Give me your gun," she says.

Zane pats his holster. "You're off duty, but if something happens to me, don't think twice about using this."

The door swings open. Natalie listens. The house is quiet. Zane tries a light switch. "No power," he whispers.

Natalie aims the flashlight into the living room. There's the sofa, and her father's chair. She wonders if the bourbon stain is still on the carpet. They move into the kitchen, where she remembers unloading those groceries and the stench of citrus from Glenn's stolen lip gloss. They sweep the first floor before moving to the stairs. "Bedroom in front," Natalie whispers. "Two more in the back."

She follows Zane. On the second floor, she aims the flashlight toward her parents' room first. When they turn, she gasps. A chain hangs from the wall by an open door, her old bedroom. She rushes to the room, sweeping the flashlight across the darkened space. Nothing here has changed, not in years. A Backstreet Boys poster still hangs over her dresser. She crouches, touching something dark and viscous. "Blood."

On the bed, Zane finds a cloth sack and zip ties that have been slashed to ribbons. "What happened here?"

Off in the distance, Natalie hears a scream. "Where the hell are the local cops?" she asks, taking off without waiting for an answer.

She slams into a wall and nearly falls down the front stairs as she dashes through the house and out the back door. Bennet's car is still parked in the driveway. She hugs the foundation and turns the corner of the house.

"Bennet," she shouts. "Come out. Show your hands. There are cops from every fucking agency in the state on their way here."

A twig snaps. She swings the flashlight like a club, only to find Zane behind her, weapon drawn.

"I'm glad you don't have a gun," he says.

"Don't shoot my niece."

"Don't run off on your own again."

"Where's the cavalry?" she asks.

"Five minutes out."

Sirens should be screaming from every direction, but it's even quieter than when they arrived. Natalie feels for her phone. It's gone.

A shriek rings through the night.

Natalie sprints toward the trees. She knows these woods. Bennet Jones doesn't stand a chance.

CHAPTER 39

DEEP IN THE WOODS, MAVIS PRESSES HER BACK TO A TREE TRUNK and tries to become part of the darkness. Fifty yards away, a light flashes. "Mavis," Bennet whispers.

She closes her eyes.

"Come out," Bennet says. "I'm not going to hurt you."

Her breathing is heavy from running. Too heavy. She listens for traffic, anything that will lead her to safety.

After she'd stabbed Bennet, she'd sprinted down the stairs and out the back door, where she recognized her grandmother's house. She ran across the yard to a neighbor and pounded on the door and punched at the bell. No lights came on. No dogs barked. No one came to let her in.

"Mavis!"

She spun around to see Bennet coming toward her, blood pouring from his broken nose where she'd kicked him.

"You have to trust me," he said, stopping a few yards from her. He still held the knife. "We need to leave."

She turned and ran, taking off into the trees.

Now Bennet whispers her name again. He lifts the light and scans the forest.

"Please, Mavis. We're in trouble."

The beam moves closer, lingering a few feet away. When it lands on Mavis, they both freeze.

"Everything's just spun out of control," Bennet says, his voice shaking.

Mavis lifts a hand to shield her eyes. She remembers Bennet coming to the house and laughing with her father. She remembers the way he'd taken the glass of eggnog from her and whispered, "I'll never tell."

"Break it down into steps," she says. "It's not that complicated. The first step is to leave."

In the distance, a single police siren blasts toward them before going silent.

"Now's your chance," Mavis says.

The light drops. Heavy footsteps pound toward her. Mavis turns and sprints, her feet crashing across the forest floor. Her head slams into a tree limb. The earth disappears from beneath her. She sprawls, arms flailing, and splashes in cold water. Bennet gasps and plunges into the water beside her. She clutches a stone from the riverbed and swings wildly. It cracks against flesh and bone. And she's on her feet again, scrambling up the other side of the riverbank and bursting through trees.

The full moon lights up a clearing. All around her, the forest is quiet, the night still. Find a place to hide. Ignore the cold. Wait for the world to find her.

But a twig snaps, and a hand covers her mouth. Steel flashes in the moonlight as a blade presses to her neck, and Bennet shoves her against a tree. "I can't go to prison," he says, his lips pressed to her ear.

Mavis's eyes fill with tears. None of this is fair. She finds that box from the back of her closet, the one with her future in it, and peeks inside. She wants to finish the soccer season, no matter what her dad did. She wants to see if Mr. Sullivan graded question four on that algebra test. She wants to graduate from the seventh grade. And she wants to be friends with Stella.

Forever.

There's way too much in there to look forward to.

But she's in these woods, and her clothes are soaking wet, and she doesn't know what she can do, how she can break this down into small enough steps to make Bennet Jones go away. His body is crushing her. She can't breathe. Not anymore. And his arm is across her windpipe. And he's really, really strong. And he's saying that he's sorry, so sorry, and she doesn't fucking want to hear it, not anymore.

She tears into his flesh with her teeth. And she doesn't let go. Not until he screams.

CHAPTER 40

EVERY LIGHT IN THE ABBOTTS' HOUSE IS ON AS ANGELA WAVES A badge at a state deputy and heads inside. Glenn Abbott sits with her attorney in the kitchen. She looks up when the door opens, and Angela recognizes the woman's expression. It's the same expression she's seen over the years from any parent missing a child. Hope. And that hope will be fleeting.

"Has Bennet Jones been in touch with you?" Angela asks.

"Why?" Glenn asks.

"He was friends with Jake, right?"

"I suppose. I'm not sure what's true anymore."

Angela meets Glenn's eyes. She wants to offer her the support she'll need. She wants to tell her that the days ahead will be tough, to steel herself, but Glenn already understands that.

"Do you have an update?" Charlotte Todd asks.

"I'll let you know as soon as I know anything," Angela says.

In the next room, she follows the sound of voices. She finds the state detective, Brock London, talking on the phone in the library. When she knocks, he glances up and waves her in.

"Any news?" Angela asks, when he finishes the call.

He doesn't answer at first, and she wonders if he plays turf wars.

"Where've you been?" he asks.

"Following up on a lead, like I told you. And it seemed as though you had things under control."

"You're investigating a murder, right?" he says. "You think it's connected to this?"

"I'd be a fool if I didn't."

"Who do you usually look at first in a homicide?" Brock asks. "With missing children, I probably look at the same people. Usually the father first, though not in this case."

"And you work your way out from there."

"Mothers, uncles." Brock raises an eyebrow. "Aunts. What do you know about Natalie Cavanaugh?"

"We've been on the force together for a while. And she works for me."

"Where is she now?"

Angela had tried to call Natalie again from the car. She still hadn't answered. Natalie hid that her niece had found Patrick Leary's body. She'd dated Bennet Jones. But Angela holds onto those cards for now. "She was following a lead. She's with another detective."

"Zane Perez."

Angela closes the door to the library and waves toward a chair. She'll be damned if she'll let this pretty boy interrogate her or question her detectives' motives. She waits till he takes a seat before joining him. Then she waits for him to fill the silence.

He says, "We got cell activity for Mavis Abbott's phone. The activity was over in Jamaica Plain."

"That makes sense," Angela says. "Mavis stayed at Natalie's house last night. Natalie lives in JP."

"Does it make sense that Mavis would send texts to her mother from Jamaica Plain at 5:30 this afternoon? That would be a half hour after a neighbor reported hearing a girl screaming by the tennis courts at West Roxbury Prep."

"Maybe she took the bus there. Maybe she's been hanging out at Starbucks this whole time. She's twelve. Twelve-year-olds do dumb things."

"Or consider this," Brock says. "She could have been at her aunt's house, while her aunt claims she didn't know where she was. She could be dead. And her mother could know about it already. Or her mother could have done it herself."

"You have a team over there?"

"On their way. They should be breaking the door down momentarily."

Angela nods. That's what she would do, too. That's what *any* detective would do. "Here's the thing," she says. "Natalie Cavanaugh's not an idiot. She knows what the steps would be in a missing child investigation, so if she were to send fake texts from a dead girl's phone, she'd do it from somewhere that wouldn't lead directly to her own house."

Brock crosses one leg over the other. The detective starts to speak, but Angela holds up a hand to stop him. An idea is starting to form, but she can't quite see its shape, not yet. "Don't move," she says.

Out in the car, she flips through the file Tom O'Neil gave her at the station in Elmhurst. She stops at the photo of Alan Cavanaugh's face, the flesh gnawed by animals, just like Patrick Leary in the factory yesterday. Then she moves on to the evidence recovered from Diane Sykes's house, the evidence that led to an arrest warrant. Back inside, she says, "Detective London, you and I, we don't know each other, but I am going to make a wild prediction about what you'll find in Natalie Cavanaugh's house, and I want you to tell me how much of it I get right. Do we have a deal?"

Brock offers a curt nod.

"Here goes," Angela says. "You'll search the house and find Mavis Abbott's phone and a valuable painting. I can't remember the artist's name, but my detective will remember. You may find other items typically associated with money laundering."

"Like cash."

"Good guess. Now you're getting into it too. But here's the big one. You'll also find trace evidence of Jake Abbott's blood, and my best guess is it will be on a partially burned piece of cloth in Natalie's fireplace."

"Pretty specific," Brock says.

Angela shows him the evidence sheet from the file. "If I'm right, it will be very similar to what was recovered in this case."

Brock sits back. He's smiling, and it tells Angela that she may have crossed a line, one that's made him respect her.

"Tell me where you went tonight," he says, "and I'd start at the beginning."

"I'll start with yesterday."

Angela tells Brock everything, and the more she speaks, the more she believes she has it mostly right. Now if she could only figure out what's still missing.

CHAPTER 41

NATALIE CRASHES THROUGH TREES, HANDS FLAILING, SWEEPING branches out of her way. She comes to the brook, swollen with rain, and leaps over it. She slows her pace and listens till another scream echoes through the night. She runs toward it and bursts into the clearing. Across the grass, trees rise around the hunters' blind. She remembers fleeing here with Glenn to escape their father and believing this was their own, secret place. Now, even in this November cold, she smells her father rotting in the August heat.

As she moves to the center of the meadow, a shadowy figure emerges from the tree line. Natalie extends her hands to her sides and says, "I'm all by myself."

Bennet steps forward, shoving Mavis in front of him. He covers her mouth with one hand and holds a kitchen knife to her throat with the other. His face is pale in the moonlight, and dried blood has caked around what looks like a broken nose. "Stay where you are," he says.

"You okay?" Natalie asks Mavis.

Mavis nods, her eyes shining.

Natalie turns her attention to Bennet. She recognizes the man she sees, one who is haunted by his own choices, one who'd give anything to go back in time and undo what's been done. "We can all leave here tonight," she says.

"Shut up," he says.

Natalie inches closer. "I don't have a gun. I don't have any weapons at all. I don't want anyone hurt, like I know you didn't mean to hurt anyone."

"I didn't," Bennet says. "I didn't want to hurt anyone."

"Tell me what happened."

"This, all of it, it just got out of hand."

"It got out of hand," Natalie says, her voice soft as she mirrors Bennet's words. "And you don't mean any of it to happen, but it does. And the only way to make it stop is to say *enough.* Isn't this enough? Haven't we gone far enough?"

"It was supposed to be easy. I was supposed to get some cash, and that's it. The rest of this. The wallet . . ."

Natalie takes a step closer. "What about the wallet?"

"I wasn't in that factory."

"Mistakes happen. We'll talk to the DA and make sure everyone understands."

Bennet's head jerks up, and his eyes focus. "I'm not going to jail. And you, don't come any closer."

Natalie holds her hands out, open, welcoming. "Would you let Mavis say something? Let her tell me she's okay."

Bennet adjusts the knife, and Mavis winces. It takes everything Natalie has not to hurl herself at him, but they're ten yards apart now. Still too far. "Why don't you put the knife down?" she says.

"Not a chance."

"You'll hurt her, and you won't mean to. At the very least, take the blade from her throat. You said it yourself. It's easy to make a mistake, one you'll regret."

Bennet looks at the knife blade as if seeing it for the first time. He lets it fall to his side.

"Thank you," Natalie says. "Now can you let her speak?"

He lifts his hand from over Mavis's mouth.

"You okay?" Natalie asks.

"I gave it my best," Mavis says.

Bennet's nose is broken, and one of the lenses on his glasses is cracked. Mavis did more than give her best.

"We all want the same thing tonight," Natalie says. "We want to go home."

Bennet laughs softly. "I don't think I'll be going home anytime soon."

Natalie steps closer. "Don't you want to leave the woods, leave the cold? This can't be it. This can't be the end."

Bennet makes a sound like a wounded animal. He's sobbing. Natalie prays that Zane doesn't choose this moment to show up. If he does, she has no doubt they'll all wind up dead. "You can leave on your own," she says. "Mavis and I, we'll stay here. I don't even have a phone with me. And if I'd come with anyone, you'd hear the sirens. You'd see the lights. The cops would be descending on these woods. It's just me, and you still have time."

Another step. Five yards.

Bennet points the knife toward her. "I told you not to move."

"Why did you do this?"

"Jake took the money. I was trying to help him out of a jam. All I did was introduce him to Patrick. That was supposed to be the end of it for me."

"That's what friends do. Right? They help each other out. And we all have secrets. I have mine, the things I carry. The things that I thought I'd buried, but they never go away, do they?" Natalie can almost touch Bennet now. "Here's one of my secrets. Dating you frightened me. I thought I might fall in love. It's something I've never let myself feel, in a lifetime of wanting it. That's why I left that morning and didn't return your calls." Natalie reaches toward him. "And I was so glad when I found you in my living room last night. But you didn't come for me. That's one of your secrets. What were you doing there?"

"Jake was going to the feds. We'd have all gone down. So I shot him. I shot him in cold blood. I came to your place for an alibi."

"But why bring Olivia into it?" Natalie asks. "Why dredge up my past?"

Bennet's eyes narrow. Natalie searches his face, trying to find the truth.

"Olivia?" he asks.

She reaches toward him. His grip on the knife softens, and for a moment, Natalie believes he might surrender. "I'm sorry," he says. "I'm not that brave."

Steel flashes in the moonlight as he raises the knife to strike. Mavis squirms away, and Natalie launches forward, tackling Bennet. She pounds his fist into the ground till the knife falls away. His knee cracks into her jaw, and her mouth fills with blood. She spits out a tooth. Beside her, Mavis claws at Bennet's face. He catches her by the hair and flings her away. And somehow, Natalie gets to her feet, Mavis at her side, and they're sprinting toward the trees. She hears water gurgling. She swears she sees light through the forest. Bennet leaps on her from behind, and they both crash into the brook.

"Run!" Natalie shouts.

Mavis disappears in the shadows.

Natalie tries to scramble to her feet as her hands slide on the smooth, wet rocks. An excruciating pain shoots from her ankle. She pivots onto her hip, kicking Bennet's knee with her good foot. He falls over her, his hands on her throat. She grabs at his broken nose, but he squeezes tighter, and her vision blurs, and she can feel herself losing strength, and the only thing she hopes is that Mavis keeps running without looking back and that her niece doesn't ever once blame herself for anything that happened tonight.

Then, suddenly, she gasps, and her lungs fill with oxygen.

Bennet topples to the side. Mavis looms over them, a tree limb clutched in both fists. "This one's for my dad," she says.

She swings again, and the limb smashes Bennet's nose. He cries out but manages to wrench the limb away. Natalie scrambles backward, but Bennet catches her and pins her with his knees. He rears back. He raises the tree limb over his head. Then he looks beyond her, his eyes filling with terror.

Natalie feels the warmth on her face first. It splatters over her skin, into her eyes, and then spreads in a pool across her chest. The tree limb falls from Bennet's fists. Blood gurgles from his mouth. He slumps forward and lands on her with a groan, and for a moment she thinks she might suffocate beneath the weight of his body. It's only when she's freed herself and water flows over her hands and knees that she begins to correlate the sounds around her, to put them in order, to trace them to their origins. The sound of the water, of course. That comes from the brook. And the screaming. That's from Mavis, who stands on the riverbank, her hands covering her face. Natalie wants to go to her, to tell her everything is okay, but she forces herself to focus, to keep parsing through the sounds till she arrives at the gunshot. It came from behind her. She turns. Zane stands by an oak tree, his weapon still drawn.

Finally, she gets to Bennet, to being trapped beneath him in his last seconds of life. He put his lips to her ear. "You're not alone," he whispered.

Thank God for that.

The world starts again. Natalie crawls through the water and up the riverbank to Mavis's side. "It's okay," she says softly. "Everything is okay."

Mavis peeks through her fingers. "I thought you were dead."

"Can't get rid of me that easily."

Zane holsters his gun and joins them. "You're a mess."

"Where the fuck have you been?" Natalie asks.

CHAPTER 42

Angela's phone rings. She tells Brock she'll be back in a moment and steps into the hallway. "What do you have?" she asks Hester Thursby.

"I corroborated Jake Abbott's story, to start. Looks like what he told his wife was true. His parents died eleven years ago in a car crash."

"Scratch that theory."

"I also traced Lindsey Sykes," Hester says. "This is what I can tell you. He moved around as a kid. He was in a series of foster homes. He stayed with one family for a couple of years, then he may have been in a group home from fifteen to seventeen. After that, nothing."

"He would have aged out of the system," Angela says.

"Yeah, he turned eighteen in 2007, but he also seems to have left the system. As in any system. It's as if he disappeared off the face of the earth."

"He could have died?"

"Sure, maybe," Hester says. "And it could have been an unidentified death. Maybe he was living off the grid. And maybe he's still living off the grid, but there's no record, at least none that I can find, so no way to prove it one way or the other."

Which brings Angela to Bennet Jones. She should have requested a background check on him yesterday, but she'd been too focused on the Abbotts as suspects. "Here's another name for you," she says, giving her Bennet's name, age, and current residence. "See if his background meshes with the Sykes kid. And tell me you started on Patrick Leary, too."

"That's part two of why I'm calling," Hester says. "What do you already know about him?"

"Long record. In and out of jail for most of his adult life."

"Here's the good part," Hester says. "Patrick Leary was also in the foster system. And he lived in the same group home as Lindsey Sykes."

"Lindsey and Patrick know each other," Angela says. "And that means Lindsey Sykes's childhood friend has been living in Glenn Abbott's cottage for the last month, which can't be accidental. Any chance you've dug up a photo of Lindsey?"

"Not yet," Hester says.

"But you'll try."

"We can always reach out to the home. It's still around."

"*We* aren't doing anything, understood?" Angela says. "Find what you can from the comforts of your own home, but no more. And let's hope this is wrapped up before I wind up having to rescue your ass. One more thing. How's Rowdy?"

"Learning to live as a pack animal but holding his own. The kittens somehow clawed their way under the sofa. They're all asleep in a pile."

"I wish I was with them."

Angela hangs up. Back in the library, she says, "Any word from the search of Natalie's house?"

"They just went in," Brock says. "And they already found the painting. It was hidden in the front closet along with a suitcase filled with money and a laptop. We haven't gotten into the laptop yet."

Angela lays out for Brock what she learned from Hester about Patrick Leary's connection to Lindsey.

He nods toward the kitchen, to where Glenn Abbott waits for news of her daughter. "Too much of this is still leading to Mrs. Abbott. Let's talk to her. We need to see what she knew."

In the kitchen, Glenn looks up from where she sits, her face pale.

"Don't say anything," Charlotte says, just as Angela's phone rings again. This time when she glances at the display, it only tells her that the call is coming from Elmhurst. She answers and can hear a siren screaming in the background.

"It's Tom O'Neil," a voice says.

Angela's already putting on her coat.

"Shots fired," Tom says. "By the old Cavanaugh house on Starling Circle. I'm two minutes out."

"On my way," Angela says.

As she gets to her car, Glenn joins her.

"You need to stay here," Angela says.

"Am I under arrest?"

"Not yet."

Glenn gets into the car. "Then I'm coming with you. And don't try to stop me."

Natalie leans on Zane, while Mavis clings to her side and they make their way toward the edge of the woods. In front of them, lights from houses blaze. It's as if every person on Starling Circle has found a way to drag themselves from bed and peer into the night. A chorus of sirens sounds in the distance. "Stay close," Natalie says to Mavis. "They'll have guns."

A local officer is the first to arrive. He swings to the side of the road and exits his cruiser, placing it between him and them. Zane raises his hands, badge out. Natalie does too.

"Boston Police," Zane says. "There's been a shooting."

"On the ground," the officer shouts. "Send the child out."

Another siren approaches, while Zane and Natalie fall to their knees. "Go to him," Natalie says.

Mavis takes a few tentative steps and then runs forward to where the officer yanks her behind the cruiser. A moment later, another cruiser arrives, followed by Tom O'Neil, driving an unmarked sedan. He confers with the officer and crosses the grass to Natalie. "Twice in a lifetime."

She allows him to help her up. "Let's agree not to see each other ever again," she says.

"You fired that gun?" Tom says to Zane, who nods.

"You know the drill," Tom says. "Officer-involved shooting."

Natalie squeezes Zane's hand as he turns over the firearm.

"The state cops'll take this when they get here," Tom says. "Anything you want to say before then?"

"The body is two hundred yards that way," Zane says. "On the banks of a brook."

Tom raises an eyebrow. "Justified shooting, no doubt."

An ambulance joins the line of vehicles. By now, neighbors have come out to stare. The deputies set up a cordon, while Natalie wonders how long it will be before the news trucks arrive, before they connect this incident to Jake and Patrick. To her father. To another lifetime.

"You look a lot worse than your niece," Tom says to her. "But my guess is that was your goal all along. Good job."

He holds out an arm. Natalie's adrenaline rush is abating, and she's beginning to feel how much of a beating she took. She leans on Tom as he helps her to the ambulance. "Anything you want to tell me?" he asks.

"Victim's name is Bennet Jones. He worked with my brother-in-law. They stole money, and it got out of hand. He confessed to shooting Jake Abbott. The rest will be for the team to figure out."

"Why'd he take your niece?"

"As much as I can tell, he panicked. He was at a party on Saturday. She saw him leaving my sister's office. My guess is he planted evidence, and he realized she could identify him. I wish I could ask him more."

"I wish I could ask him a lot of things," Tom says. "It's lucky you and your partner showed up."

One of the EMTs waits to examine Natalie. Tom helps her sit on the side of the ambulance. "Be sure to get your teeth taken care of," he says. "You always had a pretty smile." He leaves her as one of the deputies brings Mavis over. She joins Natalie while the EMT checks her vitals and bandages the cuts on her wrists. "Any pain?" he asks.

"Nothing," Mavis says.

"Did he hurt you at all?" Natalie asks.

"Not really," Mavis says.

The EMT glances over her head at Natalie. "They'll check her out at the hospital," he says.

As he speaks, the lieutenant's car turns into the circle, lights flashing. Before it comes to a stop, Glenn is out the door. She runs across the asphalt and stops in front of Mavis, just short of a hug. "I don't want to hurt you," she says, her voice barely a whisper.

"I'm fine, Mom," Mavis says.

"Did he . . ."

"No one did anything."

Natalie hopes Mavis knows what that means. And she hopes that it's true, because even if Bennet hadn't laid a finger on her, her niece will have plenty to recover from after tonight.

Glenn wraps her arms around Mavis and pulls her into a bear hug. "Ow!" Mavis shouts, and when Glenn releases her, she says, "I'm joking. Really. I'm not hurt. Nothing but a few cuts and bruises."

"Cavanaugh!"

Natalie glances up, only to see the lieutenant storming toward her, her face set in anger.

"Answer your damn phone," Angela says. "You nearly killed me tonight."

She holds Natalie by both shoulders for a moment, examining her from head to foot, and then hugs her. Unlike Mavis, every part of Natalie aches, from her broken teeth to her cracked jaw to her sprained ankle. Still, she doesn't want the lieutenant to let go.

"Don't tell anyone about this," Angela says.

"It would ruin our reputations," Natalie says.

"We should get them to the hospital," the EMT says.

"We'll meet you there," Angela says. "I'll find Perez. Make sure he's not making trouble for himself." She turns to leave. "Good job tonight," she says. "I know it doesn't seem that way right now, but this could have been so much worse."

* * *

The EMTs insist that Mavis ride a gurney. Her mother insists too. She also insists on riding in the ambulance, and Mavis gives up the fight as they hang saline for Aunt Natalie, who smiles at her through broken front teeth.

"Hold tight," the EMT says.

Aunt Natalie looks confused, as though she doesn't know who the saline is for. Her face is bruised, her ankle swollen, and she's covered with blood that may be her own or may be Bennet's. Mavis reaches across the ambulance and takes her hand. "I'm sorry about your teeth," she says.

The ambulance pulls away. Natalie closes her eyes. "I'd have gladly given up a lot more than a tooth for you tonight."

CHAPTER 43

As the ambulance drives into the bay, Glenn feels helpless. She watches as doctors and nurses descend on her daughter and her sister and rush them inside. After they all disappear behind swinging doors, Glenn stares at paperwork, unable to tackle the simplest of questions. Beyond a few cuts and bruises, Mavis looked mostly unharmed, physically at least. Natalie, though, looked as though she'd gone through a meat grinder. Glenn wishes she'd been there. She'd have blown the guy's head off herself.

"Coffee?"

She glances up to see Brock London standing over her. She nods and takes the paper cup. The warmth feels good, but when she takes a sip, it doesn't taste of anything. "Looks like I'm eternally grateful to you," she says.

"I didn't do much." Brock takes the seat beside her. "Hospitals give me the creeps, all these people, huddled here, not knowing what will happen, their fates in strangers' hands. I was in surgery last year. Got shot on the job. I remember being on the very edge of consciousness. This woman walked in, confident, talking about what would happen next. She had a purse. That's the only thing I can remember. This big shoulder bag that probably cost a month of my salary. That, and she was my surgeon, and I had to place every bit of trust I had in this complete stranger who'd open me up and take out a bullet that had lodged in my stomach and had somehow missed tearing me apart. It was one of the scariest nights of my life."

"Are you trying to make me feel better?"

"I'm trying to tell you that tonight will be over, and life will go on."

"Life will go on when the doctor gives me an update. When someone assures me that no one hurt her body. Her mind and her heart . . ."

"Kids are resilient," Brock says.

Glenn takes another sip of the coffee. She feels it land in her stomach. "Have they figured out what happened yet?"

"You tell me."

Brock waits. And Glenn realizes that he's waiting for her to fill in what she can. "It's not over, is it?" She puts the coffee aside. "There's a suitcase of money floating around somewhere. My husband was planning to leave, but someone killed him before he could. My guess is it was Bennet Jones. But confirming it, that's your job."

Brock leans forward. He suddenly seems much older. Exhausted, too. "But there's more. There has to be. What about Tonya Sykes? She's here, you know. In this hospital. She still hasn't regained consciousness. Why would someone attack her?"

"I don't know. And I hadn't given her much thought, not in years."

Now Brock turns on her. "Her mother killed your father. That doesn't sit on your conscience? It doesn't haunt you at night?"

Glenn glances at the strangers around her. Some of them turn to stare. She wonders if any of them recognize her, and if they do, if it's from before, when she'd earned it, or now, as her face hits the news.

Thankfully, a doctor appears, holding a chart. "We finished the exam," she says. "Nothing physical to worry about, though you'll need to get her into counseling right away. This has been a traumatic night."

In another lifetime, Glenn would have responded with a quip. Tonight, she simply nods.

"And we'll keep her overnight for observation, just in case," the doctor continues. "You can visit. Then try to get some rest."

"My sister?" Glenn asks.

"Someone else will have an update soon," the doctor says.

Glenn thanks her and watches her leave. "I should go," she says to Brock. "Thanks for the coffee. And for everything you did tonight. I'll be grateful forever, no matter what else happens."

"What do you think will happen?"

"That's up to you. You seem to have something to imply."

"We established a timeline," Brock says. "Bennet Jones kidnapped Mavis at about five o'clock. That's the same time your sister says she found Olivia Knowles at her house, and the same time she claims she pursued a suspect into the woods. Bennet Jones couldn't have been in two places at once. And if he didn't attack Olivia, who did? Where were you at five o'clock?"

Glenn had been outside, feeling the wind in her hair and appreciating what she believed might be her final moments as a free woman. She'd been thinking about Olivia's mother—Tonya's mother—and how she'd betrayed her. And she'd been completely alone with no one to establish her alibi.

Angela listens as the doctor talks to Natalie about her injuries, none of which are lasting, but many of which will take time to heal. After he leaves, Angela comes to the side of the bed. "Don't take the drugs they offer," she says. "That's the only advice I'll give you. And we'll start putting this mess together tomorrow and figure out what pieces we're still missing. Tonight, you need some rest. We both do."

She puts on her coat to leave, but Natalie holds her back. She winces when she speaks. "Bennet didn't know Olivia. I asked him why he attacked her. He didn't know who she was."

"He was probably lying."

Natalie shakes her head. "He wasn't. And look at the timeline. Bennet was at Mavis's school when I found Olivia. Someone else was there. Someone else attacked Olivia."

She's right, of course. And Angela will probably spend the night lying in bed and staring at the ceiling trying to work out what she's missed, but Natalie needs to focus on recovering. "Your job is done here." Angela clicks the light off by the door. "Go to sleep, Cavanaugh. That's an order."

Downstairs, in her car, she texts Cary. *We found her. All is good.*

You amaze me, Cary writes back. *Now get home.*

Angela starts the car. And her phone rings. "It's after midnight," she says to Hester Thursby. "You should be in bed, and that's where I'll be soon enough. Whatever you found can wait till morning. And by morning, I mean afternoon, because I think I'm about to sleep for the next twenty-four hours."

"Up to you," Hester says. "Call when you want to chat."

Angela clicks off. She puts the car in reverse, swears to herself, and hits redial. Hester answers before the phone even rings. "I knew you'd call back," she says.

"Get to the punchline."

"I went down a few different rabbit holes," Hester says.

"I don't need to hear about any of them."

"I researched the group home where Patrick and Lindsey lived. It's out in western Mass. A lot of kids have gone through there, and it got me thinking that maybe some of them have stayed in touch. Then I figured out that the group home had an affiliation with a summer camp that a lot of the kids attended or even worked at as counselors. I found a group on social media where people stay in touch and post photos and tag other campers. It was private, but the administrator let me join without much hassle. Patrick Leary was a camper there, and then a counselor, so there were lots of photos of him." Hester pauses. "And others."

"Punchline," Angela says.

"I'm getting there," Hester says. "I'm sending you a photo. This one is of Patrick and some counselors. Most of the counselors have been tagged, but a few have names with question marks. Like the person has disappeared or isn't on social media, so there's no profile to tag."

Angela sits up. Sleep suddenly seems very far away. "Someone wrote '*Lindsey?*'—the photo is of Lindsey Sykes."

"You got it," Hester says.

Angela's phone beeps. She opens the photo. And first her heart falls. Then she swears to herself and punches the steering wheel as she radios to dispatch. She runs toward the hospital and calls the cop on duty outside Olivia Knowles's room, but he doesn't answer. She calls Zane. He doesn't answer either.

CHAPTER 44

NATALIE'S EYES ARE CLOSED, BUT I CAN TELL SHE ISN'T ASLEEP.

Something's wrong.

She should have been arrested by now. She should be handcuffed to the bed. There's plenty of evidence connecting her to Jake, to Bennet, and to Mavis's kidnapping. "You awake?" I ask.

Her eyes open. "I ache too much to sleep."

"Hang in there," I say.

My phone beeps.

"Who's that?" she asks.

It's Lieutenant White. She knows what I've done.

"No one," I say. "I'll see you in the morning."

One flight up, a uni slouches outside my sister's room, his head nodding as he fights off sleep. "Take a break," I say to him.

He sits up. "You sure?"

"You look like you could use some coffee. And I can handle this for a few minutes."

CHAPTER 45

GLENN RUNS HER FINGERS THROUGH HER DAUGHTER'S HAIR; Mavis sleeps fitfully, fighting off real and imaginary demons in her dreams. Glenn wonders how long it will be before the memories of tonight fade, or if they ever will. No matter what's happened in these last few days, she and Mavis will have each other, they'll have Natalie. Nothing else really matters.

A nurse pops in to check on Mavis. "We can get you a bed," he says to Glenn.

"A bed would be nice," Glenn says, but once she lies down, her heart races as images flood her brain of Mavis fleeing through the woods, fighting for her life.

She gives up trying to sleep and leaves the room. It's late now, almost midnight, but staff still move through the corridors. At the nurses' station she says, "Can you tell me where Olivia Knowles is?"

"It's after visiting hours. Maybe you can see her in the morning."

Glenn leaves the station. Her arms and legs suddenly feel light, as if she's taken an Ambien. She feels as though she's lifting right out of herself and soaring through the hallways. She imagines floating right past Mavis's room and through the hospital till she finds Olivia's bedside. Tonya's bedside. She imagines begging for forgiveness.

Instead, a hand grips Glenn's arm. Brock London stands close, those steely eyes scanning the corridor. His other hand is tucked under his coat. "Where's your daughter?"

"You move like a dancer," Glenn says. "Quiet."

He doesn't smile.

"Brock London, that name can't be real."

"Take me to her. Now."

Something about his tone sobers Glenn up. She leads him down the corridor to Mavis's room. "What's going on?"

"Quiet," he whispers.

He opens the door and ushers her inside.

Natalie wishes she had her phone. She'd taken the lieutenant's advice and refused any pain meds, and now she lies in bed, wide awake, running her tongue over her broken teeth and aching from head to foot. She also keeps replaying the events of the last two days, reviewing evidence. She knows what she knows: Jake stole money and replaced it with new money; Bennet killed Jake. He confessed to that in the woods. She knows what she suspects and will need to back it up later with evidence: Jake told Bennet he was in trouble, and Bennet connected him with Patrick Leary, who used the soccer team to launder money. But who had killed Patrick Leary? Bennet hadn't laid claim to that crime. And if Bennet didn't kill Patrick, had Jake?

She rolls over, forgetting her injuries till enough pain shoots up her side to make her gasp for air. The pain also brings clarity. She sits up and fights through the pain as she stands, makes sure her gown is tied in the back, takes her badge from her coat, and heads into the corridor. A nurse sees her. "You should be in bed."

"I need to walk," Natalie says. "I'll do one loop around the floor and come back."

But as soon as she turns the corner, she leaves the unit. At another nurses' station, she flashes her badge. "I need Olivia Knowles's room number."

She can hear the lisp through her broken teeth. The nurse takes in her hospital gown and bruised face, but all Natalie can hear is Bennet's voice.

Olivia?

Natalie summons up every ounce of Detective Cavanaugh she can muster. "I need her room number," she says. "Now!"

Olivia Knowles hasn't been ready to wake. She hasn't wanted to face her truth, to be Tonya again. So she's lain in bed, eyes closed, as nurses and doctors have come in and out of the room, checking her vitals, and having discussions they think she can't hear. Now, lying here in the dark, she feels safe. She opens her eyes and listens to the beeping of the monitors beside her.

She remembers hearing a knock at the farmhouse door and seeing her brother standing on the front stoop. He'd changed, of course. His hair had darkened, his features had solidified, but even with those changes, she could still see the six-year-old who's haunted her memories.

"You came," she'd said to him.

Lindsey stepped inside the farmhouse and closed the door behind him. Olivia had thought of this moment for years. She'd imagined hugs and relief, but seeing him in her front hall, she hadn't known what to do. She hadn't expected the coldness in his eyes as she led him to the kitchen.

"I'll make some tea," she said, filling the kettle.

When she turned to face him, he stood at the wall where she'd hung the photos of Ruth. The photos of them both. Together.

"You look happy," he said. "Like you made a new life for yourself."

Olivia stepped toward him. "Ruth and I . . . it wasn't what I came looking for, but it's what I found."

"Why here? And why her, of all people? You had the whole world to choose from."

Olivia—Tonya—had returned to Elmhurst so that Lindsey could find her. And now he had.

The kettle whistled. She turned to the stove and switched the gas off.

"They're coming," Lindsey said. "They'll be here any moment. And I can't let them find out who I am."

Olivia froze, her back to him. She should have noticed the

gloves, the ones he hadn't taken off when he came inside. She should have sensed him as he came up behind her. She felt a blinding pain at the back of her head, and the world went dark.

Now the door to her hospital room opens, and the lights turn on. Natalie Cavanaugh comes into the room. She wears a hospital gown and looks as if she's been in a car wreck. "There should be a uniform out here," she says. "Where did he go?"

Olivia swallows. When she speaks, she'll revert to being Tonya Sykes again.

"Why did you have photos of my mother on your wall?"

Olivia suddenly wants nothing more than to tell this truth. She wants Natalie to know how much she loved Ruth, how much they loved each other, and to apologize for keeping that secret. But the door opens again. This time, Lindsey walks in. He holds her gaze and shakes his head almost imperceptibly, just as the loudspeaker crackles. "Code Purple. All staff and patients should shelter in place. We have a security breach."

Lindsey's phone rings. He silences it.

"What's going on?" Natalie asks. "Where did the uniform go?"

"I gave him a break," Lindsey says.

Natalie crosses the room and peeks into the hallway.

"Don't go with him," Olivia says, softly, too softly.

Lindsey takes Natalie's arm. Natalie shakes off his hand. "Zane," she says to Lindsey, "why are we on lockdown?"

"Come on." Lindsey draws his gun and leads her into the corridor. "The lieutenant needs us."

CHAPTER 46

Angela rides the elevator to the fourth floor and runs down the corridor toward Olivia Knowles's room. The officer who's supposed to be posted in the hallway is gone. A nurse approaches. "Who's been here?" Angela asks.

"Just the cop," the nurse says.

"The uniform guarding the door?"

The nurse blushes. "No," he says. "The other one. The detective. The cute one."

Angela focuses on keeping her voice steady. "When did you see him?"

"Maybe five minutes ago. I came by to check the patient, and he asked me to come back."

Angela eases the door open. The lights are on, and Olivia Knowles sits up in bed, her face blanched. "They were just here," she says. "Natalie. And my brother."

Angela turns to see the officer on duty jogging toward her.

"She okay?" he asks. "I got back as soon as I heard the alert."

"Where the hell did you go?" Angela asks.

"Perez told me to take a break."

Angela crosses the room to Olivia's bed. "Is this your brother?" she asks, flashing a photo of Zane.

Olivia nods.

"Make sure no one gets through this door," Angela says to the officer.

The elevator pings. Brock London steps off and comes toward her.

"He was here," Angela says. "He has Natalie Cavanaugh with him."

"Glenn and Mavis Abbott are safe in their room," Brock says. "SWAT's on the way and will be ready to get into position. And we're monitoring video footage. We'll find them."

Angela punches the wall. How the hell could she have missed this? She speaks into her radio. "We need a BOLO on Detective Zane Perez. Suspect should be considered armed and dangerous."

"Where are we going?" Natalie asks Zane as they step into the stairwell. He still holds his gun.

"The roof," he says, waiting for Natalie to take the lead.

She stops and grips the cold metal railing with both hands. "Why not down?"

Zane turns to her. "Because that's where they'll look first."

And then she remembers. His firearm. It was confiscated earlier, after the shooting.

As if reading her mind, he points the barrel at her. Natalie slowly releases her grip on the railing. "What do you want?"

"You don't even recognize me. Remember playing on the grass? Remember the monsters in the woods? Those were your monsters, weren't they? You created them for me. You helped me see them in my mind, even if they didn't exist."

Lindsey.

Bennet's warnings suddenly make sense, his text telling Natalie to watch her back, his whisper that she wasn't alone. Zane jabs Natalie in the ribs with the gun, and she stumbles up the stairs.

"You planted those memories for me to tell the cops," he says. "You made sure that I'd betray my mother."

"What memories?" Natalie asks.

"You remember. *They were naked. Naked, naked, naked.* What did you do? Did you tell me what you wanted me to believe till I believed it too? You were effective, I'll give you that. I can still see my mother clawing at your father's body out in the woods. I can see their bodies writhing. The state cops had a copy of the interrogation in the file. All I had to do was request it. I saw what they did, how they manipulated the interview. I saw what I did, too, how I helped them target my mother."

At the top of the stairs, he opens a fire door and shoves her into the cold night air. He forces her around an exhaust vent, where he'll be able to take cover on two sides. "Your sister started the rumors," Zane says. "And you planted the memories. You were a team."

Natalie remembers chasing Lindsey across the grass while her mother and Mrs. Sykes talked on the back porch. She remembers telling him there were monsters in the woods, but the rest he got wrong. She knows not to argue, though, not yet at least. "You killed Patrick Leary," she says. "And you tried to kill your own sister. You almost got Mavis killed too."

"Patrick was getting sloppy, trying to make a move on your sister. He was greedy too. He wanted more money, but this was never about money. I told him to cool it, but he didn't want to listen. So I shot him and covered his face with jam. Peanut butter too. I wondered if the rats would find him, like they did your father. And I got Bennet to bribe that snot-nosed kid into daring Mavis to go into the factory. Bennet wanted things to be easy."

"How did Bennet even get involved with this? He didn't know you."

"I got to know him after you ghosted him. I thought he might be a useful tool, and it turned out I was right. He told me about his boss one night after a few too many, the one who stole from a kids' soccer club. The rest of it fell into place."

"You convinced Bennet to introduce Patrick to Jake," Natalie says. "Bennet told Jake that Patrick was *his* friend, so that you could stay one step away from it all."

Zane regards Natalie with what might be contempt. Or amusement. Or respect. "He thought he'd sit on that painting and sell it in a few years, then keep the cash."

Natalie nods. "He didn't understand that once you break the rules, there's no going back."

"All I had to do was threaten him with the feds. After that, he did anything I asked. We didn't give him much choice, though, did we?"

"What do you mean, we?"

"I mean us. You and me. The moment we showed up at his apartment, he knew he was screwed. I took his wallet at the party and dropped it at the scene and told him that there was other evidence connecting him to the murder and that it was up to him whether the evidence saw the light of day or not. You should have heard him begging when you and the lieutenant went out into the hallway. He was terrified. I thought he might start sobbing right there."

"And that night, he killed Jake, like you told him to. Afterward, he snuck right into my house."

"You're getting almost all of this right," Zane says. "At the bar, I slipped a roofie into your drink when you were in the bathroom. You seemed ready enough to lie for Bennet, too, when you came to your sister's house that night. I bet he thought you would take him back, but I know you too well, Cavanaugh. You were staying close to him. You were using him, just like me. You wanted to be sure we had another suspect if we started narrowing in on your sister."

"You do know me," Natalie says. "And you should have known I'd do anything for Mavis. Why did you tell him to kidnap her? The timeline is what screwed you in the end. You can't be two places at one time."

Zane's expression falters. He adjusts the gun in his hand. "I should have killed Bennet earlier."

"Mavis wasn't part of the plan, was she? Bennet got spooked when things ran hot, when he remembered that Mavis had seen him leaving Glenn's office after he planted evidence. And I led you right to him."

Behind them, the door to the roof opens. The lieutenant's voice rings into the night. "Perez," she shouts. "Give yourself up. The SWAT team is moving into place."

Zane meets Natalie's eyes. "You and your sister would both be in jail right now if it weren't for the lieutenant. There was plenty of evidence pointing right at both of you, but she's been hovering on the edge of the truth since yesterday." Zane points the gun at Natalie. "You, your sister, your mother—you ruined my life. You killed my mother. All to protect yourselves and your little family. Your mother could have claimed self-defense, and everything would have been fine. But all three of you watched out for your family and let mine rot."

Angela shouts again. "Perez, there's nowhere to go."

Zane glances over his shoulder. "The lieutenant sent me a text when I was in Tonya's room and told me to surrender. But the game's up. I don't want to get through this. That's what makes me dangerous."

Natalie steps back.

"Don't try anything," Zane says.

She takes a deep breath. "You're right. I'm sure my mother killed my father, and I've believed it since the morning I found him lying facedown in the woods. And we all let the story about your mother take hold because it helped us, even while it hurt you. It was immoral what happened to you and your family. Your mother's name should've been cleared. But I'm not sorry for protecting my own family or watching out for my mother."

Natalie inches away. Across the roof, she sees a sharpshooter in position. Angela waits at the fire door, her gun drawn.

"Cavanaugh," Zane says, "neither of us are getting out of here tonight. We're both going to die on this roof. We both deserve to die."

Natalie takes another step. Zane levels the gun at her. She can stay here and wait for Zane to make his next move, or she can take a chance and believe in someone. "You said a moment ago that you know me. You *do* know me. And you know that I play by the book. Maybe you actually did see your mother with my father in the woods. Maybe those memories are real, and you've spent your life trying to convince yourself otherwise. Or maybe someone really did plant them. I don't know what happened. But I know it wasn't me."

For the first time, Zane's expression betrays a hint of doubt.

"I know you too," Natalie says. "Tonight, you could have let Mavis die, but you helped me find her instead. You also could have shot me in the woods and claimed friendly fire. Hell, you could have said I'd been working with Bennet all along. But you didn't."

A helicopter rises over the edge of the roof. A sniper perches in the open door.

"You told me you liked me earlier," Natalie says as hair whips into her eyes.

"I've told a lot of lies," Zane says.

"I've liked you since the day we met. I liked Lindsey, too, and I don't want him to make the same choice as his mother. I want him to live as much as I want to live myself."

Natalie turns slowly. Her legs shake as she takes one step and then another. Behind her, footsteps patter across the roof as the SWAT team fans out. She prays that she doesn't hear a gunshot. If she does, it will be from a bullet meant for someone else. In front of her, Angela closes in, gun drawn, waving Natalie toward safety.

FEBRUARY

IT'S SNOWING. GLENN LISTENS TO THE SILENCE AS SHE WALKS THE few blocks to Centre Street. She hovers outside the pub and enjoys the feeling of snowflakes pelting her face. She likes these moments by herself when no one is watching. Once inside the warm restaurant, she tugs the hat from her head and scans the room. Almost no one recognizes her anymore. Her face has disappeared from the headlines, and the brass has faded from her hair. The blog is back up, though she doesn't post as much as she used to, and while the conversation about a revised publication date for the book continues, Glenn can tell already that the passion has gone out of the work. She's had enough notoriety for a lifetime. She's considering going back to school for social work now.

At the bar, Brock waves to her. She smiles and joins him as he kisses her on the cheek.

"Brock London," she says, "you're sure that's your name?"

He lays a passport on the bar, followed by a birth certificate and a Social Security card, and cracks a rare smile. After everything that happened with Jake, it'll be some time before Glenn learns to trust again. She's glad to have Brock to practice on in the meantime.

The feds have spent the last two months reviewing every decimal point in Glenn and Jake's combined financial world, and while there will always be some people who believe Glenn was in on the Great Soccer Scam, most of the parents on the team seem to have forgiven her, even Stella's mother. It helped that the laptop the police recovered at Natalie's house, the one Bennet had planted there for the police to find, had contained so much evidence, including information on the funds Jake had hidden offshore. Glenn turned all the money over. It had only been a fraction of what he stole, but the gesture had been well received.

What hasn't been forgiven is what Glenn did to Diane Sykes and her children when she chose to start those rumors. Glenn's confessed to what she'd done. She told the Boston Police, the state cops, the feds. She even told Olivia Knowles. "This—all of it, your mother's death, everything that Zane did—everything that happened was my fault," she said.

"Kids make mistakes," Olivia said. "Find a way to forgive yourself."

That might take a lifetime. For now, Glenn will have to learn to live with the choices she made.

Stella has the camera set up and hits PLAY on her phone. When the Taylor Swift song begins, Mavis stops dancing. "Something else," she says, her smile still bright. But inside, the song reminds her too much of her dad and their last day together. She's not ready to open that box, not yet.

"You choose," Stella says.

Mavis scrolls through songs. She's packed away most of what happened in November. Every now and then, she eases the bow off an imaginary box and examines the contents, but for now, she's happy to compartmentalize it. She chooses an old song her mother likes by NSYNC, and dances beside Stella while lip-syncing along. When they're done, they post the video to TikTok and lie on the floor reading comments till Mrs. Klein calls them to dinner.

Downstairs, they giggle over other videos, till Mrs. Klein makes them put the phone away. "Your mother's out again tonight?" she asks.

A bow pops off one of Mavis's boxes. Her mother doesn't want her to know that she's dating that state detective, the one with the dumb name and the blue eyes, the one who Mavis sometimes sees slinking out of the house late at night, but she knows more than her mother could ever guess.

Mavis could snap a photo of Brock in the driveway. She could leave it lying around for her mother to find. Or she could post it to the blog's discussion boards like she did with the photo of the *bûche de Noël* from the holiday party. She could even use the same message, *I'm watching you,* but, honestly, as much as she misses her father, the state detective seems harmless. She crams Brock London away and shoves the box into her closet for another time.

The next afternoon, Natalie drives onto Starling Circle. A few cars line the driveway at the house, despite the snow that blankets the whole neighborhood. She parks on the street by the FOR SALE sign, checks the time, and decides to give it another five minutes before heading inside. She walks down the driveway and looks over the fence at the neighbor's yard, softened by the mounds of snow. Even though the pool is covered for the winter, she can smell chlorine and hear the thwack of the diving board. The tension in her stomach is still there, catching her when she least expects it, but it's abated, a little bit at least.

Zane is in prison. He confessed to killing Patrick Leary, to getting Bennet to plant evidence at Natalie's apartment, to trying to ruin Glenn's and Natalie's reputations and lives in the way that his own mother's life had been ruined. He'd also coerced Bennet into killing Jake by threatening to turn Bennet in to the feds. The painting hanging in Bennet's apartment would have been enough to implicate him, but the feds had uncovered other financial transgressions, too, certainly enough to have sent him to prison.

Zane had requested that the state police reopen the case into Alan Cavanaugh's death. Despite a written affidavit from Glenn admitting that she'd started the rumors about Diane, so far the police hadn't moved forward. No one had been convicted for the murder, and both primary suspects are now deceased. Natalie doubts they'll ever open the case again.

She's visited Zane twice now in the county jail, where he's being held before sentencing. She hasn't been able to reconcile the man who worked beside her with the man wearing prison garb, the man who will be behind bars for the rest of his life. The first time she visited, they sat in silence on opposite sides of a gray laminate table, each waiting for the other to break. When visiting hours ended, Zane said, "Nice to see you," and left. The second time she visited, Zane filled the silence at last. "It didn't seem fair," he said, "that you should be happy, that you went on with your lives while ours were destroyed. I'm a detective. I've looked at the evidence. Your mother killed your father. Anyone should have known that."

Natalie's not sure if happy is how she'd describe herself. But she wouldn't say that, not when she could walk away, and Zane couldn't.

"Why did you attack Olivia?" she asked.

"You mean Tonya?"

"Tonya."

Zane shrugged. "When I went to see her, I didn't know what I planned to do. But I saw the photos on her wall. They were of her and your mother, the woman who'd caused all of this. And they looked happy. Your mother looked content. Something inside me snapped."

He stopped.

"I didn't know about Tonya and my mother either," Natalie said. "They lived a whole lifetime without us."

She wanted to ask him if he'd considered her a friend, ever, or if it had all been an act but couldn't find the words. He met her eyes, and it was as though they were working together again, as though he could read her mind. "Not at first," he said. "I got the lieutenant to assign us to the same unit. I told her I needed a mentor and that I wanted it to be you, and the lieutenant, she liked me, and she wanted you to succeed. Once we were working together, I'd forget who you were sometimes."

A bell went off. Visiting hours were over. Suddenly, Natalie had so many questions she wanted to ask. "What about your brother and sister, Joe and Irene? What about your parents?"

Zane stood as the guard came to lead him away. "I made them up," he said.

Inside the house, Tonya—Olivia—answers questions from potential buyers. The murder's been in the news again lately, and a woman asks, "Where did it happen? Which room?"

"That was a long time ago," Olivia says. "But it didn't happen in the house."

Natalie can't tell if the woman is disappointed or not.

After the last potential buyer leaves, Natalie says, "Any takers?"

"The market's hot," Olivia says. "We'll have offers by tonight."

Natalie takes a bottle of sauvignon blanc from her bag. "Let's have a presumptive toast."

On the back porch, she pours two glasses. The winter sun hovers over the horizon, and she lifts her glass and clinks it against Olivia's. "To our mothers. They used to drink together like this when they were friends."

She sips the white wine. It smells of citrus.

"Your mother didn't kill your father," Olivia says. "No matter what anyone claims. I knew her. We loved each other. She couldn't have hurt anyone."

Natalie leans against the railing. Olivia doesn't convince her, but it's nice to hear someone defend her mother anyway. It's nice to know that someone loved Ruth Cavanaugh that much. "What was she like?"

"She was your mother," Olivia says. "You knew her."

"I knew her as my mother. But what was she like with you?"

"Oh, funny and sweet. We used to play Scrabble. She usually won. And she liked to watch seventies conspiracy movies—*The Parallax View* and *Three Days of the Condor*, that type of movie. She was kind to my son, Jason. And she loved you and Glenn. She'd have done anything for you."

Olivia holds out her glass. Natalie tops her off.

"The final year was hard," Olivia continues. "Her condition got worse. We'd leave notes all over the house to help her remember things."

Natalie remembers those notes.

Turn off the stove.
Buy Earl Grey.
Schedule a neuropsych exam.

"You were the friend. I called you the fairy." Natalie pauses before asking her next question. "Did she know who you really were?"

Olivia considers her answer for a moment. "For a long time, I wasn't sure. I think she both knew and didn't know, but my guess is her subconscious had it all figured out. I don't think she thought facing the truth was worth the consequences."

That truth would have forced Natalie's mother to finally confront her own guilt. She would have had to have admitted that she'd murdered Natalie's father and let her lover's mother take the blame. No wonder Ruth had kept her secrets.

"Toward the end," Olivia says, "when her memory was really muddled, she sometimes thought I was my mother. That's when I knew she'd known, in some way at least, the whole time. She used to talk to me as if they were out here, on the porch, gossiping."

She laughs.

"What?" Natalie asks.

Olivia shakes her head and stifles another laugh. It's contagious enough that Natalie laughs too. "Tell me," she says.

"The last time I saw Ruth, she was pissed off at Glenn. Young Glenn, though. And she thought I was my mother." Olivia laughs again. "I tried to tell her that Glenn was sweet, and Ruth said that Glenn would cut someone off at the knees to get ahead in a three-legged race."

"She knew her daughter well," Natalie says.

Olivia closes her eyes and lifts her face to the sun. "Do you remember those lip balms, the ones that tasted like candy?"

Natalie remembers them well. She can smell the citrusy lip gloss as it melted in the sun.

"They came in bright tubes," Olivia continues. "Your mother was reliving some memory, some day long ago. She told me that Glenn had stolen a lip gloss from the A&P and tried to claim it fell into the basket." Olivia opens her eyes and turns to Natalie.

"Ruth said it was easier to let Glenn get away with stealing than to suffer your father's rage. I think she was always trying to keep your father from hurting the two of you."

Natalie takes another sip of her wine. She doesn't taste the notes of citrus, not anymore. She remembers every detail of that day as though it was yesterday. "I should go," she says.

Olivia looks at her for a moment in a way that makes Natalie wonder if she knows what Natalie now finally understands.

"I'll call tonight with the offers," Olivia says.

Outside in her car, Natalie sits for a moment with the engine running.

In police work, one of the most important tools is a timeline. It's been true with this case as well: Bennet couldn't be in two places at once, so there had to be two killers.

Natalie remembers finding her father's body in the woods and telling no one, not even Glenn. She remembers going to the A&P. She remembers her mother finding that stolen lip gloss and letting Glenn keep it. No one knew that Natalie had found the body that morning, that she let it sit in the woods and rot. No one else knew that Alan Cavanaugh was already dead when Natalie's mother let Glenn keep a stolen lip gloss.

There's no reason to protect a child from the rage of a dead man. Unless you don't know he's dead.

And if Ruth Cavanaugh didn't kill her husband, who else had a motive?

Natalie puts the car in gear, drives around the corner, and waits. As she watches, Olivia takes down the OPEN HOUSE sign and stows it in the back of her sedan. Then she changes out of her shoes, puts on boots, and heads into the woods.

Olivia steps through the trees, and it's as though she's being transported back in time, as though she's transforming into Tonya Sykes right there and then.

As a sixteen-year-old, one of the things Tonya hadn't let anyone know was how well she did in school or how much she cared about her grades. Tonya was a tough girl, one who greeted the world with a snarl. The only person who knew her secret was her mother, who'd perch on her bed and whisper, "I'm proud of you, I'm proud of you, I'm proud of you," in a singsong voice, till Tonya rolled toward the wall and covered her head with a pillow. Tonya would never admit, not once, how important it was to hear those words.

Her mother had been proud, too, when Tonya enrolled in Alan Cavanaugh's summer writing course at the community college as part of the dual-enrollment program with the high school. On the first day of class, Tonya wore cutoffs and a tank top, and even though there were only twelve students, it took Alan a moment to see her. To really notice her. His voice caught on her name.

"Tell us what it's like to be published?" she said.

Alan hadn't answered. Not at first. Tonya had sensed the others in the class leaning in, waiting for his response. He'd met her eyes. "It's like being in the eye of a hurricane. Every sense is engaged. Every feeling is heightened. And it lasts for an instant."

In the woods, the snow isn't as deep. Olivia follows a familiar path, the same path she'd followed that night, though it was summer then. She wonders what Alan would claim now about the affair if he were still alive. She suspects he'd say that she targeted him, that she manipulated him. He'd probably blame her low-rise jeans and baby doll dresses and that she came to his class with cleavage spilling from her T-shirts. For a long time, Olivia had believed that too. She doesn't anymore.

Alan's the one who used to stare at her over the fence when she sat by the pool in her bathing suit and he thought no one could see. He was rakish and older, and there was something exciting about the forbidden. But Alan's the one who said yes. And no one forced him to.

Olivia leaps over the brook, crosses the clearing, and comes to where the hunter's blind used to be, where she used to meet Alan. She remembers the time Lindsey followed her. She remembers telling him later that he was mistaken, that it had been her mother wrestling with Mr. Cavanaugh. He was young and impressionable, and she remembers repeating it enough so that he believed it was true. It had seemed harmless enough at the time.

And she remembers waiting here on that specific night.

She'd told Alan about the baby right after class that afternoon. Their baby. She'd wanted him to be as excited as she was. She'd wanted him to hold her close and tell her it would all work out. Instead, he'd said, "These things are easy to take care of. We can go together. We'll say I'm your father."

Tonya hadn't wanted an abortion.

"You're sixteen," Alan said. "I'll get fired."

But they were in love. He'd told her so.

"We'll talk later. Meet me," he said, as students from his next section filtered into the room. "The usual place."

Here at the blind, she waited, listening for him to come. He was late, and when he showed up, he stumbled through the woods and into the clearing, and every ounce of Olivia's adult self wants to tell that naïve girl—to tell Tonya—to run and to never look back, to confess everything to her mother, to place the entire weight of the problem on Diane's shoulders to solve. Olivia understands that her mother would have taken the burden with ease. But Tonya didn't know that. Tonya hadn't seen enough of the world yet to understand.

He sat next to her and lit a cigarette. He had blood on his arm. "My wife threw me out," Alan said.

"Because of me?"

Tonya hoped he'd finally chosen her. As if to answer, he kissed her. His mouth tasted of bourbon and tobacco. She saw their future.

He pushed her onto her back. She enfolded him in her arms. She wanted to touch every part of him, and at first, she couldn't tell that something had gone wrong. His face was close, and his arms strong, and she struggled to get out from under him. She tried to speak, to tell him that he was hurting her because he couldn't have known that she couldn't breathe. She moved her tongue. She tried to bite down, but a rolled-up wad of paper was in her mouth, jammed into her throat, and now she tried to scream, to claw at his hands or face, at anything that would allow her to escape.

Olivia doesn't remember when Tonya found the rock. But she does remember when Alan collapsed on her. And she remembers blood pouring from the wound and oozing over her. He groaned, and she struggled to free herself.

And here's the part that's true.

She escaped.

She got out from underneath him. And she gasped for air through her wrecked throat. She backed away as Alan tried to come after her again. Beside him, his cigarette burned. And she could have run. He was too injured to pursue her. Instead, she bashed his head in with the rock. She hit him at least a dozen times, and by the time she was done, blood splatter covered her from head to toe. She took the rock with her to the brook, where she rinsed off as much as she could. She wandered home in a daze. And it didn't take much for her mother to piece together what had happened.

They burned her clothes down to nothing but the scrap the police found later. "We'll have the Cavanaughs over to the pool tomorrow," Diane said. "Ask the girls to the movies. Act as though it's any other day."

And they waited. And everything went wrong.

And now, sometimes, whole weeks go by when Olivia forgets Tonya ever existed. But maybe it's time to face her own truth.

Behind her, she hears footsteps and knows who will be there even before she turns.

Natalie stands in the snow. "My sister has a good lawyer. And I can go with you when you talk to the detectives."

"I'd like that," Olivia says. "But I should call my son first. Jason should hear this from me."

Late-afternoon sun pours through the windows in Angela's bedroom, and she can hear activity coming from downstairs. Barking, too. The clock tells her it's after noon, well after noon.

But she deserves the rest. The last two months haven't been easy. She's faced inquiries into how a murderer had hidden in her department, and how he'd continued to operate under her watch. What Angela wants to tell them is that Zane liked cosmos and baking, that he was a person, one who'd had terrible things happen to him and had made terrible decisions. She'd long ago stopped looking at the world as good and bad, and Zane's punishment will fit the crime. She hopes, eventually, she'll stop punishing herself.

She forces herself out of bed. Her whole body feels heavy, exhausted. She brushes her teeth and struggles into an old sweatshirt. She knows who's downstairs already, and they're not people who care whether she wears clean underwear.

Morgan sits by the TV, Isaiah on one side and Kate on the other, and they're playing a video game. Hester is already pouring wine and pretending to help as Cary layers a lasagna and slides it into the oven. Cary's ex, Brenda, is here too, lining a casserole with ladyfingers for a tiramisu. Hester glances up and grins. "I didn't know if we'd see you."

Angela yawns. "I wouldn't miss the game. Or my friends."

Real friends.

"Hanging in there?" Hester asks.

"Mostly," Angela says.

"It must suck, everything with Zane."

"More than I hope you ever know."

Paws thunder toward her as George barrels through the back door, leading a pack of dogs, Rowdy too.

"Rowdy's one of the gang now," Hester says. "Like the rest of us." She pours a glass of wine for Angela, not stopping till she hits the rim.

Cary turns on the radio. Madonna sings about being a Lucky Star.

"Old people music!" Isaiah shouts from the living room.

Cary takes Angela's hand and spins her through the kitchen, while Morgan joins Hester and does the same. Brenda stands off to the side, tapping a toe, till Angela relents and holds a hand out to invite her in too. They almost miss the sound of the car pulling into the driveway. Cary turns the music down and glances out the window. "It's one of your detectives."

As Angela watches, Natalie gets out of her car and looks toward the house.

"I'll be back in a moment," Angela says.

"Will you?" Cary asks.

"I promise."

Angela opens the front door and lets George and Rowdy take the lead, galloping across the snowy yard and greeting Natalie with friendly woofs and noses.

"I've been driving for the last hour," Natalie says. "Sometimes I don't know where to go anymore."

Angela leans against the car. Inside, the lights are on, and the kitchen is warm. Cary watches through the window. "How long have we known each other?" Angela asks Natalie. "Fifteen, twenty years? You've never been to my house."

Natalie's eyes fill with tears. She swipes them away with a fist. Angela would give anything to cry.

"You know what?" she says. "The rest of this crap will be here tomorrow. Right now, my friends are here for the game. Come inside. Join us. We're having lasagna."

ACKNOWLEDGMENTS

The last time I drafted acknowledgments was May 2020, when not many of us could have predicted what was to come. Here's to everyone who helped someone out in this challenging time. These are just a few of the many folks I leaned on: Michael Starr; Jack and Betty Hill; Christine Hill; all the Hills, Rowells (especially Frank, whom I miss dearly), Starrs, Miraldas, and Sullivans; early readers: Jason Allison (jason-allison. com), Beth Castrodale (bethcastrodale.com), and Gabriel Valjan (gabrielvaljan.com); fellow writers in Jenna Blum's Sunday night workshop; all the amazing writers and readers in Sisters in Crime, MWA, the New England Crime Bake, and Malice Domestic; bookstores everywhere, but especially the folks at Belmont Books, Book People, Brookline Booksmith, Ink Fish Bookstore, Mysterious Bookshop, Porter Square Books, Print, and An Unlikely Story; my agent Robert Guinsler; my editor John Scognamiglio; my publicist Larissa Ackerman; Vida Engstrand, Lauren Jernigan, Darla Freeman, Lou Malcangi, Steve Zacharius, Lynn Cully, Tracy Marx, Robin Cook, and everyone at Kensington; and all the dogs of the world, but especially Edith Ann.

And to anyone who has ever taken a chance on one of my books, thank you a million times over. I can't tell you how much it means to me.

Please be in touch!

Web: edwin-hill.com

Facebook, Instagram, and Twitter: @edwinhillauthor